*"As soon go kindle fire with snow,
As seek to quench the fire of love with words."*

William Shakespeare
Two Gentleman of Verona, Act II, Scene VII

PROVENCE FLAME

by

Kate Fitzroy

1 *'the heat of his skin against hers'*

It was a perfect day. Amber looked out of her bedroom window and down to the garden. The lawn, freshly mown in stripes, was silvery in the early summer dew. Amber yawned and then sighed impatiently… it was ridiculously early. Her breath steamed the cool window pane and her thoughts drifted back to the last hectic month. She cleared a small space in the steamed glass and strained to look down to the left… yes, she could just see the edge of the white marquee, waiting in glorious readiness. Amber smiled at her own reflection in the glass. Every girl expected to be a little busy in the final run up to that walk up the aisle. Today was her wedding day, the most important day of her life. Amber stretched and yawned again. But five am was much too early, even for her big day. She should sleep, why else was it called beauty sleep? She threw herself back on her bed and closed her eyes, concentrating on drifting gently back to sleep, but her mind was too busy, too excited to give in. Another smile crossed over her face, and she almost laughed aloud as she remembered her hen night.

'Well, we knew you wouldn't want anything too boozy.' Kim said. 'Tickets for the Taming of the Shrew seemed more you. Of course, if you ever get to arrange my hen night I shall expect the full monty night out on the tiles.'

Amber looked at Kim who was triumphantly holding up six theatre tickets. They had been best friends since school days even though it often seemed that they had nothing in common. Kim was out-going and always in a rush to grab at life. So good-looking that she never had trouble finding a man… which was a good thing as she never stayed in a relationship very long. Flying high in her career in social media, she worked as hard as she played. Under all her noisy charisma she was a completely trustworthy friend. Perhaps this was what the girls really had in common. Amber knew she could always rely on Kim and certainly there had been several times when Kim had trusted Amber to extricate her from some wild-cap scheme.

'Fantastic, Kim, only you could know exactly how I really wanted to spend an evening with my best friends. How on earth did you get tickets? It's been sold out for weeks.'

The five girls circled round Amber, enjoying the moment as the sun set, casting long shadows along the Thames embankment.

'I know, I am just the most amazing best bridesmaid ever.' Kim agreed and then added, 'But you can't have it all your own boring, serious way, Amber Marsden... the Ms.Bride soon to be Mrs. Brodie, there's a bar just behind you waiting with a cold bottle of pink champagne, and, if we go now we may even be able to make that two or three bottles before the play begins.'

Amber sat up in bed and rubbed her eyes. This idea of beauty sleep was not working. She checked her phone, no messages and now only five thirty am. Amber flicked the phone closed impatiently and threw it back on the bedside table. Still ridiculously early. Once again she lay back onto her pillows and tried to relax and think of nothing. Instead, a list of worries filed into her head. Table plan, flowers, table presents, bridesmaids' dresses, her bouquet, bridesmaids' posies, the church candles, the menu, the cake, umbrellas... words formed and disappeared at random. Amber sighed in exasperation and wondered whether Rob was wide awake too. Should she text him? She picked up her phone again and pressed his number. No, they had agreed not to speak or even text until they met in church. Amber's stomach butterflied at the very idea of seeing Rob standing at the altar, waiting for her. He would look so fine in his formal Scottish wedding tartan. She knew he was secretly pleased to have the chance to wear his kilt and a newly tailored velvet jacket. Amber smiled again and wriggled with excitement, remembering Rob's first reluctance for a formal wedding. Hadn't he wanted them just to run away together and get married up some mountain or other? Yes, that was it... Ben Nevis... or somewhere near there in the Highlands. Well, that was never going to happen. Slowly but surely Amber had managed to convince Rob that they were going to get married in her local village church and that the reception would be at her family home. Rural Sussex, not the wilds of the Highlands. As he had no close family it had to be her day. The sad lack of relations on his side would be well-balanced by Rob's numerous friends. Amber thought back to their first meeting and how sorry she had felt for this handsome young Scot, working alone in London. It had been at a friend's wedding. Another formal white wedding in Sussex, Amber's schoolfriend marrying that day. Had they been placed side by side at the wedding breakfast table by chance or had it been planned. Certainly, if it had been fate then it had been the luckiest of chances. If there was ever such a thing as love at first sight... then this was it. Amber had looked into Rob's dark, blue eyes and known that this would be the man she wanted to marry. They talked all through the meal, hardly able to wait for the speeches to end before carrying on their conversation. He told her of his dreams to travel, his love of mountaineering, his career as a surveyor bringing him to London... and finally he told her of his unhappy childhood with foster parents.

'Looking back on it, I'm sure I was an impossible brat!' Rob laughed but his eyes were sad. 'I was moved from one foster home to another, a sorry case, but I was always happy at school. I loved every subject they threw at me... maths, geography... my favourite subject... history... well, everything really but most of all the sport. Football in the winter and cricket in the summer. We do get some summer in Edinburgh, you know.' He smiled at Amber and gently took her hand. 'Would you let me show you my Scotland one day... one day soon?'

'I'd love that... yes, I would. I'm ashamed to say I have never been to Scotland... yet.' Amber let her hand rest in his and resisted a strong desire to kiss him. So this was what love at first sight was all about. All her normal reservation flew away as she looked into his eyes. Was it her imagination or did the sadness in his eyes begin to change to happiness?

From that earth-shaking moment they had seen each other nearly every day. Both working in central London, they tried to meet for quick lunches, walking in a park or sitting close together in a small café near Hanover Square. They became regulars here and the Italian owner always greeted them noisily.

'*Buon giorno*! My favourite young lovers, here, sit here in the window and I bring you your favourite panini.' And so it seemed no time at all that they were an established couple. They shared everything. Spent every weekend together, often at Amber's family home and, whenever they could get away… then they went to Scotland.

'I think you are beginning to love the Highlands as much as I do.' Rob smiled down at Amber as she sat at her painting easel. 'Will you be warm enough sitting around? Are you sure you don't want to walk up the first stretch with me?'

Amber looked up the mountain path that led to the foot of Aonach Mor. 'I am tempted but it is such a lovely day and the sun is really warm in this sheltered corner. I have such an idea for trying to catch the strong shadows on that overhanging rock. No, you go on with your group of climbers, I'll see you back at the lodge at tea-time.' Amber turned her cheek and pointed to it, 'Kiss, please!'

Rob laughed and came back to her. He held her head in both hands and kissed her mouth long and hard. 'I love you, Amber.' He said at last, as breathlessly they drew apart. 'Shall I cancel my climb today, I mean, we could…'

Amber laughed and playfully pushed him away. 'Off you go, they're all waiting for you to lead them, anyway. Tea and scones at five o'clock, it's a date!'

Rob pulled on his backpack and smiled ruefully. 'You're a hard woman, Amber Marsden. But I still love you. How about asking for tea to be served in our room?' He went off, turning for a final wave at the bend in the path. Amber smiled as she began to sort out her paints, her heart still beating strongly from their passionate kiss. How she would have loved to go back to the lodge for a whole day of lovemaking with Rob. Some ancient wisdom told her that it was better to let him go... let him go to return to love her even more.

At five o'clock, Amber was waiting in their room, watching the sky turn from the palest blue to dark red gold as the sun set behind the mountain top. She stretched luxuriously and ran her fingers through her wet hair. The table was set for tea for two, scones, cream and jam. All she had to do was boil the kettle that waited ready on the little table in the corner. Amber looked around with satisfaction. The room was large and well-heated, not deeply luxurious but not spartan either. Best of all was the addition of a small sauna room beside the shower. Amber had just emerged, her skin glowing with heat, then taken a cool perfumed shower and wrapped herself in a large, white towelling robe. Certainly, this was no ordinary climber's lodge but then, they were both working successfully in London, had only themselves to think about...so why not lavish out on a little luxury for a couple of nights? The place worked for both of them. Magnificent mountains for Amber to paint and for Rob to climb. Usually, on a day like this, they would take a stroll together in the sunset but not today. Today, they both couldn't wait to finish off that kiss. But Rob was late. Amber picked up her watercolour pad and flicked through the sketches she had made. She was unusually pleased with the bold strokes of colour that spread across the thick paper. Today and had been a very good day, her happiness seemed to show in her art. Amber threw down the pad of paintings impatiently. Where was Rob? She went back to the window and looked into the dusk. There he was, striding back toward the lodge, a few paces ahead of the small group of other climbers. As he neared the building he raised his head and looked up and saw her standing, waiting. He raised his hand and in the gathering dusk she could just make out his wide, flashing smile. Amber raised her hand in return but he was already entering the lodge doors. Her heart thumped and her stomach muscles tightened as she knew she would soon be in his arms.

The dry heat of the sauna enclosed them in silence. They sat, side by side, their shoulders lightly touching as they recovered from the storm of passion that had engulfed them. As soon as Rob had opened the bedroom door, Amber had thrown herself at him, all the tension of waiting in anticipation suddenly released as she held him in her arms. Rob threw his backpack on the floor and began to pull off his anorak with one hand as the other reached inside Amber's robe. She gave a gasp of excitement as his cold hand held her breast and caressed her nipple. Then he dropped his head and she felt the cold damp of his hair brushing both her breasts as he kissed them fiercely. She began to pull up his sweater and run her hands over the tight muscles of his chest and then down to unbutton his jeans. His breath was coming fast now and he groaned as he pulled off his clothes and then carried her to the bed.

'I've been thinking of this moment all day.' He whispered into her ear as he moved on top of her.

Now the heat of the sauna held them in peace. Amber's body ached from the weight of Rob's as she stretched luxuriously, the warmth relaxing every muscle. She turned to Rob and saw he was watching her closely. She knew by the look in his eyes that their passion was not quite spent. He reached out and lifted her onto his lap, his hands running down her back and pressing her close against him. She felt the heat of his skin against hers and threw her arms up around his strong neck as again they moved together, now in a deep, slow rhythm.

Now, once again she was waiting for Rob. Amber stood beside her father in the church porch. She closed her eyes briefly and took a deep breath, for as long as she could remember she had planned this day. She clutched her bouquet nervously and pushed her shoulders back as Kim fluttered around, arranging Amber's long veil and sweeping train.

'Where on earth can he be?' Amber said, her voice breaking under the strain and tension. 'Check your mobile, Dad.'

'I've just this minute checked and there are no messages. Don't worry, darling girl, he will be here any minute, I'm sure.' Amber's father stood calm and resolute beside her. 'He's coming down from Scotland so it could be a number of reasons. I'm sure he will be here any minute now.' Then his mobile rang and Amber snatched it from her father and read the message. Suddenly her face lost all colour and she dropped the phone onto the flagstone floor. For a long moment, her father and Kim looked at Amber, then Kim reached down for the phone. She, too, read the message and stared up at them, her mouth wide in shock as she seemed unable to speak. Then she sprang up and threw her arms around Amber and looked over her shoulder at Amber's father who was standing in shocked silence.

Kim's voice was quiet and controlled as she said quietly, 'The message says to tell Amber I am sorry but I am not coming.'

Less than an hour later, Amber was back in her bedroom. Just an hour, but her whole life had changed forever. She had no idea how she was here, how she had left the church, how she had climbed the stairs... how she was now sitting on her bed, her wedding dress crushed and creased, tears streaking her face with make-up, her veil pulled off with such anger that it lay torn across the floor. She was crying, her breath coming in uneven sobs, her head throbbing as she tried to make some sense of what was happening to her. Kim sat beside her on the bed, unusually silent, her arm resting lightly round Amber's shoulders.

'Is there anything I can do?' Kim asked quietly,'Anything at all, I just can't think what to say?'

'Nothing, nothing...' Amber's voice was a new sound in her ears. She didn't recognise herself. Even the words seemed to come from somewhere faraway. There was no reality. Panic rose within her as, once again, wild uncontrollable sobs racked her whole body. She doubled up, as though she had been physically winded and then, curled into a tight miserable ball, she lay on the bed. Kim gently removed Amber's satin shoes and pulled the quilt over her. She stroked back Amber's hair and said, 'I'll get you a glass of water.'

For a brief second Amber surfaced from her misery to say, 'Don't let anyone in my room, not even Mum. I just can't face anyone.' And then the relentless tears began again and consumed her with misery.

Kim returned with a glass of water and a pill. 'Amber, try to drink some water, you should. Your Mum said to take a headache pill. Here.' Kim held out the glass and Amber slowly raised herself onto her elbow and took the glass. Her hand shook so much that Kim steadied the glass as Amber sipped the cold water and swallowed the pill.

'Is Mum all right?' Kim mumbled as she sank back onto the pillows.

'She said to tell you that she would take care of everything. Not to worry and... well, she didn't really say anything else.' Kim faltered to an awkward silence.

'There is nothing to say, is there? Kim, thanks for everything but I think I want to be alone now... just for a while.'

Kim looked at Amber doubtfully and then nodded. 'I'll go downstairs and check on your Mum, see if I can make myself useful. Maybe you can sleep or rest a little.' Kim blew Amber a small kiss and then quietly left the room.

Whether it was the pill or nervous exhaustion but Amber did slip into a dreamless sleep. When she awoke, a few hours later, the house seemed silent and sad. Amber sat up in bed and rocked back and forward, her grief and lost dreams hitting her like a sledgehammer. She felt a spasm of sobs rising in her throat. Quickly she threw back the quilt and stood shakily beside the bed, one hand steadying herself against the wall. Slowly she took a few paces and stood in front of the long mirror. There she was, a wrecked image of a bride. A jilted, unwanted bride in a crumpled silk dress. What was so wrong with her? Her light, blue eyes look back at her reproachfully. Normally a striking turquoise blue, her eyes were now pink-rimmed and blurred with crying. Amber reached up and pulled her hair back from face and held it in a tight bunch. Good thick hair, naturally shiny with health, pale ash brown. Amber let her hands drop to her sides and her long hair fell down across her shoulders. She reached up and slid the ivory silk of her dress off her shoulders. Good breasts, high and firm pushed against the silk of her camisole. Amber felt her knees almost give way as she remembered how Rob had loved her breasts. So, was it all to be in the past tense now, whenever she remembered him… no future? Amber sat back on the bed, feeling too weak to stand, too miserable to remain upright in a world where Rob no longer wanted her. She pulled off the wide tartan sash that now hung round her hips and stepped out of her dress. Suddenly she stamped on the pile of crumpled silk and then kicked it across the room. Now her misery was turning to anger. She looked down at the large amber ring glinting on her finger, the third finger on her left hand. Her mind flashed back with a filmic image of the moment that Rob had placed it on her finger. Valentine's night, two years ago when her whole world had seemed so beautiful. Furiously she pulled the ring from her finger and threw it across the room. Just then, there was a light tap on the door and her mother's voice, soft and familiar, called her name.

'Come in, Mum, I'm awake.' Amber sighed, knowing it would be unreasonable not to talk with her mother but somehow dreading her sympathy. Her mother's first words surprised her,

'This is a hard blow, Amber, my darling girl, but you will have to get over it. Why don't you go for one of your long runs in the country?'

Amber looked at her mother in surprise. 'Go for a run?' she repeated idiotically as though this was not what she did nearly every other day of her life. But this had been her wedding day not any day, not a normal day, this was to have been the day to start her new life.

'You go and wash your face and I'll dig out your tracks and trainers. Go on, Amber, it will do you good.'

Suddenly Amber knew her mother was right. What she needed was fresh air in her lungs and to remember that the world did still exist out there in the June sunshine.

As her feet pounded the dry Sussex soil, Amber breathed in an even rhythm and her head began to clear. The events of the day rolled away as she enjoyed the consolation and beauty of nature. Following her usual route, she circled a ploughed field and then took the path that led into Ashdown forest. Here the land rose steeply and Amber struggled to maintain her pace. Finally, she reached the top of the hill and as the trees cleared she looked down into the valley. Suddenly, she knew just where she was going. Veering away from her usual path she headed downhill toward a cottage that nestled into the scenery as though it had always been there. Amber saw smoke curling up from the one chimney in the centre of the red-tiled roof. She smiled to herself, even in mid-summer her grandfather would have the Aga smouldering and a kettle hissing on the top.

'I just can't believe it's happened.' Amber said, probably for the tenth time. She sat with her grandfather in the small, sunny courtyard that overlooked the forest.

'Have another piece of toast, my dear, honey or marmalade?' Amber's grandfather pushed the plate of toast toward her and refrained, yet again, from making a comment. Amber took a large piece of buttery toast and began to spread it with honey. She took a large bite and then nearly choked as she heard her grandfather finally begin to talk.

'Well, I know you won't want to hear this and you probably won't believe me, but I have to say I think you have just had a very lucky escape.'

'Escape, Grandy? How can you say that?' Amber spluttered with anger, as she replied through a mouthful of toast and honey. 'I loved Rob.'

'Ah, now it begins… listen to yourself. You said you loved him, not that you love him. Now what does that tell you?'

'Well…' words momentarily failed Amber as she tried to pull her thoughts together before continuing. 'I mean, I do love him… no, actually… truly… I can't say that now, can I? But Grandy, I did so love him only this morning, how can I bear it… I mean how can I believe what has happened?'

'Now you are returning to where you started. Let's think things through. I'm going to top up the tea pot while you just think about it all for a while.'

Amber sat very still, looking across the tranquil valley and over to the light summer greens of the forest. It was a beautiful world and should a moment be wasted in tears? Her troubles were so minuscule in the grand scale of things. But how could she bear it, how could she stand losing Rob from her life? Her eyes began to fill with tears and she brushed them away angrily. How could he do this to her… after all the happy times he had spent with her family… how could he hurt them too? Anger now flooded through her and she stood up quickly and went into the cottage to find her grandfather.

'Grandy, there's another thing! I am so, so angry. I have never felt so angry in all my life.' Her grandfather turned round from where he stood at the old Aga. He smiled as he said, 'Ah, now that's what I wanted to hear you say. You're angry and so you should be, my love, mighty angry. Now, anger comes with its own energy and you should use it all up.'

'What do you mean? How can I use this engulfing rage I feel?'

'Well, the sun is not so warm now so let's go into the conservatory. You bring the tea tray and I'll bring pen and paper.'

So, Amber and her grandfather sat together again, now in the late afternoon sun that filtered through the large, leafed plants in the conservatory.

'What did you mean… use my anger, Grandy?' asked Amber, sitting with her head in her hands and her elbows on the table. 'I just feel exhausted by it all. My whole future lies ahead empty without Rob.'

'What you say is partly true, I can see that. Your future lies ahead without Rob… but, empty, no, no, I can't accept that. You have more courage in you than you think.'

'I wish I could agree, but you know if he walked through the door right now…' Amber swallowed hard, a huge lump forming in her throat at the mere idea of seeing the familiar shape of Rob in the doorway, but she struggled to carry on, '… I know I would just throw myself into his arms.'

'Hmm,' Her grandfather stirred his tea thoughtfully, 'well, I think it much more likely you'd throw your cup of tea at him. Don't forget I've known you all your life. As a child you were a ball of energy and courage and I don't think you have changed that much.'

Amber sat for a moment and then looked across the table at her grandfather and gave a wide, beautiful smile. Her face was still marked by tears but suddenly there was the light of hope in her eyes as she said.

'You know what, Grandy, you're so right! I'd love to be able to throw my tea at him right now, followed by the whole tea tray and all your flower pots.'

Grandy gave a sudden laugh and then they were both laughing. New tears filled Amber's eyes as she said, 'Do you remember when I smashed up my own doll's tea party. Oh goodness, I must have been a terrible child.'

'Well, we cleared that up and only one tea cup broken in the end.' Grandy continued to laugh, his shoulders heaving as he put his cup down on its saucer for fear of spilling his tea.

'And you made me mend it very, very carefully. I remember that afternoon… although I have no idea now why I had thrown such a tantrum… but yes, I remember the smell of that glue and the tweezers you gave me to pick up the pieces. I think I enjoyed mending that little cup more than the actual tea party.'

Amber's grandfather stood up and went into the kitchen, returning a minute later holding out his closed hands to Amber. 'Which hand, Amber, left or right?'

Amber laughed again, remembering how her grandfather had always held one hand a little in front of the other so that she could always choose the hand holding the surprise. So, she tapped the hand nearer to her and he opened it. There lying in the palm of his large hand lay the small mended tea-cup.

'I don't believe it! You still have it, Grandy.' Amber took the cup carefully and examined it. 'The very cup! I must say I did a fine job on the repair.'

'It's always kept on the top shelf of the dresser. I enjoyed that day, too. I knew then you were going to be a girl with fine qualities. Of course, I may be a little biased.' Grandy smiled fondly at Amber and sat down again next to her and took up his pen. 'So, let's begin, let's pick up the pieces you are in and carefully put them back together.'

'Why the pen and paper?' asked Amber, still examining the little cup.

'Well, you know I am a self-made business man and never had much education...'

'That never stopped you from being a huge success,' Amber interrupted, 'your name, William Marsden, is stamped on nearly every cardboard carton flying around the world!'

'True, it was a strange way to make my fortune... empty boxes... folding flat... but I don't want to talk about my life. We just don't have the time and after all, cardboard boxes may be useful and made my fortune but they are not truly interesting. My point is that, as I didn't have a degree in business or anything else for that matter, I used to make long lists and plans. You know, pros and cons, that sort of thing.'

'Yes, I see what you mean, but... sorry Grandy, can't think of many pros in my future at the moment... more cons.'

'Well, let's have a think.' Grandy tapped the table with his pencil. 'Right, give me a practical disadvantage...

something more concrete… not… Oh, Grandy my heart is broken in two!'

Amber couldn't resist a smile as her grandfather spoke the last words in a silly falsetto voice. Then anger welled up in her again as reality hit her in the face.

'I've handed in my notice at work. Oh my god, Grandy, I don't have a job. We were moving to Glasgow together. Rob has a new job starting next month and I was… well, just going to look for something up there.'

'Hmm, well, you see I'd like to put that under disadvantage on this clean piece of paper in front of me but then it does seem like something of a big advantage not to be job-seeking in lovely Glasgow. Especially as your field of work in art restoration is so specialised.' His pencil hovered over the paper and he looked across at Amber with a wicked smile. 'I'll keep that on hold for a while. Give me something better… a bigger disadvantage, please, keep it practical, not emotional.'

'Well,' Amber struggled to think of something more in line with her grandfather's way of thinking. 'Well, Mum and Dad have spent a fortune on the wedding day and now…' Amber exhaled a long breath at the thought of all the wasted wedding plans.

'True, I could write that down. Not sure though… not altogether a disadvantage and I will happily pick up the bill. One of the advantages of my cardboard box empire and happily? Because my lovely grand-daughter has just escaped a life of misery.'

'Life of misery? What do you mean, Grandy?'

'Well, any man who could not turn up on his wedding day is not exactly reliable. You have to agree, Amber, and how could you ever trust a man like that again? If he had walked through the door and survived you throwing my tea tray at him…well, you would never be able to truly rely on him. Imagine, he could be half an hour late home any night and your heart would be trembling, thinking he had walked out on you. No, no… the biggest advantage I would write so far are these two words… lucky escape.'

Amber watched in silence as her grandfather wrote the two words in capitals under his advantage column. Before she could object or even think about it, he was carrying on.

'Right, we've made a start, now what next?'

Amber searched wildly for something tangible, something that would make her grandfather realise the mess she was in. 'I've spent all my savings on the honeymoon,' she said in a small voice, 'I know it's not what you'd expect in your day, Grandy. I mean, I know traditionally the groom pays for the honeymoon and all that stuff but, well...' Amber struggled to think how it had come about, 'I did all the planning and so I just booked and paid for things as they came up. Rob was so busy applying for his new job lately and I enjoyed the planning... oh dear, I do sound such a fool.'

'So where was this honeymoon to be?' Grandy asked in a straightforward way, ignoring Amber's eyes filling with tears once again.

Amber sniffed and pulled out a tissue to mop the hot tears rolling down her cheeks.

'P...P...Pr... Provence' she stuttered miserably and burst into loud sobs.

3   *'a small attic room under the Parisian stars'*

To: amber@hotmail.com
Cc:
Subject: TELL ME
From: Kim Simpson - kimS@gmail.com

Amber, where are you... tell me it's not true and that you are not on your honeymoon with your grandfather? best love/luck wotever, Kim

To: kimS@gmail.com
Cc:
Subject: TRUE!!
From: Amber Marsden - amber@hotmail.com
Just reached Avignon, having a great journey down south. Will explain all soon x

Amber smiled as she closed down her iPad. How to explain it all to Kim, her closest friend, or anyone at all? Even her mother had shaken her head and looked worried when Kim had told her. And yet, Amber was so sure it had been the best thing to do. The day following the day that should have been her wedding day, Amber had driven round to pick up her grandfather and they had set off together for Dover. Of course, it hadn't been quite that simple. Amber sighed as she remembered her family and friends closing round her, sympathetic and loving, offering to do anything at all to help. For a while she had thought she would drown in their sympathy and sink back into tears and misery. Then, she remembered Grandy's last words of advice, when she had finally left his cottage as the sun set behind the forest.

'Go home now and face the music. It will be hard to look in the face of everyone you love best in the world, very hard but not impossible. They will all want to help you through this… so, take them at their word and let them. Leave all the worry of returning presents and clearing up the debris of this non-event to them.'

It had been difficult, he was right there, but, also, it had not been impossible. Grandy had played his part, there had been a very long phone call to her mother. Then her parents had gone over to his cottage. Amber had no idea what had been said but by the time they returned the mood had changed. Amber was packed and ready to leave early the next day and her parents reluctantly accepted that was how it was going to be. Even more reluctantly that she was going to travel with Grandy.

Now here they were in a small hotel in Avignon. Grandy was resting before they met for dinner. He had arranged everything, cancelling hotel bookings and changing the hotel accommodation to suit their new route south. The first night they had stayed with his friends in Paris. Nothing could have been more different from the first night of the honeymoon that Amber had planned so carefully. Amber had driven through the mad rush of Parisian traffic, following the frantic voice of the sat-nav to the address that Grandy had keyed in. He had then tilted his seat back as far as it would go, pulled his old panama hat over his eyes and fallen asleep. He awoke just as the voice advised them they had reached their destination. Amber had hardly time to recover from the stress of the journey before being immersed in the large and noisy family life of Grandy's friends. The apartment was huge and yet still seemed filled with life and laughter. Over a wonderful long dinner, everyone had seemed so interested in Amber's work as an art restorer. She couldn't remember ever talking so much about herself before. Offers were made to show her around galleries and museums the next day but Grandy said they had plans to move on south. Amber had sighed with relief, as now did not seem the time for an extensive Parisian art tour. She had sipped her coffee and felt exhaustion creep over. That night, in a small attic room under the Parisian stars, she had slept better than she had slept in months… or maybe the last few years.

Now, sitting in Avignon, she thought again how easy it had been to leave Grandy to make all the arrangements. She reluctantly admitted to herself once more that Rob had taken no part in the planning of the honeymoon. She hadn't minded, knowing his work was more demanding than her quiet museum work. Only now was she beginning to question everything. Had he ever intended to marry her? Amber pushed the unhappy thought away and looked out of the window and down to the tree-lined square below. Yes, there was just time to make a brief water-colour sketch. Amber opened up her small leather bag of paints and brushes. She sighed again, this time with satisfaction, as she slowly mixed the perfect green to outline the leaves blowing gently in the breeze.

'hills fading away into the blue of the sky'

To: amber@hotmail.com
Cc:
Subject: okaaaay…so it is TRUE
From: Kim Simpson - kimS@gmail.com

Amber, I think I get it… not a bad idea in the grand scheme of disaster. Let me know what I can do back here, best love/luck as ever, Kim

To: kimS@gmail.com
Cc:
Subject: THANKS
From: Amber Marsden amber@hotmail.com
All going well… have started painting and have a hundred new ideas for more… will let you know when we arrive at the coast. Weather brilliant and impossible to be miserable in magic Provence. Thanks again and love, Amber

   Amber and her grandfather were back in the car again, heading further south. The morning sun lit the fields on each side of the road with a pink glow. The rich, red soil of Provence folded away to a distant line of pale blue hills.
   'Oh Grandy, isn't it just so beautiful. Look at those hills fading away into the blue of the sky.'
   'Beautiful indeed. Do you mind if we stop? I'd like to take a few photos. Look, there's a small lay-by coming up on this side of the road.'
   Amber pulled into the lay-by and parked under the shade of some pine trees. The morning air was still cool but she had begun to worry that her grandfather should not stay too long in the sun. She watched as he strode away from the car, camera in hand, his old panama hat firmly in place. A wave of fondness and gratitude swept over her and she quickly took a photo of him in the middle of the wild landscape. She

looked down at the image in the small screen on her camera and smiled. It was a really good shot. She'd post it on Facebook later and show the world that she was having a good time in a special way. Not a honeymoon but a great journey with her loving grandfather. She looked up again and saw that he was waving his hat to catch her attention. She locked the car and ran over to where he stood.

'Take a deep breath!' Grandy said, 'The air is full of the perfume of wild herbs… rosemary, thyme and… is that lavender?'

'Oh my, isn't it splendid, better than any perfume from a bottle. Better than medicine. Fantastic, yes, I think I do smell lavender.'

'Maybe there are some lavender fields near here and we are smelling the perfume in the light breeze? Why don't you take some time off and go for a walk… take your paints?'

'What about you Grandy?'

'Oh, my old knees don't think it a good idea. I'll look at your photos and sketches later.'

'But it will get hot back in the car.' Amber looked back at the car parked in the scanty shade of the few pine trees. The idea of a few hours alone and painting was almost irresistible and yet she would be worried to leave Grandy in the rising heat of the day.

'Don't worry about me, didn't you notice that just before we pulled off the road we passed a small hotel, Hotel Lavande, I think. I thought I'd drive back and have a cold drink and see what it's like. I think I caught the glimpse of a blue swimming pool.'

'Is there anything you don't notice?' Amber laughed.

'Well, you had your eyes on the road. Anyway, I have your mobile number in mine so we can always contact each other. Do you see that pale, pink roof just peeping over the next line of pine trees? That's where I'll be. You take your old painting bag and we can meet there for lunch.'

Together they walked slowly back to the car. Amber took her grandfather's arm, not sure if she was supporting him or the other way round.

'Here, take your sunhat.' Grandy threw the hat like a frisbee at Amber as she set off with her ruck-sack. 'Do you have your bottle of water?' Amber raised a hand in farewell and smiled ruefully as she accepted the fact that he was definitely still looking after her.

Two hours later, even where she was sitting in the shade of an outcrop of rock, she was hot and grateful for the water. Some she had carefully poured onto her mixing palette but now she was drinking the last drop. She began to pack away her paints and brushes and then looked at her three paintings before placing them into a folder. Never had she known paint dry so quickly on paper. Her work restoring art at the museum in London now seemed more than a thousand miles away. Another lifetime. The small, dark studio where she had spent her days, the tiny painstaking brush marks that she made on great works of art, the careful colour mixing to another artist's original work, the stages of waiting for the oil paint to dry before adding another layer. Nothing could be more different to the work she had just finished. Now she had three large sheets of heavy watercolour paper, filled with bold strokes of bright colour. Amber sighed with satisfaction and then, shouldering her bag, she headed in the direction of the distant pink roof of the Hotel Lavande.

An hour later she was sitting under a very large, pink parasol, sipping a glass of cold rosé wine. 'Everything seems to be pink in Provence!' Amber raised her glass to her grandfather.

'Doesn't it just! No need for rose-tinted glasses around here. Even the lavender fields look pink.'

'I was so surprised when I reached the top of that small hill behind the hotel and suddenly saw the lavender fields stretching away as far as the eye can see. The light is so strong the purple of the lavender is bleached out to pink. I can't wait to paint it all. No wonder it's called the Hotel Lavande. And to think I had been looking in the opposite direction all morning. Although, you were right, there was definitely the perfume of lavender in the air.'

'The land here is deceptive, hillier than it looks. But you can't have been more surprised than I was to find how lovely this place turned out to be. Four stars and worth more, I should say!'

'Absolutely! It's like finding heaven on earth. I'd wandered further than I realised and the last stretch down the hill was quite a slog.'

'Lesson learnt then. One bottle of water may not be enough… especially if you use it for painting. Anyway, you had a good, long drink of water when you did get here and now you deserve your glass of wine. In fact, I was wondering what you thought about staying here tonight? I could go and see if they have rooms?'

'I can't think of anything I'd like more.' Amber stretched lazily and watched her grandfather march into the hotel. He didn't seem to have any trouble with his knees when he was on a mission. She took another sip of wine and then nibbled one of the shiny, black olives that had been placed on the table with their drinks. Then she picked up the olive dish and examined it. The dark terracotta was beautifully shaped into an off-centre heart. How romantic, she thought to herself. Everything today had seemed to throw the pleasure of art and living at her. She carefully placed the little dish back on the table. Would Rob have loved it here? Would he have enjoyed the spontaneity of deciding to stay the night? Her own lop-sided heart lurched and missed a beat as she realised the harsh truth. He would have hated it.

5 *'it was impossible not to be a little envious'*

To: amber@hotmail.com
Cc:
Subject: pouring with icy rain here amber@
From: Kim Simpson - kimS@gmail.com

Amber, you just can't believe how cold it is for June…some sort of record, I'm told. So it seems you are in the right place.
Enjoy the sunshine and glad to hear you're painting again.
Love from your shivering friend, Kim

To: kimS@gmail.com
Cc:
Subject: Impossible to believe it's rainy and cold in London
From: Amber Marsden - amber@hotmail.com

This land is rosy pink and perfect… I am just the pink bit… sun very hot so have to be careful not to burn. Grandy found this amazing little hotel not far from Aix en Provence so we are staying on. It seems strange to be able to just change plans so easily. We were heading for the coast. But then, Grandy makes everything easy… I am so lucky. Hope it stops raining soon, Amber x

'That was quite definitely the best meal I have ever, ever eaten' Amber folded her napkin and patted he stomach.
'I agree, and I have eaten a great deal more meals than you, my dear. I think the flavours were quite extraordinary. I spoke with the owner this afternoon, a most charming young woman. She and her husband have set this place up all on their own. Not just the hotel, but a thriving pottery and five studios for resident artists. I thought you'd be interested, so they're going to try and join us for coffee on the terrace later.'
'Wow, when did you find all that out?'

'Probably when you were dozing on that very nice lounger by the swimming pool. You're looking all the better for a swim and some sunshine.'

'I feel great, but I'll have to be careful I don't turn as pink as everything else around here. It is so, so hot.'

'Yes, too hot for me out there this afternoon. The bedrooms are very cool though, excellent air-con… ah, there they are!' Grandy waved his hand in the air and stood to greet a young couple that were making their way across the restaurant toward their table. As they drew near, Amber realised that the girl was holding a baby in the folds of her long cotton shawl.

'Now who do we have here?' Grandy asked, forgoing any formal greeting and looking straight at the baby.'

The young couple smiled happily and the girl very gently moved the soft voile cotton away so that they could admire the sleeping child.

'This is our little Fleur.' the young woman spoke quietly.

Amber moved closer to peep at the baby. 'Oh, she is so beautiful, absolutely perfect. How old is she?'

'Just three months. Pleased to meet you, my name is Calinda Rabin and this is my husband, Daniel.'

They all shook hands formally and then moved away from the table and out to the long terrace that ran along the back wall of the hotel.

Calinda and Daniel sat close together, Fleur still sleeping in her mother's arms.
Amber looked at them with an artist's eye, thinking they were almost too beautiful. Daniel was of medium height, muscled and very tanned. His dark hair cut very short, his strong eyebrows like straight dark lines over his dark brown eyes. Calinda was slightly taller but very delicately boned. Her long arms so graceful as she enfolded Fleur close to her, that she had a Madonna-like dignity. Amber had worked on several old masters depicting the Madonna and here, outlined against the dark, dusky blue Provençal night it was as though she was faced with the real thing. Much as she loved painting

landscapes, she sat wondering whether this was an opportunity to think about portraiture. Lost in her own thoughts, Amber gave a small start as she realised her grandfather was saying her name.

'Amber, come back from your dream world!' Grandy turned to Calinda and Daniel and smiled benignly, 'I'm afraid my grand-daughter is often dreaming… or rather she did as a child.'

Amber smiled at his words but before she could begin to apologise she had a momentary thought, a realisation that she had indeed stopped dreaming for some time now. Being with Rob was all she had thought about. There had been no time for her own thoughts, even her Scottish watercolours were just efficient paintings. Good enough in technique, but with no soul, no life. The work she had done today had pleased her more than anything she had done since she left uni. Or rather, when she had met Rob. The thought took only a moment but the truth made her draw in her breath in shock. Then, pulling back her shoulders resolutely, she joined the conversation.

'How long have you had the Hotel Lavande?' she asked and was surprised at their laughter.

'Do you see what I mean?' Grandy said, 'Completely in her own world. Amber we have just been through all that. The Rabins have been here for six years, Calinda was a model in London and came out here for a photo shoot. It was love at first sight when they met and…'

'Oh my goodness, of course…' Amber interrupted, 'You are the Calinda, the super-model who over-night disappeared off the catwalk scene. There was a huge furore in the media about you!'

Calinda waved one long, dark hand elegantly in the air above her head and gave a flashing smile. 'So much hot air… that was the world I had fallen into. Three months or so later they forgot all about me. Now I am just the name of a perfume.'

'Well, not quite true, you are still the most iconic image in the world of photography.' Amber said, looking admiringly at Calinda's cool elegance.

'Luckily I still receive royalties, too!' Calinda laughed and looked at Daniel. 'But running away from all that madness was the best thing I ever did. I had never intended to be a model. I came to London from Tunis, I had won an art scholarship to the Slade but then this talent-spotter guy came along and well, offered me a small fortune to work as a model. My family are very poor and it did mean I could send money home… well, that was then. Now, we make our own money and we live happily together with our little Fleur.' Calinda looked down at the baby in her arms and smiled, then looked at Daniel. Amber nodded and smiled, too, but it was impossible not to be a little envious.

'It looks like a very successful business to me.' Said Grandy, as he looked along the candlelit terrace, every table now filled with people drinking coffee and digestifs. The warm evening air was filled with the sound of voices and laughter. 'Yes, you have some very happy customers… and believe me, that it what business is all about.'

'My grandfather is a very successful business man, self-made, so if he compliments you then you can be sure he means it… or he is thinking of buying you out!'

They all laughed and the baby stirred in Calinda's arms. She stood up, tall and very beautiful. 'I shall take a stroll around the gardens. Amber, would you like to join me?'

Amber stood up quickly, 'I'd love to, I've been so lazy all afternoon and I need a walk after that fantastic meal. Yes, that would be great!' Amber followed Calinda and saw how the terrace could become a catwalk. Amber's own athletic, long-legged walk seemed nothing compared to the cat-like smooth way that Calinda weaved between the tables. Following in her wake, Amber caught the looks of admiration, from men and women. There was no doubt that Calinda had a magnetic attraction.Turning left, at the end of the terrace, they were soon away from the small crowd of people and walking across a cobbled courtyard.

'Daniel restored all these barns and stables… so much of the work he did himself. The first year was very hard. Now, we are established it is a little easier, we take resident guests for pottery courses, so there is always work, of course. Since I had Fleur, Daniel has taken on more and more… he works so very hard.' Calinda looked down at her baby now settled back to sleep and added softly, 'Your Papa does all the work for us, *n'est ce pas?'*

'Your English is so perfect that I had almost forgotten I was in France.' Amber said, then added, 'Daniel, too. Although he does have more of a French accent.'

'Well, of course, I studied English at school in Tunis and then I lived and worked in London before coming here. Daniel didn't speak a word of English when we met but he determined to learn… and when he decides to do something there is no stopping him. Now, of course, it is very useful with the ceramic classes and our hotel guests. They are nearly all English or American.'

'You certainly do have your hands full, apart from Fleur, I mean!' Amber laughed, trying to subdue the annoying feeling of envy that kept rising within her. How perfect a life could be when you married the right man, she thought to herself.

'And I haven't told you about the lavender farm yet. On the north side of the hotel we have fifty hectares of lavandin… and bee hives, too. Tomorrow, if you like, we could take a grand tour.'

'I'd love that… should we go early if it is going to be hot?'

'Yes, the earlier the better and you can be sure it is going to be very hot.'

6   'impatient with her own thoughts'

To: amber@hotmail.com
Cc:
Subject: still raining
From: Kim Simpson - kimS@gmail.com

Amber, I think you might be cross with me. I just took it into my head to go and see your old boss at the museum. Anyway, to cut a long story short and after he had bored my socks off with kindness, coffee and a tour of the archives… he said you could have your job back any time. They miss you and he said there is no-one that can do your work so well. OK, it looks boring to me, working at a little desk under a spotlight but… well, that's it really. Hope you're not cross with me. Everyone misses you here. x Kim

To: kimS@gmail.com
Cc:
Subject:_Not cross but…
From: Amber Marsden - amber@hotmail.com

of course I'm not cross… it was a very kind idea and has given me something to think about but…well, at the moment I'm having a great time here. This place is run by an amazing couple… sort of hotel and pottery studios. Will tell you more about everything next time I write. x Amber

    Amber woke early but the sun was already glinting through the louvred shutters. She stretched and thought back over the day before. So much that was new. From the moment she had pulled off into that lay-by it was as though she had slipped into another world. A beautiful, perfumed land of deep blue skies and bright sunshine. How could it be that only four… no, was it really only three… days ago she had been waiting in the church for Rob. Amber closed her eyes and tried to feel some trace of the anger she had felt then. Had the hot Provencal sun burnt the bitterness from her? She lay still for a moment longer and thought of her grandfather's words. A lucky escape. Would she have lived happily with Rob and was this her escape now, here in the hot Provençal landscape? Amber stretched and jumped out of bed, suddenly impatient with her own thoughts.

Half an hour later she was jogging along the track that led away from the hotel. The air was still cool but she could feel the heat of the sun on her shoulders. She turned off the track and followed a narrow path that led into a small pine forest. Now the land began to rise gently and her breathing quickened as she kept the same pace, her feet pounding rhythmically. Still running she glanced quickly to her left and took in the view across the lavender fields. The brilliant purple rows stretched away to a blue haze of infinity. Amber gave a short, whistling exhale of breath as she carried on running, almost a gasp of exasperation, as she wondered if there was any corner she could turn where there wasn't a landscape begging to be painted.

That question was abruptly answered as she came back to the hotel and ran into the courtyard. There in a shaft of sunlight, a young man, stripped to the waist, was leaning into a fountain of sparkling water. His strong muscled arms cupped the water and threw it over his head, then he turned toward Amber. It was Daniel, of course, it was Daniel. Amber, already breathless from her run, struggled to reply to his cheery greeting. Wasn't it hard enough to stand being jilted without this perfect specimen of manhood being thrust in her path?

Amber returned to her room and quickly ran a shower. The cool water ran over her as her tears streamed down her face. This was a new grief overwhelming her. The tears now were not for the loss of Rob but more the pain of thinking what might have been. Amber slowly massaged the lavender perfumed shampoo through her long hair and then stood quite still, letting the water run and run. Finally, she turned off the tap and, wrapped in the hotel's fluffy white towelling robe, she went out onto the small balcony. She vigorously rubbed her hair and her courage slowly returned. Such a beautiful day, the sun still rising, the small birds singing and flitting from tree to tree… it was impossible to remain truly miserable.

Amber's grandfather was already seated at a breakfast table on the terrace. He stood up as she approached and pulled out a chair for her.

'Bonjour, Amber! My goodness, you look rosy-cheeked. Have you been for a run already?'

'Yes, Just up to the pine forest and back round the edge of the lavender field. I've never run anywhere like it in my life. I used to think it lucky to be living near enough to run in the parks and squares of Bloomsbury. It's another planet here.' They both sat silent for a moment, each with their own thoughts of life in England carrying on without them. Then Amber added, 'I had email from Kim, she went to the museum to ask if I could have my job back.'

'Typical Kim!' Grandy laughed, 'Spontaneous, kind, loyal and totally out of order!'

'I know, but I'm so used to her being like that. Of course she shouldn't have asked without even telling me but, as you say, typical Kim.' Again there was silence. Then the waiter came up to the table and they left the subject whilst they ordered breakfast.

'Now, that's another thing I like about this place, no dreary line-up for a buffet breakfast. Proper service. That's just how it should be.'

'It is a treat, isn't it. I agree, it's not a great start to a day queuing for a bowl of cereal out of a plastic dome… I wonder if they have fresh pressed orange juice here?' Amber's question was soon answered. The waiter returned with a large silver tray laid with a pink cloth, a basket of warm croissants, a large jug of coffee, a jug of frothy milk, a small pottery bowl of jam, a pat of butter and yes, two tall glasses of fresh orange juice.

'I knew I was old but I now think I may have died and gone to a Provençal heaven!' Grandy surveyed the tray with satisfaction and began to sip the juice. 'So how do you feel about going back to your old job?'

Amber had just bitten into a flaky crescent of buttery croissant when Grandy's question suddenly fell into the air. Almost choking, Amber picked up her napkin and dabbed her mouth, playing for time before she answered. 'Actually, Grandy, the honest answer is, I just don't know. This morning seems full of confusion.'

'Hmm,' Grandy answered with his mouth full, 'There's only one thing to do in a state of confusion.'

'Do tell me!' Amber smiled, 'I am sure you are going to as soon as you have finished your second croissant, anyway.'

'You're counting, are you? Can't an old man even enjoy his breakfast in peace?' Grandy poured the coffee and passed a cup to Amber. 'This place is really stylish. Even the coffee cups are customised.'

'Are you changing the subject? Are you going to give me that gem of wisdom or not?'

'Very tempting to say - not. But, as you're my favourite grand-daughter I may reconsider.'

'Grandy, I'm your only grand-daughter.'

'True enough, well then, in my humble opinion, when feeling confused it is better to do nothing at all. Stay cool and collected and wait for the dust to settle. There, will that do for worldly wisdom? And would you pass me that bowl of cherries.'

'Maybe life is a bowl of cherries.' Amber looked at the shiny fruits filling the pale pink bowl, a perfection for a still life study.

'Now you're going all metaphysical on me, Amber. I know you... off dreaming again. What is it? An idea for another painting?'

Amber suddenly shook her head, her long damp hair flying around her shoulders as her mood lifted. Quickly she pulled her camera out of bag and before her grandfather could change his expression she clicked the shot. She looked down at the image in the small screen and laughed with delight. It was exactly the look she had wanted to catch. Her grandfather looking at her with fond intolerance.

'Ha ha, you see, I was not dreaming of a painting. Now I have you... looking at me as though I am a hopeless case.'

'And so you are, completely hopeless. Always have been. No respect for my considerable age... taking a paparazzi shot when I probably have crumbs all over me. You're a bad girl, and always have been... you just look like an angel.'

They both laughed and drank their coffee in companionable silence until Amber said in a more serious voice. 'But you're right, Grandy, I should let the dust settle. Right now I just want to enjoy things day by day.'

'Exactly, and looks as though the day is really beginning now. I can see Calinda coming toward us and we have a tour of the hotel planned.'

Amber turned and watched Calinda advance, even more beautiful in the morning sunshine, her dark skin glistening, her silky, black hair shimmering as she turned from side to side to greet her clients. She moved through the tables, charming but slightly aloof, not stopping, raising a long elegant hand occasionally in greeting and the other hand nestling her baby. Amber sighed as she thought that Calinda was possibly the most beautiful young woman she had ever known. A perfect match to Daniel. Then, her thoughts were broken into as her grandfather stood up to hold a chair ready for Calinda.

'*Bonjour*! Will you join us for a coffee?' Grandy asked as Calinda stood at the table beside them.'

'*Bonjour, mais non*, if you don't mind I should like to begin our tour as soon as possible. If you are ready, of course?' Calinda asked the question politely, her delicate eyebrows raised, but there was something about the way she spoke that made it something of an order, a royal command.

Amber smiled and stood up quickly, 'No, that would be perfect, we have finished breakfast and were just chatting. Anyway, it will be so hot soon.'

Calinda gave a flashing smile and said, 'Good, follow me, we will begin then. Daniel told me he was going to show your grandfather the lavender farm. We'll go and find him first.'

They left the terrace and Amber was very aware that all eyes were on them. It seemed that Calinda's celebrity was still a strong influence even here in the remote fields of Provence. They crossed the shady courtyard behind the hotel and then across what would have been a farmyard to a collection of barns.

'You and Daniel must have done a great deal of restoration work to get the place to this high standard.' Grandy said, as he looked admiringly at the timbered barns.

'Oh so much work, you can't imagine. All done by Daniel. He worked with a team of local men while I finished a year of my contract modelling. I came here every minute I could but that was not so very often. And, each time I did get here, there seemed to have been another transformation. He works like a trojan… and here he is!'

Daniel, hearing their voices, emerged from the nearest barn. Amber took a small breath inwards as she tried to stop her stomach butterflying madly. This was another woman's man, the father of a beautiful child, a family man… way off limits. Surely she could be allowed to admire the way his immaculate white t-shirt showed every muscle in his chest, the way his strong dark hair shone in the sunlight… no, not a good idea. Not even admiration could be allowed as now he was looking straight at her and shaking her hand. His gaze was direct and friendly with not a hint or suggestion of anything more, but still Amber's heart beat too fast for comfort. She was relieved when she realised that Calinda was talking again and quietly outlining the route of their tour.

'If Daniel and Mr. Marsden want to visit the lavender farm then Amber, Fleur and I could go through the ceramic studios… then in an hour we can all meet in the cool of the hotel lobby.'

'That sounds a very good plan, except for one thing.' Calinda looked up sharply at Grandy's words as though not expecting any objections. Grandy continued, 'I may be ancient and I am definitely a grandfather, known as Grandy, but I do possess a first name. So, in order not to make me feel even more decrepit than I am, I wish you and Daniel would call me William!'

Calinda smiled with delight, 'William, it is! Now, shall we begin?' She strode off in the direction of another barn. Amber exchanged a quick smile of amusement with her grandfather before hurrying to catch up with Calinda and Fleur.

7   *'his strong hands shaped the clay'*

To: amber@hotmail.com
Cc:
Subject: so…what?
From: Kim Simpson - kimS@gmail.com
so what do you want me to do? Shall I go and see your old boss again?

To: kimS@gmail.com
Cc:
Subject: Nothing
From: Amber Marsden - amber@hotmail.com
no… no need…not making any plans yet. Thanks anyway.

Amber knew she should write more to Kim but somehow she didn't have the energy. Lying under a large pink umbrella at the side of a sparkling blue swimming pool was just so much easier. She knew she couldn't put off making decisions forever but today was not a day to even begin. There was so much new to think about. If she had a remnant of energy she would go up to her room and find her paints. Even that, tempting as it was, seemed just a little too much trouble. Amber slid her iPad into her bag and closed her eyes. In the background she could hear the voices of children playing in the pool. Everything seemed a long way off and it would be so easy to drift into sleep. She opened one eye and looked sideways, warily checking on her grandfather. He had found a copy of yesterday's Times and was happily reading every word. The wine at lunch didn't seem to have made him sleepy. As though he sensed she was peeping at him he said,

'Are you drifting off to sleep, Amber. Why don't you have a quick dip and wake yourself up.'

'Don't you feel tired, Grandy. The wine at lunch and the heat of the sun… I can hardly keep my eyes open.'

'Plenty of time to sleep when I'm dead,' he replied, 'Seven hours a night is enough for me. There were times when I didn't need more than four or five. Go on, have a swim.'

Amber reluctantly sat up and looked at the shimmering water of the pool. It was tempting. 'Well, if I sink to the bottom like a stone you can jolly well rescue me then.'

Amber stood up and made a perfect shallow dive into the cool water. She swam under water for a few more strokes and then surfaced. She looked back to wave at her grandfather and then saw he had been joined by Daniel. Daniel in immaculate white swimming shorts, his tanned legs proving to be as muscled as his torso. Amber sank under the water and swam to the far end. As forbidden fruit went he was just about as tempting as she could bear. Sitting on the far side of the pool she started up a conversation with the mother of the children playing in the shallow end. Anything rather than return to her sun-lounger and stretch out close to where Daniel was standing. At last, Grandy raised a hand as though in agreement and Daniel turned and quickly dived into the pool. Amber watched mesmerised as his body slipped through the blue water with the agility of a fish. Was there anything wrong with this man apart from the fact he was happily married? Refreshed by her swim determined not to think one more minute about the unobtainable Daniel, Amber returned to her room and found her paints.

'We haven't discussed it, Amber, but I wonder if you want to stay on here for a few days or head on down to the coast?'

Amber looked at her grandfather in surprise.

'Goodness, I hadn't thought about it? What do you want to do, Grandy?' They were sitting after dinner, enjoying the warm night air.

'No, no, completely your decision. I am happy to do either.'

Amber thought for a moment. The day had been perfect. Calinda has shown her the artist's studios and she had met a few of the residents. The ceramic work was more advanced than she had imagined. Several potters were working on large sculptural pieces, others were throwing perfect pots on the wheel. Nothing was further than the typical Provencal pottery she had expected to find. Daniel, in particular, had been working on a large construction for a fountain. She had watched fascinated as his strong hands shaped the clay leaves that were part of the design. Yes, fascinated.

'I do love it here,' Amber replied, hastily dragging her thoughts away from the image of Daniel. 'But maybe we should carry on south tomorrow. What do you really think, Grandy?'

'Well, I could happily spend the rest of my life here but I was thinking we could go down to the coast for a few days and book rooms here next week. Come back this way? Would that work, do you think?'

'Sounds a perfect plan. Should I go and get my iPad and look for a hotel on the coast?'

'Well, actually… ' Grandy hesitated and then gave one of his wicked smiles, 'I was talking to Calinda earlier and she recommended a place in La Ciotat.'

'So I am guessing you booked it, right?'

'Well, only provisionally, of course, I was waiting to see what you wanted to do.'

'Of course you did. Grandy, you're a dreadful schemer but it is very relaxing and I am truly grateful.'

'Jolly good. After what you've been through I think it's a good idea just to let go and relax.'

Amber was about to thank him again when she saw Calinda making her way toward them. 'Calinda's coming our way. Little Fleur in her sling as usual. Do you think it's a good idea, Grandy, carrying her baby around all the time?'

'I think it's an excellent idea. It seems to me that Calinda is a very intelligent and determined young woman. I saw her practicing yoga with Fleur earlier this afternoon.'

'Really!' Amber opened her eyes wide at the thought, but before she could reply, Calinda had joined them.

'*Bonsoir*, William, *bonsoir* Amber! I hope you have enjoyed your meal?'

'The meal was perfect. Will you join us for coffee?' Grandy stood up and held a chair in readiness.

'Actually, I was wondering if you would come to our apartment and take coffee there. Daniel is still out delivering but he should be back soon. There is something I should like to ask your advice about, William.'

'Delighted!' Grandy looked enquiringly at Amber and she stood up quickly.

'Of course, that would be great!'

Once again they followed in Calinda's path and then to the lift in the hotel lobby.

'We have turned the attic floor into our own living accommodation.' Calinda said as the lift whisked them up three floors. The doors then opened straight into a stunning hallway, paved with creamy, white tiles and opening onto a huge, open-plan living area. Amber drew in her breath in surprise and admiration. The whole area was cool and silent. '*Bienvenus!* This is where we hide out from our guests. It is our retreat!' Calinda waved her long arm around her head and for the first time began to slowly unwind the soft cotton sling that held the sleeping Fleur. Carefully, Calinda laid the baby in the middle of a very large, white sofa. She turned to Amber and her grandfather and said with a flashing smile.

'Isn't she just perfect!'

They slowly advanced and looked at the baby lying so quietly, one arm outstretched toward Calinda.

'I don't think I've ever seen a more beautiful and contented baby before.' Amber said, her voice quiet and thoughtful.

'That is because we never let her cry. She is always happy. That is how I want her to grow up.' Calinda spoke with an even more determined voice than usual.

'She certainly seems happy, but you know, you mustn't worry too much. I know it's difficult with a first baby.' Said Grandy thoughtfully.

'Ah, you understand exactly!' Calinda turned to Amber, 'How lucky you are to have such a grandfather,'

'Indeed I am,' agreed Amber.

'Now, why don't you girls go and make the coffee and I'll sit right here beside Fleur and keep a good eye on her.'

Calinda drew in her breath sharply. 'I have never let her out of my sight yet.'

'Well, now is a good chance. I am perfectly used to handling babies but anyway, she is sound asleep and you will be nearby.'

Calinda looked startled, her dark eyes regarding Grandy with alarm, then, biting her lip, she nodded and walked slowly away. Amber followed her in some confusion. When they reached the kitchen, just a narrow galley off the side of the living area, Calinda spoke quietly.

'I think your grandfather understands everything. He has guessed that I had a very difficult childhood. It is almost as though he knows all my fears.'

Amber reached out and rested her hand lightly on Calinda's slender shoulder. 'Talk about it if you want, you can trust me. What is it that worries you so much?'

Calinda busied herself with making coffee and then quickly looked round the corner of the kitchen to check on Fleur. 'She is still asleep and your grandfather is watching over her. This is a big moment for me. I know it is hard to understand. Daniel is the only person in the world who knows everything in my past. But I will tell you one day. It is not a happy story.'

Amber remained silent, waiting for Calinda to continue, but at that moment the lift doors opened and Daniel came into sight.

'*Bonsoir, tout le monde!*' he called out, his loud, happy voice filling the quiet space and dispersing the dark troubles that hung around Calinda. Her face lit with joy and she ran to greet him.

'*Regardes, Daniel!* Fleur is so happy sleeping with William looking after her!'

Daniel looked down fondly at the sleeping baby. '*Bravo*, William! I have been trying for three months now to persuade my beautiful wife that Fleur will survive for five minutes without her!'

They all laughed and the atmosphere lightened. Calinda brought through the coffee tray and they sat round a low table. Amber noticed that Calinda sat very close to her baby but she seemed more relaxed now that Daniel was back home. Momentarily she wondered what could have happened in Calinda's childhood that had made her so insecure. It was so opposite to her general composure and confidence. Then she realised the conversation had turned to business.

'When we realised that you were the William Marsden, we thought it too good an opportunity to miss. I know it very cheeky of us but we are in serious need of some business advice right now.I hope you don't mind?' Daniel leaned forward and spoke earnestly, his dark eyebrows drawn into a worried frown.

'Not at all, an old man like me enjoys the attention. So, what is your problem. It seems to me that you are running a very good business here already… is it cash flow?'

'No, we are doing very well, better than we had dreamed. But, well, the thing is we have had an offer from a chain of hotels… it seems a good offer but…'

Calinda interrupted Daniel. 'Yes, it seems a good offer but we really don't know if it is. We have put everything into this place… not just every cent of our money but all our energy and ideas. Daniel has worked so hard and…'

Now Daniel interrupted Calinda. 'But the money has been all Calinda's, the small fortune she made from modelling and still makes from sponsorship and advertising… she has put everything into this place.'

'Stop, hold on a moment,' Grandy held up his hand and, at the same moment, Fleur stirred. Calinda quickly picked her up and moved across the room and sat in a chair by the window to feed her. Daniel looked across at them and continued to talk in a quieter voice.

'We are very tempted, William. The work here is tremendous, completely time-consuming. We have very little time together now. When we began we thought it would be a quiet life. A life we were both seeking together. As Fleur gets older and maybe we have more children, we want to have time to simply play with them and enjoy our family life. Here, at the hotel it is very difficult to have any privacy, Calinda particularly needs that. The life she led in London was frantic. Even here she is a famous figure, everybody wants a moment with her… still the exotic Calinda of the world's catwalk.' Daniel spoke even more quietly, 'And she had a very hard childhood in Tunis. All I want is for her to be quiet, safe and happy.'

Amber looked at his serious face, now without the slightest feeling of desire. This man belonged to Calinda and Fleur, he belonged to them more than she could possibly imagine. She was about to say something when Grandy spoke first.

'I can see you are going through some sort of dilemma. I was only saying to Amber, earlier today, when there are hard decisions to be made it is best to be calm and think things through quietly. I suggest that you and Calinda write down as many things about this offer that you can think of… not just the exact financial terms but every last thing you can think of… everything.'

'Make a list of pros and cons!' Amber added, 'that's a good start.'

'Exactly,' Grandy looked at Amber and nodded, 'Amber and I are going to leave in the morning and, if you can fit us in, then we should like to come back again after a few days. That will give you time to get everything sorted in your own minds and prepare a resumé of your accounts, put together anything at all that you think relevant. Then we'll have a proper meeting and I'll give you as good advice as I possibly can. How does that seem?'

'there are some advantages of being wealthy'

To: amber@hotmail.com
Cc:
Subject: still raining
From: Kim Simpson - kimS@gmail.com
See the same heading as my last…yes, it is still like monsoon without the heat here in dear old Blighty. So little news from you that I am just hoping its because you're having a good time. Our flat… you do remember our little flat, don't you… was so empty without you that I have let Mike sort of move in. Don't worry he is under threat of death not to touch anything of yours. I keep your bedroom like a shrine, of course. When do you expect to be back? x

To: kimS@gmail.com
Cc:
Subject: hi
From: Amber Marsden - amber@hotmail.com
sorry not to have written but there is just so much going on here. We've been staying on at the same hotel… very friendly with the owners now. Grandy has been asked to give them some business advice. I guess that may happen often although I had never realised before how successful in business he was/is - he seemed quite ok about it anyway. We are moving on today in the direction of the blue Med and then plan to come back here next week. Sorry not to be able to give return date to London but I am also taking Grandy's advice and doing nothing except let the dust settle. Very relaxing and I am very lucky to have such a grandfather and also a friend like you. Good luck with living with Mike - don't do anything I would do - like get engaged x Amber

Amber closed down her iPad and placed it in her bag. She was packed, ready to go. She looked around the room to check she hadn't left anything. Although she was looking forward to getting to the sea she felt a strong reluctance to leave. She sat on the balcony for a while, thinking back through the last few days and then her thoughts turned to Kim's last email. The truth was, she realised suddenly, Kim was right to ask if she remembered the little flat they shared. It did seem ridiculously hard to imagine living again in Bloomsbury, running every day in the leafy squares, the cold London climate, the traffic and noise. Amber shook her head, impatient with her own thoughts. Of course she would return and yes, probably retrieve her old job and work again under that spotlight in the dark museum studio. Of course she would… but when? That was a question she just could not answer. Amber stood up quickly and, with a last fond glance at her room, she ran downstairs to join her grandfather for breakfast.

An hour later they were bowling along a small country road in the general direction of the Mediterranean sea.

'I love these gadgets,' Grandy said as he fiddled around with the sat-nav. 'Ah, this is it, I've keyed in 'scenic route'. Is that all right with you? We're in no hurry and the motorway south is a boring way to go.'

'I'm just the driver, you're the navigator, I realise that.' Amber smiled, not realising that her smile was a younger, prettier version of her grandfather's wicked smiles.

'I hope, young madam, that you are not inferring that I boss you around?'

'Not at all, you don't boss, you just manipulate.'
'Now that is downright slanderous!'

'You don't really think I am so stupid as not to realise you had planned to stay at that hotel… that you knew exactly where it was and just pretended to find it by chance?"

'Hmm, all right, you have found me out there. I have to admit that maybe I had a little idea before we left that it might just be a good place to stay… break our journey south…' Grandy's words petered out.

'Little idea? Grandy, just admit it… you knew the place was on the market. I bet you found it somehow on the internet. You knew a bid had been made on it.'

'Very well, I confess, I break down under your interrogation! I do actually know the boss of the hotel chain that are making the take-over bid. I've known him quite a while and he is a slippery character. We used to play poker together in my wilder days.'

'Poker, yes, I can see that you would have been very good at playing poker, keeping all your cards close to your chest.'

'Well, I certainly wouldn't have wanted to see you across the table. You may be a dreamer but you're a shrewd young woman. Maybe that dreamy look is just a double bluff?'

'Well, I was taken in by Rob, wasn't I? I can't be that shrewd. I realise each day that passes that I was a complete fool, an idiot.' Amber slammed her hand on the driving wheel in anger.

'Maybe, but probably a young girl's prerogative to be a little foolish in love. We'd better talk about that another time. I know I said it was good to use your anger but please don't take it out on the car. Look, just by chance, there's a roadside café coming up in five hundred metres, perhaps we should stop until you cool down.'

'No way, Grandy, no more of your just-by-chances, I'm on to you now. Don't worry that was only a brief moment of self hate and anger. I'm fine now and if I am not mistaken I just caught a glimpse of a very deep, blue sea on the horizon.' As the car rounded the top of a hill the glimpse suddenly became a breath-taking wide view of the sparkling Mediterranean.

'Now that is what I call a sea!' Grandy said with a sigh of satisfaction. 'Ah, there's nothing quite like the Med, your grandmother and I mis-spent our youth along this trashy stretch of coast. Whatever is thrown at it somehow it manages to hang on to its very own magic.'

'I know, of course there are many less spoilt parts of Europe but the Côte d'Azur, the French Riviera... just the names are exciting. Oh Grandy, how you must miss Grandma.'

'Every single day, my dear, every morning when I awake and every night just before I fall asleep. The hours in between pass by happily enough and I am lucky to have you to remind me of her. Such a strong family resemblance that has emerged, skipping a generation.'

'I know, Dad always says we look alike but sadly I hardly remember Grandma, I was too young when she died so suddenly.'

'I know, I know, and how she adored you, Amber. She gave you that little doll's tea-set. Do you remember that?'

'Strangely enough I do have some sort of memory of her, just a vague image of her face looking at me as I opened the box. Yes, I do sort of... it's so frustrating not remembering clearly though.'

'All family memories are important.' Grandy paused briefly and then added, 'I feel so deeply sorry for Calinda.'

The change in the subject of their conversation made Amber give a quick glance to her grandfather. She saw his face was very sad and serious.

'What do you mean, Grandy?' Amber concentrated on the road ahead which was now weaving downhill.

'When you had your early morning run this morning, I met up with Calinda picking cherries in the orchard behind the farm. We had a long chat.'

'Was she still carrying Fleur in her sling even when she was picking cherries?'

'Oh yes, she has to keep her close and now I begin to understand why... it's a sad story.'

'I realised there was something in her childhood that made her so... well, not exactly neurotic but so very anxious.'

'She told me that when she was a child, living in a village near Tunis, that her little sister went missing.'

Amber gasped with shock. 'Do you mean she was never found?'

'Never found.' Grandy spoke the two words so quietly and sadly that Amber hardly heard him. 'We'll speak of it again later as I am still thinking it all through. Right now, we have arrived at your Côte d'Azur. Let's hope that Calinda's hotel recommendation is good. Has the sat-nav given up on us or what? Shall I…'

'You have arrived at your destination. Hotel de la Plage.' The precise voice of the sat-nav interrupted him and Amber drew the car in to the side of the road. There was a shabby hotel overlooking a good stretch of sandy beach.

'Do you think this is it then?' Amber asked doubtfully, well aware that her grandfather was used to the best in hotels.

'Afraid so… yes, Hotel de la Plage, this is it. Now, trust me for a while longer. Why don't you take your swim things straight to the beach and I'll go and see about checking in. Then…'

'No need to tell me, Grandy, then we can meet for lunch at that restaurant on the beach, just in sight. What exactly are you up to now?'

'Nothing my dear, nothing at all. Just have a good swim and we'll talk over lunch. How can you resist all that sparkling, blue water stretching as far as Africa?'

'It certainly does look tempting. OK, Grandy, you win. I'll just grab my beach bag and off you go to cook up your next plot. See you for lunch then.' Amber threw her grandfather the car keys and, grabbing her beach bag, she jumped out of the car and ran across the sand. She turned to wave but her grandfather had already turned the car and was heading for the hotel entrance. She waved her sunhat in the air, enjoying the heat of the sun and the sand beneath her bare feet. There was an answering toot of a car horn and Amber laughed aloud, thinking there was nothing that Grandy ever missed.

The sea was simply perfect. Warm enough to relax and float and yet with cool, deep undercurrents. Amber was a strong swimmer and moved easily through the gentle waves. She swam underwater, watching the myriad of tiny, silver fish that swirled around her. Surfacing she trod water and looked back to the coast and to the inland hills. Somewhere up there, Calinda, Daniel and little Fleur were carrying on with their daily life at the Hotel Lavande. Then she looked at the Hotel de la Plage. If location was everything then this place had it. Surrounded by palm trees and luxuriant green vegetation, it looked as though it had been there since the heydays of life on the Riviera. Possibly built in the 1920's, Amber thought, and maybe not painted since. The pale, pink walls were peeling and, even from this distance, she could tell the place was dreadfully neglected. Idly, as she began to swim slowly through the water, she wondered why Calinda had recommended it. Then she fastened her pace and began a long swim parallel to the coast. As she worked her muscles and forced her way faster and faster through the sea she forgot to think about anything else... just the movement and the sea.

An hour later, pleasantly exhausted and very hungry she was sitting in the beach restaurant waiting for her grandfather. It was the sort of restaurant that any hungry traveller would dream of finding. Blue and white striped awning, small wooden tables covered with white cotton tablecloths, slatted wooden deck flooring just above the sand... the smell of garlic and charcoal grilled food. Amber sat at a table for two, close to the water's edge and luxuriated in the moment. A waiter hovered and she ordered a carafe of wine and a bottle of Evian. Then she saw Grandy making his way from the hotel, along the beach toward her. This time he waved his old panama in the air and she stood up and went to meet him.

'I've taken a table... you did want to eat here, didn't you?' Amber asked.

'It looks to me as if it would be a big mistake in life not to eat right here! Jolly good, some cold wine waiting. Pour me a glass, I could do with it, I can tell you!'

'What's up, Grandy, you're not usually so desperate for a slug of alcohol! What on earth have you been up to now?'

'Well, this time I'm going to come clean straightaway but it's quite a long story so let's order lunch. I'm starving and you must be too.'

'Ravenous, I had a great swim, the water is perfect.'

They ordered quickly, deciding to share a local speciality called *bourride*. 'Are you sure it's like paella?' Amber asked, wrinkling her forehead as she looked again at the menu. 'You know it's as though we have really just arrived in France. At the hotel with Calinda and Daniel speaking English all the time and with most of their clients being English or American, it just didn't strike me as very French.'

'Well, you'll know we're truly in France at the Hotel de la Plage. Ah, here it comes, that was fast service… ah yes, not paella, more like *bouillabaisse*, that's what I meant.'

Amber breathed in the delicate aroma of seafood and herbs that rose from the large tureen that had been placed ceremoniously on the table between them.

'It smells fantastic and right now I don't care what it's called! Lovely new bread, too.' Amber took up the large ladle and served her grandfather and then herself. They both ate in silence for a moment.

'Mmm, mmm, so yummy! Now Grandy, just what exactly did you mean about this hotel being truly French?'

'Well, it's no good pretending it's luxurious. I suppose it was, once upon a time, now it hangs onto a little faded elegance but…'

'Grandy had you better start by telling me why we are staying there and why Calinda recommended it especially.'

'Well, to cut to the chase, as they say in the movies, Calinda and Daniel are thinking of buying it. Calinda rather hoped I would give it a try and see what I thought.'

'Buy it! But… I mean…wouldn't it cost a small fortune here right on the coast…even though it does look dilapidated.'

'Yes, you're right of course, and it all depends on the offer made on the Hotel Lavande. Calinda longs to be by the sea and Daniel seems to want to give her everything he can. He's a great guy. Kind and strong. He understands Calinda.'

'You haven't finished telling me about her sister.'

'There is little more to be said. But I have the beginning of an idea in my old head.'

'What do you mean?'

'Well, there are some advantages of being wealthy.'

'I don't get it, Grandy. I mean, I know you made a lot of money with your old boxes but what does that have to do with it? It's been strange these last few days being with you and realising how much you have done with your life. I suppose I have always just thought of you as Grandy, kind and generous, but just my Grandy living in a cottage in our valley in Sussex.'

'Then your Mum and Dad have made a very good job of doing exactly as I asked them on the day you were born. The fact is, Amber, I made a ridiculous amount of money out of my boxes and then I went in to biodegradable and then waste disposal... and at just the right time... so you see, I am seriously rich. However, and your Mum and Dad agree with me on this, we never wanted you to have a trust fund. We all agree that it is best you make your own way in life. When I pop my clogs my money will be going to charities across the globe.'

Amber looked at her grandfather in astonishment, her fork held in suspense above her food.

'You look shocked but it's time you knew. The rest of the world probably know more about my money than you do. You do understand about my leaving everything to charity, don't you. I know it may seem hard but...'

'No, no, Grandy, of course I understand and it is absolutely the right thing to do. I'm just so shocked. I had no idea you were really rich.'

'Well, that's exactly how I wanted it to be. I have several friends in the same echelons of money, some self-made like me, and I have seen the disastrous effect a trust fund can have on a kid. The expectation, the waiting for an inheritance... all leading to a dreadful uselessness of their own young lives. I hope you do understand. Of course, you'll never be penniless... when I go I intend to leave you the cottage and a few keepsakes… like that old broken tea cup. Now, let me finish my lunch, because I have a whole lot more to tell you yet.'

Amber sat back in her seat looking across the table at her grandfather. He looked just the same as ever as he spooned his soup and chewed his bread. But she realised she was also looking at an experienced business tycoon, a man who gained respect and admiration all over the world.

'This is going to take me a while to understand, Grandy. How on earth could I have been so naive not to realise your place in the world. You're just my Grandy!'

'True on two counts, my dear. Now I want to get over telling you something rather more difficult. But I want to get it over with now. Yes, it is true you have been rather naive and of course, I am just your old adoring Grandy. That's why it makes it hard to tell you something more.'

Amber was about to make a joke but she saw her grandfather's face was very serious and stern in a way she hadn't seen before.

'Go on, Grandy, you're scaring me now.'

'Nothing to be scared of, my dear, no, no… but it's a hard truth about Rob.'

'Rob, how on earth does he come into the picture?' Amber felt herself losing touch with reality as she sat in the beach restaurant with her life revolving around her. Rob, the man she should have married only a few days ago. Not even a week had gone by yet. What had he to do with anything that Grandy had just told her?

'Yes, Rob Brodie, your ex-fiancé.' Grandy reached out and gently took Amber's hand in his own as he continued quietly, 'Did you ever discuss a pre-nuptial agreement with Rob?'

Amber shook her head and then nodded as she suddenly remembered. There had been a night, before they were engaged, when they had talked about some friends who were marrying with a pre-nuptial agreement. They had both laughed and agreed that neither of them had any money to worry about. With the memory came a sudden dreadful but slow realisation. Amber pressed Grandy's hand but made no reply.

'Actually, my dear girl, I know you didn't. In my position I have people around me who find out these things and act accordingly. I'm afraid to say that Rob Brodie was allowed to discover that my will left all my wealth to charity.'

Amber jumped up from the table and ran across the beach. She ran the entire sweep of the bay before she threw herself down on the sand. She cried until her tears ran dry and then slowly she walked into the sea and swam calmly back until she was parallel to the beach restaurant. She walked slowly out of the sea and stood for a while in the shallows, feeling completely exhausted. She looked up to the blue and white striped awnings and saw her grandfather was still there, sitting at the table waiting for her. She raised a tired arm in greeting and saw him raise his hat in return.

9   *'wasn't exactly attractive but then he wasn't unattractive either'*

To: amber@hotmail.com
Cc:
Subject: at last…some pale sunshine in London
From: Kim Simpson - kimS@gmail.com
Still no news from you. I called your mother today and she said you did call her most evenings and that you were fine.
Thanks for telling me! No, only joking, Amber. I absolutely understand if you don't write … just hope you are having a good time. Love, Kim

To: kimS@gmail.com
Cc:
Subject: hi
From: Amber Marsden - amber@hotmail.com
Thanks for understanding. It's not that I don't want to tell you everything more that I don't know where to begin. Grandy has filled me in today on a few home truths. One thing for sure, I am no longer the smallest bit in love with Rob. I'll explain more when I see you but just to say he was more of an effing b*stard than I thought possible. It's going to be a very long time before I let myself get involved again. I am just going to enjoy myself and not care about anything. Anyway, it is much too wonderful over here to be miserable. Sun, sea, sand and… well, that's enough for now.
x Amber

Amber and her grandfather spent a quiet afternoon in the gardens of the hotel. Amber had set up her small painting easel and made several watercolours, detailed studies of the tropical jungle of vibrant flowers and large leafed plants. As she worked, concentrating on mixing the colours and closely studying the beauty of nature, she felt a return to calm after the earlier shock and emotion. The horrid idea that Rob, the man she had loved so well, was actually a gold-digger was hard to bear. She needed time to accept the whole dreadful idea. Time was what she had been given like a magic gift from her grandfather. She looked across to him where he lay stretched out of a dilapidated rattan lounger, reading the Financial Times. He looked up at her across the top of the newspaper.

'Better outside than in, this place!'

'Certainly is!' Amber laughed, 'Did you try the plumbing in the shower yet?'

'What plumbing? You have plumbing in your bathroom? I knew I should have taken that suite all decked out in gold and pink!'

'Ah well, famous film stars have slept in my room!'

'So they said, silent movie film stars, I should think, and they haven't decorated since.'

Amber laughed and picked up her brush again and Grandy returned to his close examination of the world's finances. They passed another hour in happy silence and then Grandy made a move.

'If I stay here any longer I shall turn into an antique statue. I think I'll give another go at taking a shower. Don't stay too long down here, now that the sun is going down the bugs are beginning to bite.'

'I'm packing up right now. If I have any luck with my shower I'll come and tell you.'

'Just give a light tap on the wall, I can hear everything… I even heard your music earlier! 'Take me to Church' indeed. I wondered how you could play that track?'

'Fortunately I have a very black sense of humour.' Amber pulled a grimace at her grandfather and then changed it to one of her own wicked smiles. 'I probably inherited it from you. By the way, before you start planning our evening, I am way ahead of you. We're going to take a taxi into Cassis… I've looked it up and booked a table at a well-reviewed restaurant, Le Bateau Noir, and tonight is live jazz night. No arguments, Grandy, it's my turn to boss.'

Her grandfather raised his arms in mock submission. 'Absolutely delighted, my dear, I certainly hadn't planned on eating in the hotel here tonight. Delighted to accept.' He bowed and then walked slowly into the shabby doorway of the hotel.

'Taxi at seven!' Amber called after him. Then she quickly pulled out her camera and managed to take a shot of her grandfather, just as he turned to raise his panama hat at her. Amber smiled with satisfaction as she looked at the image held for a moment in the camera screen.

The taxi was punctual. The taxi was also driven fast and furiously by a wild-haired, young man wearing a Gothic cross.

'You want autoroute or old road to Cassis?' He turned to ask them, as he swung the taxi around a roundabout. Amber glanced hastily at her grandfather but he was saying nothing,

'The old road, *s'il vous plaît!*' she answered quickly, grabbing the leather strap that swung beside her head. The car lurched as the taxi driver turned to look back at the road ahead and swerved to narrowly avoid an oncoming lorry.

'Ok, no problem!' Route des Crêtes! The taxi driver replied cheerily and then, turning the radio on full blast he settled happily into his seat. They drove through the port and then the road began to climb and get narrower. Still the pop music was blaring and the car was travelling too fast for the small road.

Grandy leant forward and tapped the driver firmly on the shoulder, saying in a quiet commanding voice, 'No music, slow speed, extra ten euros in Cassis, OK, no problem?'

Amber caught a glimpse in the driving mirror of the astonished face of the driver. She almost laughed aloud as the driver raised his hand to his wild hair as though to touch his non-existent cap.

'Yes sir, slow slow sir. I am very good driver.' He switched off the music and settled to a slow speed.

'Now we can enjoy the views, look down there, Amber, we're above the port and you can see the huge, white cliffs ahead.'

The narrow road was now so high that the view down could have been from an aeroplane. Amber craned her neck to look from side to side and remarkably it seemed the sea was spread wide on both sides. Were they soaring across the Mediterranean? The car began to gather speed and drew uncomfortably close to the rear of a motor-caravan in front of them. The taxi driver began to weave in and out, attempting to overtake, at moments so close that Amber could see every detail of the bikes strapped to the back of the van. She clutched the seat in front of her and held her breath. Grandy leaned forward and tapped the driver again on his shoulder. Immediately the taxi slowed and the van drew ahead. Amber sighed with relief and once again began to take in the incredible views on both sides. Grandy laughed and patted her hand,

'Didn't you ever see a film called Taxi 2? I suddenly remembered it when the driver suggested the Route des Crêtes. I had a suspicion we were in for a very scenic ride.'

'No, don't think I know the film but you were right about scenic... it's simply amazing. I didn't know any stretch of the Med round here was so rocky... wonderful red rocks mixed with creamy white. I have to bring my camera up here... and my paints.'

'And why not? The whole world is here for the taking, Amber. Anyway, we seem to be going downhill now and that must be Cassis, the harbour at the bottom of those cliffs.'

'So beautiful... with the sun just setting now. No wonder it was chosen for a film setting. Was it romantic?'

'Hmm, not as I recall... more Marseilles gangs and Japanese crime scene. But I am sure there is romance to be found.'

'Don't even think about it, please Grandy. I've had enough romance to last me a life time.' Amber gave a heavy sigh and allowed her thoughts to slide back a week to the happy time when she was so in love with Rob. The sad thoughts were still with her when they were sitting in a restaurant on the edge of the small harbour of Cassis. She watched the boats bobbing up and down in a sea turned to dark gold as the sun made its final bid to heat the day.

Her grandfather poured her a large glass of cold wine and raised his glass to her. 'Good choice, Amber, really great little restaurant, couldn't be better, good health.' Amber was about to raise her glass to his when a voice from the next table interrupted,

'Good to hear a Brit voice! Cheers!' It was a very American voice belonging to a young man at the next table. He continued, 'Sorry to interrupt, very American of me, I know.'

Amber sighed as her grandfather took up the conversation. 'Not at all! Pleased to meet you. Are you on holiday here?'

'No, working like dogs in fact and this is an unusual night out. My name's Sam Robinson and this is my friend and colleague, Matt Winston. We are working in Sophia Antipolis just up the road.'

'Ah, of course, the silicon valley of the Côte d'Azur. Have you worked there long? Grandy began a friendly conversation with the two young men about their work. Amber remained silent but gave a quick glance through her lashes at the two men as they answered her grandfather's questions. Obviously very well-mannered and educated in a smooth American way. It seemed one did all the talking whilst the other smiled and nodded. The one called Sam wasn't exactly attractive but then he wasn't unattractive either. He caught her eye and she realised that Grandy was now introducing her.

'This is Amber and my name is William, we're just here on holiday.' Amber forced a smile and took up the menu, pointedly hiding behind it, in an attempt to end the conversation. There was no stopping Sam the talker. 'Did you come here for the music tonight?'

'Well, Amber made the booking, is that why you chose this place?' Her grandfather looked at her and she was forced to reply.

'Well partly, the place has good reviews online. Is there often live music?'

'Oh yeh, every Friday night there's a great soul band that plays here. Do you like soul, Amber?'

'Well, yes, actually I do.' Amber finally looked at Sam and was surprised to find his eyes were an unusual pale grey and that he was more attractive than she had realised. 'I didn't expect to find it here.' She looked back at the menu, trying to hide her confusion. Not only were his eyes fascinating but the way he drawled her name was strangely appealing. Then the waiter appeared and they ordered their food. Grandy continued the conversation about the new technology and research that the young men were working on. Amber stayed silent again, trying to remind herself that she was the walking wounded in the land of sunsets, bobbing fishing boats and young American men. When their food arrived Sam politely wished them '*bon appetit'* in a good French-sounding accent and then left them to eat. When their desserts were served the two young men had finished and paid their bill. Sam stood up and Amber couldn't help but glance at his commanding height and big-boned frame as he leant over their table and said,

'Hope to see you later, the music starts about ten usually… we'll be back for that.'

Amber watched as they walked away across the harbour. Sam was much taller than Matt and walked with a confident stride.

'Nice young men, both of them… obviously experts in their field.'

'Yes,' Amber agreed, 'what exactly is this Sophia place they were talking about?'

'It's a huge development near or rather behind Antibes, a technology park surrounded by high rise apartment blocks. I've never been there but I think JG Ballard's great book Super Cannes is based on the community there.'

'Oh, right, I remember reading that. Wow, must be a strange place to work.'

'They seemed fairy archetypical Harvard lads, don't you think? Very Ivy League!'

Amber laughed, 'Very typical, both wearing short sleeved, nicely ironed Tommy Hilfiger check shirts, chinos… also well-pressed …and the obligatory Gucci loafers… very shiny.' They both laughed and began to sip the coffee that had now been brought to their table. Amber's laughter turned to a smile as she allowed herself a small moment to wonder whether Sam was attractive or... or not?

An hour later she was dancing with Matt while Sam watched from the bar. Matt had some good moves and, whether it was the vodka and orange, he now seemed to have lost his shyness. A small band played at the far end of the crowded cellar and Amber could only just see over the tops of the heads of the other dancers. There was a girl vocalist and a saxophonist who seemed to be leading. The music was very loud, reverberating off the vaulted walls and low ceiling. Amber gave herself up to the joy of the moment, moving to the strong beat with a feeling of liberation. Life was sweeping her along, the beauty of the Provencal scenery, new friends, the hot sun, Grandy's love and now the strong rhythm of the music. She closed her eyes and danced as she had never danced before. When the music ended she joined in the applause and calls for an encore. She looked at Matt and smiled but he was looking toward Sam who seemed to be propping up the bar. As the music began again Amber began to dance, not caring now if she was dancing all on her own. Then Matt was joined by a pretty girl in a vibrant pink dress and suddenly, Sam was standing in front of her, smiling and holding out his hand. She moved into his arms as the music took on a new, slow tempo. Sam held her lightly, not too close, but with a strong hand on her back. Amber was aware of the heat of his hand through the thin cotton of her dress. Before she had time to even question whether she liked the feeling or not, he was talking in his low, soft drawl.

'Amber, you're quite a mover. Matt loves to dance, too. I have two left feet so be gentle with me please!'

Amber arched her back and looked up at him. He was very tall and his eyes really were very grey and fringed with dark lashes. Yes, she thought to herself, he could definitely be classed as attractive.

'It seems to me that you are a very smooth mover, Sam.' Amber smiled and allowed herself to flirt. Why not?

They danced together for the next two songs, hardly moving around the small cellar dance floor. Slowly Sam drew her nearer to him and Amber rested her head on his chest, letting the music take her away from everything. When the piece ended they drew apart and joined the clapping.

'I must get back to my grandfather.'

Sam looked at her in surprise, 'Your grandfather, William is your grandfather? I thought…'

Amber's cheeks flushed pink, 'Oh my god, you thought I was…well, with him? You thought he was my sugar-daddy? They both burst out laughing at the word and her indignation.

'I'm sorry, I don't know what I thought, I mean, he is obviously old but he's a good-looking, powerful old guy…' Sam faltered to a halt.

'Don't worry, I can see where you are coming from although obviously…' Amber was about to continue when suddenly she stopped short, her face registering shock. The dance floor had begun to clear and Amber saw the band for the first time. The girl singer was chatting to the saxophonist and standing close beside her was none other than Daniel. Amber raised her hand and was about to call out when Daniel put his arm around the girl and kissed her. Not a friendly kiss but a passionate, long embrace. Amber felt sick and hurriedly moved out of sight to the other side of the bar. Sam followed her and she realised he was looking at her anxiously.

'Are you OK? You're very pale.' Sam stood beside her and then ordered a glass of water. Amber sipped it gratefully as she tried to take in what she had witnessed. Her thoughts flew up to the hills where the fragile Calinda would be sitting, holding Fleur close. Sam was still looking at her with a frown on his wide, smooth forehead.

'I'm sorry, I just thought I saw someone I knew.' Amber could think of nothing more to say.

'Amber, you're a girl of mystery. Come on, let's go and find your grandfather.' He put his arm gently around her shoulders and steered her toward the cellar stairs. When they emerged into the restaurant, the tables were still full of people laughing and talking. Amber looked across to the table where she had left her grandfather and was surprised to see him talking animatedly to a group of people. As she approached with Sam, Grandy stood up,

'Ah, here is my grand-daughter at last. Just before midnight, like Cinderella!' The group all laughed and looked up at Amber. She smiled and raised a hand in a general form of greeting, then took Grandy's arm.

'We should be going, Grandy, sorry to keep you waiting.'

'Hey there, Cinderella… you can't escape just like that. You haven't even left me a shoe… how can I find you again?' Sam smiled at Amber and then at her grandfather. 'Do you have any plans for tomorrow? Matt and I have a boat in the harbour here and we mean to take a picnic and swim a little. Would you join us?' Sam addressed the invitation more to Grandy than directly to Amber and he answered first,

'That sounds like a very tempting idea… can I call you in the morning?'

'Absolutely, here's my card.' Sam quickly pulled a card from his wallet and then smiled at Amber. 'Thank you for making my evening outstanding and I hope to see you tomorrow. There are some wonderful deep bays just round the corner from Cassis. The swimming is great.'

'Thanks, as my grandfather said, very tempting indeed. We'll call you in the morning… is ten too early?'

'Not at all, I shall be up and running at eight am at the latest. I'll be waiting for your call. Phone as early as you like.' He ducked his head down suddenly and gave Amber a light kiss on her cheek.

10 *'the drops of water, like teardrops in his dark lashes'*

To: amber@hotmail.com
Cc:
Subject: raining again
From: Kim Simpson - kimS@gmail.com
Amber, you sure know how to be annoying....ok ...joking again... but saying you have so much to tell me and then not telling me... well, it is just a tad annoying. Here I am stuck in grey and grimy London... give me a break... tell me something/anything interesting. x Kim

To: kimS@gmail.com
Cc:
Subject: hi
From: Amber Marsden - amber@hotmail.com
OKAAAY. you asked for interesting... here goes. I've met an American guy named Sam, very classy Harvard type, works near Antibes, has boat... going out with him tomorrow... Grandy too! Ha ha...is that good enough for you?
x Amber

Amber had slept badly, tossing and turning all night trying to decide what she should do about seeing Daniel with another woman. All the way home in the taxi she had pretended to be asleep as she couldn't even decide whether to tell Grandy about what she had seen. The taxi had taken the autoroute back to La Ciotat and it had been easy to pretend to doze on the smooth journey. Once back at the hotel they had both been eager to get to their rooms and sleep. Now, waking early after a bad night, Amber decided to go for a run on the beach. In the bright light of the morning it seemed almost impossible to believe that it had been Daniel she had seen. As she ran, she played the scene over and over again in her mind. Could it have been someone that just looked like Daniel. She dismissed the idea almost as soon as she had thought it. Much as she would like to believe it, she knew it couldn't be true. The way he held his head, the wide, muscular shoulders, every detail was clear, especially Daniel's hand on the girl's back, sliding down as he propelled her from the club. Amber's eyes filled with tears of anger and she stopped running and, with her hands resting on her knees, bent over and tried to catch her breath. Slowly her heart stopped thumping and she ran slowly back to the hotel. Grandy was already sitting at the breakfast table in the shade of a palm tree.

'Good morning, Amber, you look wild-eyed... did you have a long run?' He looked at her closely, waiting for her to reply.

Amber jogged on the spot for a moment, giving herself time to think.

'I'll take a quick shower and join you for breakfast, won't be long.' Amber ran off and into the hotel before he could reply. This was not the time, she thought to herself, to tell Grandy about Daniel. There were some things that she had to resolve for herself. She managed to take a quick shower in the slow trickle of water running from the ancient plumbing, then hurried down to join her grandfather. He looked up at her as he poured her a coffee.

'Well, it's nearly ten o'clock and I'm going to call Sam. What do you want to do today, Amber? Do you want to go out on his boat?' Grandy looked closely at Amber again as though trying to read her thoughts.

'Do you know what, Grandy? There's nothing I'd like more!' Amber answered quickly and as she spoke she realised it was the truth. She felt a shiver of excitement at the thought of seeing Sam again.

'Shall I ring him or do you want to?' Grandy held out his mobile toward her.

'Oh no, you make the call... is it OK with you?'

'Well, I was thinking it might be a good idea for you to go and I'll hang around here and make some more enquiries about the hotel.'

Amber looked at her grandfather in surprise. 'But Sam invited you, too, definitely... you must come. I mean, you love being on the water and it sounds great… please come Grandy.'

'Well, I just thought it would be a bit ridiculous, you going on a date and taking your old grandfather with you.'

'Exactly why I want you to come. I don't want it to be like a date, just a fun day out, please Grandy.'

Her grandfather sighed and began to dial the number whilst giving Amber a hard look and shaking his head in mock despair.

'Hello, Sam? How are you this lovely morning? Yes, yes, thanks, we'd love to… fine…see you outside the restaurant at eleven then. Is there anything I can bring? Yes, I will be bringing my lovely grand-daughter…' Grandy laughed and raised his eyebrows as he looked at Amber again, 'I meant anything like food or wine… anything for the picnic? Right, fine. Good, see you soon. Bye.' Grandy shut his phone and put it in his jacket pocket. 'Well, looks like I shall be playing gooseberry all day. Sam seemed to be expecting me to come. By the way, he said if you have a snorkel and flippers you should bring them with you.'

'Great, I'll go and get ready now. I saw a shop selling masks and stuff on the front here. I'll go and buy some. We had better get going.' With a sudden surge of energy, Amber ran back into the hotel, aware that her grandfather was looking at her with some amusement.

Half and hour later they were in the car park and ready to go.

'I think it's best we go in my car and not a taxi today… but which route do you want me to take, Grandy?'

'Oh, definitely the grand scenic route round the cliff tops. You can take it at a steady speed and it's too good a view to miss on a day like this. I have every confidence in your driving, Amber.'

'OK, let's go… I agree, it's a fantastic road.'

Today the sun was even hotter than ever. Already at mid-morning the heat was shimmering off the tarmac as they made their way at a steady speed up and away from La Ciotat.

'I saw a lay-by on the right as we were careering around a bend with that mad taxi driver. If you see it and have time to pull in, Amber, I'd like to take a photo or two.'

'It's not one of your tricks, is it, Grandy. Not a secret property you have your eye on?'

'No, seriously not this time. Anyway, I think I have enough on my plate sorting out the idea of the Hotel de la Plage and the Hotel Lavande. I spoke with Calinda this morning and she said the prospective buyers had been back to them asking for an answer to their offer.'

'Did you speak with Daniel?' Amber asked, trying to keep her voice casual.

'No, Calinda said he was out delivering again. Anyway, I told her to hang on and do nothing and that we would be back soon.'

Amber's heart sank as she thought of all the excuses Daniel might have made when he said he was out delivering. At that moment, the lay-by came into sight and Amber pulled in and parked. Grandy took his camera and went to look at the view.

'You have to see this, Amber, come and look.' Amber took her own camera and snapped a shot of Grandy outlined against the deep blue sky. As she drew near the cliff edge she took in a deep breath of fresh air. It was such a beautiful world laid out in front of her. The sky and the sea seemed to fuse into one at the horizon. The water was completely calm. Amber felt the tension drain away and her shoulders relaxed. There was nothing she could do to help Calinda at this moment. She resolved that she would confront Daniel when they returned to the Hotel Lavande. However difficult it became she would stand by Calinda and little Fleur. That was all she could think at the moment but as for today…today was her day and she was determined to enjoy every moment.

When they arrived at the harbour in Cassis, Sam and Matt were waiting for them, sitting in the same restaurant, drinking large cups of white coffee. Sam stood up as soon as he saw them, his face alight with pleasure and his hand outstretched in greeting. 'Hi, good to see you! Would you like a coffee? You can guess we're drinking Americanos!'

'Good morning, I'll just take a small black coffee, please. How about you, Amber?'

'I'll have an orange juice, I think I've drunk enough coffee for a week.'

Sam went over to the bar to give their order and Amber watched him. He was tall and athletic, well-tanned and well... well everything, Amber thought to herself with a smile.

After they had finished their drinks they made their way toward the long pontoon that stretched out between the moored boats. Matt waved to a girl standing near the end and Amber recognised her as the girl he had been dancing with. She was standing, waiting beside a very large and glamorous cabin cruiser. Sam moved ahead and dumped his backpack down on the wooden boards of the pontoon. 'This is Yvette, a lovely young French woman who is brave enough to go out with Matt.' The girl laughed and punched Sam lightly in the stomach,

'Why do you always tease my Matt? Pleased to meet you.' They all shook hands and then Matt waved an idle hand toward the shining sleek boat,

'And this is Sophocles, welcome aboard.'

'My goodness!' said Grandy, 'She's splendid, must be nearly 40 feet?' Amber looked at her grandfather in surprise and then smiled as she jumped aboard. Hadn't she learnt yet never to be surprised at what her wily old grandfather knew?

Sam edged the boat slowly away from the mooring and then headed toward the harbour entrance. He raised a hand at the coastguard as they passed.

'How long have you sailed, Sam?' Grandy asked, sitting back comfortably in the white leather seating next to the helm.

'Well, I have sailed my entire twenty-eight years, I guess. I was brought up with sail boats, my family have a place on Long Island and then at Harvard I was in the sailing team. Relax, sir, you and Amber are in safe hands!' As he spoke the boat gathered speed and cut a swathe through the blue water. Amber, sitting at the stern, looked down at the curling white wake stretching behind them toward the coast. Now they were far enough out at sea to see the small harbour of La Ciotat and the hills behind. Amber could just make out the Hotel de la Plage. From this distance it looked an elegant building, its peeling paintwork just showing a delicate pink in the sunshine, framed by tall palms. It was certainly a great location with its gardens down to the beach. Amber sighed, wondering how to tell Grandy about Daniel. Somehow she knew she had to do it, especially as he was about to advise Calinda and Daniel on their future business plans. Once again she looked up at the distant hills and wondered how life was going on at the Hotel Lavande. Then she heard her name being called. She turned round and realised that Yvette was holding out a glass of orange juice. Amber reached out and took it carefully, there was a slight swell now as they left the shelter of the harbour walls.

'Thank you, lovely!' she said hastily, 'Sorry, I was miles away, admiring the view of the coast.'

'Well, it is beautiful, isn't it. I come out here most weekends and I always find it wonderful… even in the bad weather.' Yvette raised her own glass to Amber. 'Welcome aboard the Sophocles. It's very good to have some feminine support!'

Amber took in the fact quietly and decided not to ask more but to change the subject.

'Do you live near here, Yvette?'

'Well, I live and work at Sophia Antipolis, my family home is in Paris.'

'So what's your field of work? I hadn't even heard about Sophia Antipolis until last night.'

'Well, it's a huge technology park and the University of Nice is on site. We are all marine biologists. Matt and Sam studied together at Harvard and I met them when they came here a year ago. Sam specialises in the responses of temperate marine symbioses to climate warming but Matt and I work together on a project on seascape analysis, particularly the genus Diplodus found in this area of Les Calanques.'

'Phew, I am not sure I have understood a word of all that.' Amber laughed, 'but it sounds interesting work and in an amazing place. Did you say Les Calanques? Is that the cliffs round here?' At that moment the engine slowed and the boat began to slowly turn back toward land. Amber looked forward and realised they had rounded the headland. She gasped with amazement at the beautiful, deep creek that they were slowly entering. Steep white cliffs were on both sides of them now, soaring up into the blue sky.

'It's simply amazing!' Amber grabbed the chrome bar that ran around the boat's edge and looked all around her, blue water, blue sea, white cliffs dotted with a few sparse green trees. Then looking in to the boat she looked at Sam, he had swivelled round in his seat at the helm and was watching her. He saluted her and called back,

'*Bienvenu*, Les Calanques! I'll putter along a few more minutes and then we'll drop anchor.' He smiled at her and then turned again toward the prow of the boat. Grandy waved his hat in the air and called back to Amber.

'Paradise, we've found paradise-on-sea. I had no idea this area existed… like the fiords of Norway with a Mediterranean climate. Paradise!'

A few minutes later, Matt and Yvette moved efficiently around the deck, lowering the anchor and checking the instrument panel before Sam cut the engine. As the noise died down they all stood still, quietly enjoying the new silence. Nothing apart from the gently lapping of the water and the cries of seagulls overhead.

Sam spoke first, 'Anyone for a swim before lunch?' He pulled his t-shirt over his head and turned to Amber. His body was lean and long, lightly muscled and very tanned. Amber could find no fault with the marine biologist in front of her, no fault at all. She stood up, steadying herself against the gentle rise and fall of the sea.

'I can't wait to swim,' Amber said, pulling her dress over her head and facing Sam. She had a moment to be grateful that she had worn her navy one-piece costume under her dress and not one of her usual skimpy bikinis. The navy blue suit was well cut and had the advantage of staying on when she dived. Sam looked at her for a long moment and then turned to Grandy.

'How about you, sir? Will you join us for a swim. The water will be about twenty degrees right now.'

'Hmm, I'd love to but one thing I have learnt over the years, is that it is a lot easier to get into water, hot or cold, than it is to get out.' Grandy peered over the steep white sides of the cruiser. 'My knees are telling me that the little ladder hanging there is not for me.'

'No sir,' Matt interrupted, 'I'll lower the stern deck, of course.' He moved swiftly to the rear of the boat and pressed a button. Slowly a small platform lowered to the level of the water. He turned to Grandy and smiled, 'What do you think, sir?'

Amber smiled as Grandy walked carefully over to inspect the flat deck. These Harvard boys with all their deferent sir this and that certainly had an appeal. She turned to Yvette who was now standing on the lowered deck, wearing a neat black swimsuit and carrying a pair of ordinary swimming goggles. Yvette raised a hand and smiled at Amber, then turned quickly and made a perfect dive into the sea. Amber watched the small figure swimming under the clear water until she surfaced. Then she heard a small splash and turned to see Grandy bobbing into the sea. He raised his hand to Amber and called out,

'Wonderful, Amber, come on, what are you waiting for?' He swam a few strokes and then floated on his back. Amber walked down to the lowered deck and stood a moment between Sam and Matt. Then Matt gave a small jump and made a perfect jack knife dive into the water and swam to join Yvette.

'Our turn now… are you happy with diving in, Amber?' Sam turned to her, his face wrinkled as he looked into the sun.

'Oh yes,' Amber replied and the next instant made her own perfect entry into the water. As she surfaced she had a moment to think that Sam had some charming freckles across his cheekbones and then he was surfacing close beside her.

They both trod water as they looked at each other. She could see the sea reflected in his pale grey eyes and the drops of water, like teardrops in his dark lashes. Then with a quick duck dive she swam under water to her grandfather.

'The water is refreshing but not very warm, Grandy! Do you think you should stay in long?

'No, I'm going to tootle back to the deck right now and warm my old bones in the sun. Don't worry about me, you have a good swim. Have you got your mask and snorkel, what about your flippers?'

'I'll come back with you and get them. I feel a bit of an amateur with these professional marine biologists.'

'Well, at least you're a good swimmer and you did take that sub-aqua course, didn't you?'

They were sitting back on the low deck, the sun already drying the salt water on their skin.

'Fancy you remembering that… yes, I was only about fifteen years old and the highlight of the course was to get away from practicing in the school pool and have a day out at a local gravel pit.', Amber looked around her, 'Still, I always dreamed of diving somewhere like this one day.'

'You should always strive to make your dreams come true. Right now, I am dreaming of a black coffee with a dash of cognac. Sam kindly told me where to find everything in the galley, so off you go again. Dive into that dream!'

11   *'there is nothing more in the world'*

To: amber@hotmail.com
Cc:
Subject: Amber …you are SO so annoying
From: Kim Simpson - kimS@gmail.com
American guy… tell all or I may never e you again. BTW all
going well here in 'our' flat Mike is very cute and very
sweet… definitely not American from Harvard…more lively
lad from Hackney … but we do get on really well. So, are you
moving on or WHAT???

To: kimS@gmail.com
Cc:
Subject: hi
From: Amber Marsden - amber@hotmail.com
Glad you are having a good time with Mike. I have to confess
that it is hard to remember I have half a flat in Bloomsbury.
That's all I have time to confess right now… just to say I had a
fantastic day yesterday with Sam… and his friends Matt and
Yvette… and Grandy too, of course… managed to get him to
float around the Med for five minutes or so. Such fun. Now
packing as we are going back to Hotel Lavande later today. So
much to sort out… too much to tell you and I am already late
for breakfast.
x Amber

Indeed, the day did had passed with a dreamlike
quality. As Amber swam idly through the calm water toward
Sam she had thought for a brief moment that she might wake
up and find herself back at the church door waiting for Rob.
She gave a small duck dive and swam underwater for a
moment to dispel the thought. This was the new reality, here in
the blue waters of the Mediterranean. Then she realised that

Sam was swimming alongside, smiling at her, his grey eyes looking at her through his mask, and he was gesturing to her to follow him. Amber pulled on her snorkel and waved a hand back and then, with a strong kick with her flippers, she followed his path. They were swimming just under the surface of the water through shoals of minute fish, electric blue in the rays of sun that penetrated the surface. Amber followed, fascinated as they made their way over some rocks. Then Sam was gesturing upward and they both broke the surface of the water. Sam pulled off his mask and shook his head, water spraying in the bright sunshine.

'There are some good flat rocks over there, do you want to sit for a while?'

'Yes, just for a while, I can't stay in the sun too long though.'

They swam side by side to some smooth, white rocks that reached into the sea from a small beach. Sam held out his hand to steady Amber as they clambered over the slippery pebbles and reached a large flat rock that was partly in the shade from the over-hanging cliff edge. Amber dropped his hand as soon as they were sitting safely on the rock. Suddenly there was nothing around, the boat was out of sight from the bend in the creek and Matt and Yvette had swum in a different direction. Amber felt a shiver of excitement as she looked around.

'It's like being on a desert island, as though there is nothing more in the world.' She smiled with delight and rested back on her elbow.

'Isn't it just! I'm glad you like it. Sometimes I like to get away from everything. You're a very good swimmer, Amber. Have you swum a lot?'

'Oh, I used to swim in races and stuff. Now, I don't swim often enough.' Amber had a sudden vision of Rob. He had hated the water and always wanted to head for the mountains. Had they always done what he wanted them to do? Had she let herself be drawn into his world? Then she realised that Sam was talking.

'My world is mainly under the water. I spend a great deal of time lugging an aqua lung around. Have you ever done any scuba diving?'

'Well, I did the British sub-aqua course when I was still at school, but I never really had time or opportunity to use it.' Again, Amber thought of Rob and how they had met that day in the refectory. Was that when she had given up on her ambition to dive all over the world when she graduated? Struggling to push away the memories she shook her hair and moved into the shade. 'I seem to remember my last attempt was in a horrid gravel pit. I passed the test and that was that.' Amber laughed and finally dismissed her thoughts of the past.

'A gravel pit… well, I think I could improve on that if you have some time free. There are some underwater paths here, marked out for sub-aqua enthusiasts. Simple to follow if you are interested. Or, better still you could join Matt, Yvette and me on one of our day research trips.'

'It must be amazing to work like that, you're very lucky.'

'I expect you are thinking I am a typical American spoilt brat. In a way, it's true. But you would understand, I guess. Your grandfather is William Marsden, isn't he? The WM trademark on practically every cardboard box in the world. You must be very proud of him… he seems a great guy.'

'Yes, I am… although you might find it hard to believe that I have always thought of him as just my grandfather. Only recently, very recently in fact, have I come to realise how very rich he is.'

'So you're a trust fund kid, too?"

Amber laughed, 'Oh no, that's all been sorted out. Grandy doesn't believe in inherited wealth so he has left the lot to various charities. I must say I am very relieved.'

'Yeh, way to go. Your grandfather is so right. Trust funds can be a double-edged sword, that's for sure. Maybe being a self-made man made him realise that. My family money is what is known as, at least in the USA, old money. They take it very seriously indeed.' Sam suddenly laughed, '

But I have put a stop to that before it could begin. I've managed a big fall-out with my dear Pa and he has disinherited me.' He stretched and looked up at the sky. 'Suits me just fine. I've seen what a trust fund looming in the future did to my friend, Matt.'

'You make it sound dreadful. How can money really be so evil.'

'Oh, it's too lovely a day to worry about it. Look up at the rocks opposite, Amber, can you see that nest in the crevice. Looks like a peregrine falcon, there's a whole department at Sophia Antipolis devoted to the conservation of nesting sites that lie in these cliffs. There! Do you see now? There's some movement, you can see a wing flapping…'

Amber tried to follow the line where he was pointing. 'No, I can't see anything. Where do you mean?'
Sam slipped his arm around her shoulders and took Amber's arm to point in the right direction. 'Do you see the scrubby tree hanging on to that outcrop? There, look to the left, the nest is just in the shade. Can you see it now?'

'Yes, yes… I see it now. Oh look, the bird is just flying off.' She turned to Sam and found he was looking at her, his grey eyes seemed darker and his eyelashes so black that they stood out against his tanned skin. He moved closer and then he kissed her, just a soft brush of his lips against her cheek.

'You're so beautiful, Amber. I just couldn't help that!' Sam gently stroked her damp hair away from her forehead and looked at her in silence. Amber's emotions were running wild, her heart beating as she wondered what to do next. She took his hand and then looked back at the bird's nest. So many thoughts were seething through her head that she was lost for words. Finally, she managed to break the silence hanging in the air between them, 'No need to apologise, Sam. It was a perfectly lovely kiss and perfect for this wonderful day. I feel as though we are on some magical part of the world where nothing else exists.'

'I know what you mean, but I can sense you holding back in some way… and to be truthful, so am I. I may as well tell you that I am just about recovering from a very painful break-up. My fiancée, Marianne, was here last week, she came all the way from New York to bring back my ring and tell me she had fallen in love with someone else.' Sam looked down at the rock and ran his hand lightly over the surface.

'Strange, I know all about this limestone rock and everything about what lies under the sea all around us and absolutely nothing about human nature.' He laughed and stood up.

Amber hesitated, wondering whether to tell him about Rob. She stood up and they stayed side by side, looking out to the bright sunshine on the calm, blue water.

'I'm very sorry, Sam. Believe me, I not only sympathise but completely understand. One day I'll tell you why you were right to think I was holding back too.'

Sam took her hand and gave it a soft, long kiss, 'I hope that it will be soon, Amber, very soon. Right now I guess we had better get back to the Sophocles and get lunch going.' Then, still holding her hand in his, he led the way back across the rocks until they were paddling in the warm waves that lapped the stones. They looked at each other for a moment and then both smiled and dived into the shallow water and swam back to the boat.

Yvette and Matt were already on board, chatting with Amber's grandfather and laying out the table with the picnic lunch.

'Hi there!' Matt greeted them as they pulled themselves back onto the deck. 'I thought Sam would smell the chicken a mile off.' He waved a chicken leg in the air as he spoke. 'Come on, or we'll start without you.'

Yvette threw Amber a towel and held out a glass, 'Would you like a fruit juice, Amber? We don't carry booze on board, apart from cognac for medicinal purpose!' She laughed and her pretty face shone in the sunlight.

'I had to have a small dose of medicine this morning, after my swim,' Grandy admitted, 'the water was colder than I thought. You have to be young and hot-blooded to stay out as long as you did.'

'Yes, well it's still only 23 degrees now at the peak of the day, but that's average for this time of the year.' Sam was looking at the instrument panel beside the wheel.

'Don't let him start on averages or we'll never get lunch,' Matt laughed, 'Sam can bore for the whole of the United States on the stats of Les Calanques.'

'Well, you can certainly match him as far as that goes,' said Yvette turning to Amber, 'you may as well know that these two American lads are married to the sea. They have no time for anything or anyone else on the earth.'

'Well, the earth is very boring in comparison with the sea.' Sam smiled and began to pass the salad around as they all took their seats. 'For a long while I thought that there was nothing better in the world than skimming across the surface of the waves and then I found out it was a whole lot more interesting underneath.'

'Yeh, I remember that,' Matt grinned, 'and he dragged me down with him so that we both ended up studying it… in depth, you could say.'

'That's a terrible pun.' said Yvette, pulling a face.

'I love bad puns and this chicken is fantastic. I didn't realise how hungry I was.' Amber smiled and began to devour the chicken and salad. It was true she thought… she hadn't realised just how hungry she was… but not just for food. Suddenly she thought how she had missed being on the sea, in the sunshine and with friends, just friends. She looked across at her grandfather. He was now in deep conversation with Sam, but he caught her glance and raised his panama. Amber grabbed her camera from her bag and was just in time for another perfect shot.

'wearing his family tartan'

To: amber@hotmail.com
Cc:
Subject: raining again
From: Kim Simpson - kimS@gmail.com
Spoke to your Ma last night and she told me you're having a great time. I am beginning to feel deeply jealous. Work is frantic and weather is dire. So far going well with Mike… can't believe we haven't had a row yet and… guess what… he actually likes cooking. How great is that? Let me know how your glamorous escape is going… did you get out on that boat with the Preppy Guy?   x Kim

---

To: kimS@gmail.com
Cc:
Subject: hi
From: Amber Marsden - amber@hotmail.com
Oh yes indeedy! Boat was a splendid cabin cruiser…all pale wooden decks and white leather seating. And yes, we swam off the boat and yes, Sam kissed me… but before you go hyper… it was sort of a friendly kiss and then we went back to the boat. Oh, did I forget to tell you that we had landed on this miniature desert island… just the two of us, like Adam and Eve… ok … ha ha joking… but almost true.
x Amber

Amber logged off and slipped her iPad into her handbag. She looked around the room to check she hadn't left anything. The early morning sun was filtering through the shutters and the ceiling was rippled with the reflections of the sea. She had grown to love the faded elegance of the room in the last few days. The wide view of the sea stretching to a hazy horizon brought a sense of calm. The top of two tall palm trees, were just level with the balcony and Amber stood for a last moment to watch the small birds that flitted busily from one fronded branch to the next. She wondered idly for a moment whether the room was even lovelier that her room at the Hotel Lavande. But the soft lapping sound of the sea gave the answer. No wonder that Calinda, having spent her early childhood in a seaside village in Tunisia... Amber's tranquil thoughts suddenly shattered. How could she hang around dreaming when she should be helping Calinda? The beautiful Calinda with such a troubled past and now... now, was her married life to be ruined by Daniel's philandering? Amber grabbed her bag and practically ran from the room.

'You seem in a hurry to leave, Amber. Finish your orange juice while I settle the bill. I thought the charming Sam might have tempted you to stay on here for a few days?' Grandy looked across the breakfast table at Amber, his eyebrows raised in question and his eyes twinkling.

'I know, Grandy, it is seriously tempting. He's going out diving today with Yvette and Matt.' Amber looked wistfully toward the blue sea and though of Sam, his grey eyes fringed with black lashes, his quiet and gentle manner. Amber sighed, everything about him really, well, nearly everything.

'Sam began to tell me that his fiancée had just broken off his engagement. I think he's still trying to get over it and as for me...well, I didn't even begin to tell him that I had gone as far as the church door. It's all to much.' Amber sighed again.

'Matt filled me in with some of the detail when you and Sam were swimming... or whatever it was you were doing...'

'Grandy, it was all perfectly innocent... we just swam along the creek and sat on a small outcrop of stones. It was so peaceful. We watched a peregrine nest and then, OK, Sam did kiss me but it was so brief and so... I don't know... sort of sweet. Nothing more.'

'He seems a very kind guy. Matt also told me that Sam had pulled him through a year of rehab. Apparently Matt's parents are very wealthy and have always given him everything in the world, well, the material world anyway. Matt went right off the rails in his first year at Harvard and it was only with Sam's help that he pulled through. Yvette knows the story too and she's another good kid. I think they are both still keeping a watchful eye on Matt.'

'Really? I hadn't realised it… Matt seems sort of a quiet type. Mind you, when we danced together he certainly had some wild moves.' Amber was quiet for a moment. 'People are so often not what they seem at first.'

'Well, life just comes along and hits you sometimes. You're thinking of Rob, of course. I think it may take a time but one day you will feel sorry for him. He had a dreadful start in life, shifting from one unhappy foster home to another. No wonder he was seeking security in a financial way. All that business with wearing his family tartan when the sad truth was he had no family. One day you may be able to forgive and forget him.'

Amber nodded and remained silent. For once her grandfather had misread her thoughts. It was not Rob she had been thinking of but Daniel. She stood up quickly. 'Anyway, Grandy, we're booked in at the Hotel Lavande tonight and we ought to get going. They are awaiting your business advice.'

Grandy looked up at Amber and smiled. 'I can see you're ready for the off and I have checked out everything I can here for the time being. The place has been quietly on the market for a year already but the state it is in has put people off and they are asking too much for it, of course.' He looked up at the peeling plasterwork and the rotting wooden shutters. 'I'm surprised my old poker-playing enemy hasn't heard of it and snapped it up for his chain of hotels?

'Do I sense rivalry between you and this hotel guy?'

'Oh yes, rivalry verging on war!' Grandy laughed and they went together into the hotel.

On the journey back inland they listened to music and spoke little. Maybe they were both too occupied with their own thoughts to want to talk. Amber concentrated on the driving as the road wound uphill between silvery olive groves and stretches of neat vineyards. Every inch of the rich, red soil had been carefully cultivated, the only exception came when the earth turned to rugged rock and even here, wild herbs managed to find root. Grandy wound down his window and broke the silence with a sigh of pleasure.

'Breathe in Amber, smell the perfume of the wild herbs. A bit different from your Bloomsbury air. Have you heard from Kim today?'

'Yes, so far she haa emailed me every day before work. She's a good friend, that's for sure. I feel sort of guilty as I know she is probably worried about me and here I am having such a great time.' Amber took in a deep breath of the fresh perfumed air that was blowing through the car. 'Still, she's happy and in love so that's good.'

'Is that Mike? The boy she was with at the wedding?' Grandy's last word fell into the air like a heavy weight and he looked anxiously at Amber.

'You mean the non-wedding, don't you, Grandy? The non-event of the year. I've talked to Mum about it, nearly every night on the phone. I wish everyone would just understand that I am over it, so very over it.'

'Good, then we can all stop tip-toeing around the whole thing. When you get back to London you can wipe the slate clean.'

'I'm not going back to London, Grandy.' The words slipped from Amber's mouth as though she had thought them to herself. The truth was she was shocked at her own words. They reverberated in her ears and suddenly she knew they were true. Before her grandfather could speak she carried on hurriedly, not wanting to lose the momentum of truth. 'I mean, I haven't worked it all out yet but, as you said, I'm just letting the dust settle. The museum is stillI paying me up to the end of June, officially I am on holiday for another two weeks. I think Kim really wants Mike to move in permanently so he will probably take over my half of the rent. I think it can all be worked out. Next week I shall start looking for work here. My art restoration has to be useful in a museum or gallery… somewhere.' Amber took one hand off the driving wheel and waved it vaguely around her head. Then she took the wheel in both hands, pulled back her shoulders and looked straight ahead with a determined smile on her face. Grandy's laughter filled the car as they carried on their journey together.

They arrived at the Hotel Lavande just before lunch time. The terrace was filling with guest as they took their places under the row of pink parasols. There was no sign of Calinda or Daniel in the reception so they signed in and the staff took care of their luggage.

'Do you want to meet in half an hour or so for lunch?' Grandy asked as they took the lift to their new rooms.

'I was wondering if I have time for a half hour run first?'

'In the mid-day sun? What are you… a mad dog or an English girl?'

'I'll run through the pine forest and then take a quick dip in the pool… unless you're starving now?'

'No, no, I'd like half an hour to relax and unpack a bit. I'll make my way down to the poolside bar in an hour and I'll book a table for one thirty… how about that?

'Perfect, thanks Grandy. I need to move a bit after the journey.'

'Absolutely, and I need not to move a bit so that will be fine.'

Amber hastily went to her room. It was a larger suite this time with views over the lavender fields. She stood on the balcony for a moment, shading her eyes against the sun that shone high in the sky. The lines of purple flowers stretched in neat rows away to the horizon. Amber breathed in the perfume and began to relax then, suddenly, she realised that there was a man walking between the rows of flowers, inspecting the blooms. The man was Daniel. Amber turned quickly back in to the room and pulled open her bag.

In less than five minutes she was jogging round the back of the hotel, through the cobbled courtyard between the barns and heading for the lavender fields. Grandy was right, it was extraordinarily hot. She ran on, pacing herself although every fibre in her body wanted to run, sprint as fast as she could to confront Daniel. This was the moment she had been waiting for, the moment of truth. Then, she was running between the lavender and drawing close. Daniel turned at the sound of her pounding feet and a wide smile of welcome passed over his handsome face.

'*Bonjour, Amber, bon retour!* We were expecting you later today.'

Amber drew to an abrupt halt in front of him, her feet planted in the earth, her hands on her hips. Any plans she had made of how to tackle the situation fled from her mind. Anger filled her and she stamped her foot on the dry earth.

'How could you?' She shouted the words, she wanted to hit him, she wanted to hit him for all the other cheating men and women in the world. Time stood still as her temper took hold. 'How could you do it to Calinda and little Fleur? You vile, rotten piece of...' and then, unable to restrain herself any longer, she slapped him hard across the face.

'*Qu'est ce que c'est? Amber, tu es complètement folle ou quoi?* Have you gone mad?' Daniel easily caught Amber's hand and held her back from him. She felt the frustration of her weakness against his muscled strength and she struggled to pull away from him but he held her shoulders now in a firm grip. Amber kicked out but he dodged her foot.

'*Amber, Amber, calme-toi.* Tell me what it is?'

'You know quite well, you two-timing piece of garbage. I saw you with that singer in the club at Cassis. You were all over her.' Once again, Amber struggled to get away from Daniel, trying to kick and hit out at him. Then, suddenly he was laughing, laughing in her face.

'*Mon frère jumeau*, you must have seen Luc, my twin brother. When he is in France he often hangs out on the coast around Cassis.'

'Your twin brother?' Amber gasped and all her energy dissipated and she sank down on the ground as Daniel released her from his grip. 'You have a twin brother?'

'Yes, an identical twin brother. This sort of thing has been happening all our lives.' He rubbed his face and smiled down at her, 'Well, not usually quite so dramatically.' He held out his hand to her and pulled her to her feet. Amber stood for a moment in silence as she thought it through. Then relief welled over her and she doubled over, resting her hands on her knees, she mumbled, 'I am so sorry, Daniel, and I am so, so relieved. I have been worried sick about it all, bottling it up. I didn't even tell my grandfather. It just seemed so horrible that you could go with another woman.'

'Well, now I know you must be mad! How could any man lucky enough to win the heart of the most beautiful and sweet woman in the world ever want more?' Daniel picked a few sprigs of lavender and gave them to Amber. 'Here, lavender is renowned for its calming qualities, take a good sniff!' He laughed and Amber took the bunch of fragrant flowers.

'I am truly sorry, Daniel, sorry I hit you, too!' Amber looked at him cautiously, but there was no sign of a red hand-mark on his cheek, just a very wide smile. It was as though he couldn't contain laughing out loud. Amber gave a small smile and then looked away to the rows of lavender.

'That's better, Amber, just forget it. I've had harder knocks than that, I used to box when I was a kid… and my brother, Luc. Our saintly mother made us take up boxing to try and stop us from fighting each other. We must have driven her mad with our constant battles. Although we are identical twins we are … how do you say in English, cheese and chalk. I am still learning your sayings.'

'Chalk and cheese,' Amber said quietly, 'Your English is amazing, Daniel. Calinda told me you studied very hard, in fact she said that everything you do, you do very well.'

'Did she say that? Good to know. I try but she is a hard act to follow. She is so perfect that I wake every day and thank my lucky stars. So you see, I am never going to be found in a club in Cassis unless I am dancing with my Calinda.'

'I am so truly sorry, Daniel. I feel dreadful about all this. I should have known.…' Amber was lost for words. Daniel laughed again and they began to walk slowly back toward the hotel. 'By the way, Amber, in the circumstances, may I tell you…what is it in English… a home truth?

'Yes, I deserve any home truth you have to tell me.' Amber sighed and waited to be told off in some way for her impulsive temper.

'Well, you know that old thing they do in the movies… when the man tells the woman that she is more beautiful than ever when she is angry… well, I just want to tell you that it really isn't true in your case. Your little nose was all red and it just didn't suit you. You are so beautiful when you are in your usual calm, dreaming mode. I think you should stick with it!' Daniel laughed aloud and this time with such gusto that Amber joined in and by the time they reached the pottery barns they were chatting like the best of friends. When they reached the shade of the buildings, Daniel stopped and said to Amber,

'Anyway, thank you for keeping your fears to yourself, even though you were so mistaken. It must have been hard. Your grandfather is a very attentive and observant man. I'm glad he wasn't involved in hating me too. Anyway, let's forget it… we are looking forward to meeting you both this evening for that meeting. Would you both join us to dine in our apartment… say seven o'clock?'

'That would be lovely, thank you, Daniel, I'll tell Grandy now.' Amber nodded and gave Daniel one last smile, as thought to acknowledge her dreadful mistake and then ran round to the pool area. She ran straight into the standing shower that stood amongst some tall plants at the end of the pool. She let the cold water run over her and take with it all the fears of the last few days. Calinda was secure in the love of Daniel, he obviously adored her. The water ran a long time as she let it wash away every last remnant of her anger. Her thoughts moved on to Sam… he had to recover from his broken engagement just as she had to recover from Rob's treachery, but they were young and fortunate in so many ways. Calinda and baby Fleur needed the love of a good man and that is obviously what they had found in Daniel. Amber pulled her streaming wet hair back from her face and sighed with relief as the water ran over her face. Even with her eyes tight closed she could sense the bright, blue sky above her.

Provence was all around her and right now she was determined to find a little corner of it for herself.

13 *'her cheeks burned as she thought of it'*

To: amber@hotmail.com
Cc:
Subject: pale sunshine today
From: Kim Simpson - kimS@gmail.com

Yes, the sun has finally decided to pretend it is summer in London. I've put your pot plants out on the window ledge to try and bring them back to life. Sorry, but you know I am hopeless with anything with leaves on… or rather off. Sorry, but it is all your own fault if they die as you have deserted them. The plants miss you and so do I! Do you have any plans to ever return? Work as hectic as ever and everything going amazingly well with Mike. It is so good to get back here in the evening and find he has cooked dinner for me. Domestic god that he is. However, don't think that I am not still jealous of your Provence stuff… all that sunshine plus american hunk… let me know more asap. x Kim

To: kimS@gmail.com
Cc:
Subject: hi
From: Amber Marsden - amber@hotmail.com

You need to be very jealous… it is like paradise here. Now we are back at the Hotel Lavande and I am writing this just before dinner. Grandy and I are invited to eat chez Rabin in their top floor apartment. I have already resolved one problem that I didn't even have time to tell you about. Feeling very happy now and… sorry… not sure when I shall return. I really have until the end of June to decide my next move but I will let you know asap. In the meantime, could you ask your domestic god to take over the pot plant care? I have a feeling he would make a better job of it. Also tell him that you are the craziest girl on earth but also the best of friends.

x Amber

Amber closed down her email and threw her iPad on the bed. She did feel a pang of guilt, thinking about Kim in their little flat in Bloomsbury. She must make up her mind what to do as soon as possible. Now that she had every intention of staying in Provence, then she had to do something about the rent and all her belongings in the flat. Still thinking it all through, she opened the wardrobe and flicked through the few dresses hanging there. She picked out an ice-blue shift that was dressy in a simple way. She was about to slip it on when her phone bleeped with a message. She picked it up, expecting to see a message from Kim. She nearly dropped the phone when she saw Rob's name on the screen. She looked at it for a long moment, not sure whether to even read the message. She held the phone away from her as though it were toxic. Then, she quickly tapped the screen and read the message.

'can you forgive me - I miss you.'

Amber snapped the message closed and deleted it. She found she was breathing fast and her heart was thumping in her chest. There were so many angry replies that she could make, words formed and dissolved as she stared at the screen. What was it Grandy had said about being able to forgive Rob one day? Amber exhaled sharply and then deleted Rob's name and number from her contact list. There was no need for an answer, silence was the best reply and today was definitely not the day she was ready to forgive him. Right now she was going to carry on getting ready for dinner with Grandy and her new-found friends.

When the lift arrived at the top floor, Amber had recovered her calm once more. She held Grandy's arm as the lift doors open and they entered the cool, white space of the apartment entrance hall. Calinda came to meet them, wearing a white dress and as graceful as a swan gliding across a lake. They exchanged greetings and then Amber asked,

'Do you learn to walk like that or was it how you always walked, Calinda?'

Calinda laughed, 'I don't know any longer… I suppose my long legs make me walk in a certain way, I take long strides and, of course, in the first few months of my career I had training on the catwalk, how to turn… how to smile, pout, frown and look into the audience.' She whirled around and her white dress swirled as she walked the length of the apartment and then turned back to them laughing. 'Like that! You try, Amber, you have long legs and the perfect figure for a model.'

Amber laughed and then gave an exaggerated walk toward Calinda, swinging her slim hips.

'No, much too much movement, just one foot in front of the other, slowly and don't bob up and down!'

Amber reached the end of the room and gave a twirl, trying to imitate Calinda. Both girls stood together laughing and Grandy joined them.

'Enough walking, we should be drinking!' Calinda gave a radiant smile, the smile that had been on thousands of magazine covers. 'Now, what can I offer you, Monsieur Marsden… sorry, William. Cold rosé, gin and tonic, vodka…'

'Stop right there, I should love a glass of cold wine. I never realised rosé could be so delicious. Never drink it at home, just wouldn't do somehow… but here it seems to touch the spot.' Grandy took his glass from Calinda. 'Where's Daniel, still out delivering? And where's the little Fleur?'

'Daniel is in the kitchen, he has cooked for us tonight and Fleur is sleeping. Daniel has persuaded me to leave her sometimes for an hour or so in her new cot. It is so hot and I think he is right. She seems very happy on her own. it is me that misses her, of course.'

'Ah well, you may as well start getting used to that idea, believe me. So many times ahead of you… first day at school, first time she wants to go somewhere on her own, first school outing … all building up to the day they leave home. It's all very scary indeed. Off they go, happy as larks while you stay behind with nothing but your worries.'

'You make it sound so dreadful!' Calinda laughed, 'But you are right, of course. I remember how my own mother cried when I left to go to college in London. I felt so bad because the truth was that I just couldn't wait to get away. Yes, I must remember all these things.'

'Anyway, I am exaggerating, of course. There are all the happy times in between. If you are very lucky then you may one day have a grand-daughter who lets you go on holiday with her. Ah, here comes Daniel. *Bonsoir*, Daniel.'

So the evening began, they moved out to sit on the candle-lit roof terrace, talking and laughing as they ate the small canapés that Daniel had prepared. The moon hung like a silver globe, high in the sky, so bright that is was almost like daylight.

'Such an evening!' Amber leaned her head back to look up at the scatter of stars above them.

'Indeed, and even up here the perfume of lavender is in the air.' Agreed Grandy.

'That might be enhanced by my wife's own fragrance,' laughed Daniel. 'Her perfume '*Calinda*' has some overtones of wild herbs and lavender. It was designed in a perfumery not far from here, le Chateau de Fleurenne . I was working on their flower harvest when I met Calinda. She had come over from London for a fashion shoot and was sitting elegantly… well, she can only sit elegantly… on a bale of hay, looking very bored.'

'I was bored to tears!' agreed Calinda, I just wanted to get the day over and get back to Nice airport… that was until I spotted Daniel and we started chatting.'

'You mean you chatted me up… isn't that the English expression for it?'

They all laughed and Daniel topped up their glasses.

'That must have been a mighty big change in life style for you, Calinda?' said Grandy.

'Oh, I couldn't wait to get off the catwalk… more like a treadmill. We work hard here but it is all for ourselves.'

'Well, that leads me to what we should perhaps be talking about. The evening seems to be too fine for a real business talk, but I will just say that I inspected the Hotel de la Plage as best I could whilst we were there. You're right, Calinda it has enormous potential. Which is another way of saying that it needs absolutely everything done to it. However, the one thing that can't ever be changed is also the best thing about the place. The location... right on the edge of the Med. Fantastic!'

'*Pieds dans l'eau*, feet in the water... exactly Calinda's dream.' Daniel sat forward in his seat, his face alight with enthusiasm. 'She was brought up in Nabeul, a small seaside village near Tunis.'

Amber looked at Calinda and wondered if it was her imagination or not, was there a shadow across Calinda's face as she thought back to her childhood? But Daniel was carrying on talking.

'It is a dream though... we can't believe we will make enough money on selling this place in order to buy the Hotel de la Plage, even in its derelict state. We have had our accounts prepared up to date and some valuation figures and the Sylvestre chain are still holding out their offer to buy us out... but ...'

'Hold on a moment, Daniel. Let me take a look at the paperwork tomorrow morning. I have a few ideas up my sleeve but I need to think it through and check the figures. I know the big boss of the Sylvestre chain of hotels. Don't let him bully you. If he really wants the Hotel Lavande he won't go away in a hurry.'

'Of course, you're right, William.' Calinda nodded thoughtfully, 'It is a huge decision for us so we mustn't be too hasty. It would be very kind of you to look through our accounts... I feel bad asking you, William. I know exactly what it is like to be pursued when you are trying to get away from everything. Are you sure you don't mind... after all, you are on holiday here.'

'I shouldn't worry about that for a moment,' Amber laughed, 'Business accounts and statistics are Grandy's idea of ideal escapist holiday reading.'

Calinda folded away the papers into a large folder and put them aside. 'Well, if you are really sure, thank you again. Now, I'll go and get Fleur and we should all eat. Dani, is it ready to serve?'

Daniel stood up and gave a mock bow to Calinda. 'To the point of perfection, *ma chère princesse.*'

'Hmm, well, maybe you should check it as I think I smell burning.' Calinda swept out from the terrace blowing a kiss to Daniel as she went. Daniel ran after her and Grandy and Amber smiled at each other as they heard them carry on talking.

'*Peutêtre…* maybe it was my imagination, I don't smell burning now, *mon cher*. Don't panic!'

'*Tu es méchante, Calinda, très méchante.* Wicked woman!'

'Aren't you a lucky man then.' Their voices died away and Grandy turned to Amber,

'Now that seems to be a very good marriage. They are so happy together.'

Amber took in a deep breath, thinking how nearly she had worried Grandy about Daniel being unfaithful to Calinda. Her cheeks burned as she thought of it. But how could she have possible guessed that Daniel had an identical twin brother? Maybe she would meet him one day?

14 *'dipping their spoons into a raspberry coated cheesecake'*

To: amber@hotmail.com
Cc:
Subject: be warned
From: Kim Simpson - kimS@gmail.com
Thought I should warn you that Rob sent me a text today… wanted to know where you are etc…of course I did NOT reply… in fact wiped him from my contacts list as couldn't find a trash box labelled effing s**thead. Apart from that horrid moment my day has been routinely dull but sweet Mike has promised lasagna tonight so that keeps me going. How are things with you…are you floating around on a cruiser or wandering through the lavender fields… get a life, Amber! Way to go … enjoy! x

To: kimS@gmail.com
Cc:
Subject: hi
From: Amber Marsden - amber@hotmail.com
I know, Rob sent me a text too. I deleted just like you and didn't answer. Hanging on to remnant of my dignity, I guess. I'll tell you more when I see you but basically he was a sleazy gold-digger who dumped me at the altar when he found out I wasn't ever going to inherit Grandy's wealth. Well, you wanted some news so get yourself over that one. I have. It is so great out here that none of all that mess at the non-wedding seems real … I have to warn you that I just LOVE it here and can't imagine coming back to the old smoke. But will talk it through properly asap. Promise. x Amber

Amber stretched out luxuriously under a pink parasol by the pool. Grandy was sitting on the next lounger, under another umbrella, and sifting through a file of paperwork. Amber lay for a moment thinking back over the evening before. It had been a very relaxed meal. Daniel had cooked an excellent leg of lamb and served it with a simple green salad. There was something about the simplicity of the meal that had made it so perfect. Calinda had sat quietly nursing Fleur and letting the conversation drift over her until near the end of the meal. As they were dipping their spoons into a raspberry coated cheesecake she had joined into the conversation again. Amber felt a small pang of jealousy at the obvious happiness of Calinda and Daniel. She knew it was wrong and illogical to feel envy, but it was such a short time ago that she had thought she was about to enter that realm of married bliss. For a moment she allowed herself to envisage a domestic scene, Rob cooking a meal, herself nursing a baby of her own. Tears that she thought had run dry, began to form in her eyes. How could it hurt so much when she knew the truth of Rob's deceit? She pulled on her sunglasses and reached for her Kindle to read. She sifted through the list of her stored books, carefully avoiding any title involved with romance. She was surprised how few books were left and felt angry with herself all over again. Had she been living in some unreal world of dreamy love? She looked across the pool to the distant view of the hills. There was a beautiful world spread in front of her and all she could do was to wallow in self-pity. How could she be the slightest bit jealous of Calinda who had suffered such a sad childhood? Amber closed her Kindle impatiently and began to fold up her towel. Grandy looked up and said,

'Have you had enough of lolling around the pool?'

'Yes, I think I'll go and find my paints, I may try a few sketches of the lavender fields. I can sit in the shade of the barns. You're busy too.'

'Well, I've nearly finished looking through the accounts but I have been thinking about something else. Let me just ask you about it before you go. I'd like your advice. Do you mind?'

'Of course not!' Amber looked at her grandfather in surprise, 'I just hope I can give you advice about anything.'

'Come and sit close by me, I don't want anyone overhearing.' Grandy patted the end of his lounger and Amber moved over and sat at the foot of his chair.

'Whatever is it? Is there a problem with their accounts or something?'

'No, no, nothing like that. I can work easily with the figures they gave me and we'll talk with them about that later. No, this is about Calinda's sister.'

Amber's eyes stretched wide in surprise at his words. 'Whatever do you mean, Grandy. Calinda's missing baby sister?'

'Yes, exactly.' Grandy spoke quietly and there was a serious look in his eye as he looked at Amber and added, 'I told you that I support various charities, well, one of them is closely involved with finding children who have been abducted. I have been making a few enquiries and, of course, it was nearly twenty years ago so it is a very difficult project… but, well, there is a small chance that we may be able to trace her. There was a gang working in that area near Nabeul, where Calinda lived around that time. They were all arrested many years ago and now one of them, it seems, has been facing his demons and confessing. It is still a very long shot but there is some small hope that the evidence will show the names of target families. I have sent a serious private detective out to the prison in Tunis to interview this man.' Grandy nodded and took Amber's hand in his, 'I know it's a shock but I wanted to ask you what you thought about it all. Am I interfering… should I be even thinking about it all?'

'Phew, Grandy, you have taken my breath away. My immediate reaction is that it would be an incredible thing to find Calinda's sister and then a hundred other thoughts rush into my head.'

'Exactly, well, we shall think about it quietly for a day or so. Of course, there must be no mention of it to Calinda or even to Daniel. It would be too cruel to give her any glimmer of false hope if the search all comes to nothing. The agency has warned me that this could be the outcome. As you rightly say, there are at least a hundred issues that could arise.

But I have been thinking over what you said about my manipulating life… perhaps I do?'

'Oh no, don't think that Grandy, everything you do is done out of kindness. But you're right, we'll keep it a complete secret. Some things are better like that at least until the truth is certain.'

'Right, that's what we'll do then and I'll let the search go ahead. Now, off you go to find your paint pots and I'll tot up a few more figures. Then I shall take an idle swim, my goodness, it's hot today. Make sure you stay in the shade!'

Amber set up her easel in the deep shade of a barn at the rear of the hotel. She had already learnt that complete shade was better than the shifting shade of trees, especially as the mid-day sun reached full strength. As she laid out the small tubes of paint her mind was still full of her conversation with Grandy and his plan to find Calinda's long lost sister. She was touched that he should ask her advice but even more so that he should worry about being too manipulative. Amber smiled as she thought of it. Her grandfather was a remarkable man with a mind open to anything, even self examination at his age. How lucky she was to have him in her life and how much more she had discovered about him on this chance holiday. She looked to the horizon, shimmering in the heat, and began to mix the first colour. As her brush began to swirl the strong indigo blue into the dab of cobalt, she sighed with pleasure and immediately forgot everything except her work.

Two hours passed and it wasn't until she ran out of paper that Amber finally put down her brush. She wriggled her fingers, cramped from gripping the brush, and then stood up and stretched her back. She was used to working long hours over a painting in the museum in London, but this seemed more exhausting. She looked down at the pages of paper laid out in the sun around her. Nine paintings, no wonder she was tired, she had worked at a furious pace, wide, brush strokes swept across each page. Nothing like the detailed work of restoring an old master. She was checking the paintings to see if they were completely dry when Calinda came round the corner of the barn.

'Hi Amber, am I disturbing you? Your grandfather told me you might be round here.'

'No, it's good to see you. I was just packing up. I hadn't realised how the time had passed.'

'Why, Amber, these are fantastic! I had no idea you worked like this… so dramatic and the colours so exactly right. I love this one.' Calinda put her arm around Fleur, once again asleep in her sling, and leant over to pick up one of the paintings. 'This one is so amazing. Abstract in every way and yet I can recognise our lavender fields in such detail. How do you do that?'

Amber smiled with pleasure and hesitated before she answered, 'Actually I'm not quite sure how I came out with these… it must be the heat and the perfume of lavender. My work in London is very detailed and painstaking. This lot have just been fun.'

Calinda helped Amber pick up the paintings and then stopped to look at the last one, 'I love this one, with the more detailed lavender stalks and flowers in the foreground. You've really made it stand out.' Calinda peered closely at the sprigs of lavender that filled the lower part of the landscape, then passed it to Amber.

'That's is the last one I did and it's dry already. I'm not used to working in such heat. Drying so quickly means I can overlay another colour almost immediately. I think it helps the spontaneity of the whole thing.' Amber ran her hand lightly over the surface of the painting.

Calinda spoke quietly, 'I see your new sun tan has covered the line of the ring you no longer wear, Amber. Is that a good thing?'

Amber started at Calinda's words and hurriedly took her hand away from the painting they were both studying. There was a short silence between them and then Amber spoke,

'You're very observant, Calinda. Yes, I was engaged to be married, in fact my wedding should have been last week.'

Calinda gasped and said, 'I'm so sorry, Amber, I shouldn't have spoken. Please forgive me.'

'No, actually I am pleased you know, Calinda, it's rather a relief. I mean, I don't exactly want to go round with a label saying I was left standing at the altar but I do want to start being able to cope with it.'

'That's a sad story, but you know, with a talent such as yours you should be painting, not messing around marrying too young and to the wrong person.'

'I suppose so, but of course I didn't think he was the wrong person… not until recently anyway. As for my talent, I don't know about that.'

'Then let me tell you! This work is exceptional… I would like to buy the whole series for the hotel entrance foyer. They would look fabulous and I have been looking over a year now for something that is the essence of Provence without being the usual touristy stuff. In fact, why don't I hang them around the hotel with small 'for sale' stickers. I think you may be surprised at how they may sell.'

'Sell! Oh no, they're just rough sketches… I couldn't sell them.'

'You don't need to because I am sure I could. One thing I learnt when I was at art college … know when to stop on a piece of work… don't go past the high point. There is an exciting spontaneity in these paintings… you may think they are rough or even unfinished but why not let me try? I have good instincts for this sort of thing.'

'Well, if you're sure, of course you can take them all.' Amber stacked the paintings together and slipped them into her portfolio. 'Anyway, I'd better get back to Grandy, he'll be wondering where on earth I am… he may be waiting for lunch. I had no idea I had been out here so long.'

'Don't worry about your grandfather, he sent me out to find you and I left him talking with Daniel. They're sitting in the poolside cafe and probably planning our lives for us.'

'You're so right. I can't think why I ever worry about Grandy, he's always in the background pulling strings. We're probably just puppets!' Amber laughed but couldn't help thinking back to her conversation earlier with Grandy. How would Calinda feel if she knew exactly how Grandy was involving himself in her life? Not wanting to even think about the matter whilst hiding it from Calinda, Amber hurried to continue, 'But I'm sure Daniel doesn't control your life, Calinda. It seems more that you make all the decisions.'

'Hmm, well maybe, or maybe it's just my clever husband making it seem that way. There maybe a double bluff going on too! Let's go and find them and see what they have cooked up!'

Grandy and Daniel were sitting in the poolside café with a pile of paperwork on the table.

'Ah, you have come back to us at last!' Daniel stood up and smiled at Calinda and then to Amber. 'Your grandfather has been simply amazing and has explained so much to me. Here, Calinda, pass Fleur to me, I'll hold her for a while.'

'Would you let me hold her?' Amber asked. Her words fell into a small silence so she continued hurriedly, 'I'll just go and wash and brush up first.' Amber hurried into the changing rooms and then took a long, cold shower. She was beginning to really enjoy showering outside in the fresh air. She let the water run over her as she thought about her paintings and Calinda's praise. Then she dived into the pool and swam back to where Calinda and Daniel were sitting with Grandy.

'Shall I order you a sandwich, Amber? We're all going to eat here while we carry on talking. Ok with you? Your usual goat's cheese and tomato?'

Amber nodded and then with a quick duck dive she swam under water back to the other end of the pool. Grabbing her beach towel she quickly dried herself and then ran up to her room. She put on a cotton t-shirt style dress and pulled her wet hair back with a wide bandana. She glanced at herself in the mirror and approved the new clean and efficient image of herself. Surely Calinda would allow her to hold the baby Fleur.

As soon as she was back at their table, she quickly repeated her question.

'Would you let me hold, Fleur?' Daniel was now holding Fleur and he glanced at Calinda. Calinda was looking at Amber, her fine, dark eyebrows drawn together with a frown.   'Well…' Calinda hesitated and then seemed to make up her mind, 'if you sit down.' Amber sat down promptly and held out her arms as Daniel carefully passed the sleeping baby to her. Amber looked down at the baby and felt her weight in her arms. Without looking up, she said, 'She is so beautiful and so peaceful. Thank you for letting me hold her.'

'She seems contented with you, at least.' Calinda said grudgingly. 'I'll just eat my salad, then, while you hold her.'

'I read up about these baby slings, Calinda.' said Grandy thoughtfully as he munched his sandwich. 'Some research by a developmental neuropsychologist and his theory on developing basic trust. The bonding, as we have learnt to call it, apparently could be the foundation for future human relationships. I think the idea is very sound. Amber here is living proof, in fact. Being the one and only child and grandchild in our family she was never allowed to cry or want for a thing. She's certainly turned out confident enough. In fact, I think we may have overdone it… she can be a stong-willed little rebel!'

They all laughed and the serious tone turned to general banter. Amber continued to hold the sleeping Fleur and Calinda pecked at her salad, glancing frequently at Fleur. Finally, she put down her fork and came round the table to Amber.

'I'll take her now, thank you, Amber. You eat your lunch now. You must be starving after all the work you have done. She scooped Fleur back into her arms and gently rocked her as she continued, 'I hadn't realised your grand-daughter has such talent, William! You should just see her paintings, Dani, they're fantastic. I'm going to have them framed, very simply behind non-reflective glass, and hang them around the entrance lobby. I told Amber I would put price tags on them but really, I don't want to sell them!'

'They're just water-colour sketches… I'm not sure they're good enough to hang on any wall, let alone your magnificent entrance. I remember when we arrived at the hotel, how impressed I was with the stone-flagged floor and the pale beamed ceiling. So cool in every sense.'

'Believe me, Amber, if my wife thinks they're what she wants in the lobby then you don't stand a chance of getting them back. Better to go back tomorrow and paint another lot, because if she thinks they'll sell, they will! Calinda has an uncanny way of knowing what the general public want in their lives.'

'That's a huge skill, you know.' Grandy finished the last crumbs of his sandwich and tapped the pile of paperwork in front of him. 'You can read any amount of accounts, projects and stats but the bottom line is knowing what people want. I would say, having looked at the figures that it is very obvious you both know what you're doing. The Hotel Lavande is doing extremely well. Couldn't do better in fact… apart from a small shortage in cash flow. You're stretched but pulling through well and next year all your efforts are going to reap benefit. It would be a big mistake to sell out now and let someone else profit from all your hard work.'

Calinda and Daniel looked at Grandy and then at each other.

'Do you mean we should turn down the Sylvestre hotel take-over offer and stay as we are?' Daniel asked, taking Calinda's hand in his as he continued, 'I mean, I understand what you say but Calinda so very much wants to live by the sea. Selling here means we could make an offer for the Hotel de la Plage.'

'Well now, that's another issue altogether,' Grandy smiled at them both,'You should always follow your dream, but I think we could come to an arrangement where you can do both. I know that Calinda feels, in a way, suffocated by her success as a model. This needs some thought between you both, of course, but in my opinion she should be royally proud of the name she has created for herself. Calinda, the name is a huge asset. Just looking at the revenue it brings in from your perfume… it says everything. Sales haven't dropped since you hid from the public eye… they have doubled each year.'

'I know, and it is a very useful income but…' Calinda sighed, 'it's hard living in the glare of the public eye.'

'I can imagine that it is,' agreed Grandy, 'my life is nothing to compare with the glamour of all that media interest but I still like to remain private in my own way. By the way, you must have had a very good lawyer working for you when you were a top model, your intellectual property rights are very well sewn up. That's important because, much as you may not like my idea, I think you should make more use of your name. Develop it like a brand.'

'A brand? You mean, extend my perfume into make-up or something?' Calinda asked, and she looked at Daniel, shaking her head.

'Well, of course, the possibilities are endless, but all that can be left to a marketing team. I was thinking first, with your pottery talents, you should develop *Calinda* tableware. I mean, that's just an idea… pie in the sky.'

Daniel suddenly sat up straight and said, 'That I can imagine… maybe a simple tin glaze with some cobalt underglaze… very simple design…'

'Maybe a suggestion of lavender flowers?' Amber entered the conversation for the first time, 'I can imagine a cobalt blue fusing into the white glaze… it could be lovely.'

'Stop, wait a moment for an old man to catch up with all you artists. Hang on to the business matter for a moment longer. You see, I was thinking of offering Calinda and Daniel an interest free loan, with the Hotel de la Plage as security and a share to go to Amber. This is not an unusual offer in this economic climate. The banks are not worth investing in and the stock market has its own problems so, business men like myself, are beginning to invest in young businesses instead.'

Now, Calinda, Daniel and Amber were all staring at Grandy in astonishment. Then, suddenly they were all talking at once. The questions and answers went on until the sun began to sink toward the dark red earth of Provence.

15 *'she turned a cartwheel and then another'*

To: amber@hotmail.com
Cc:
Subject: be warned
From: Kim Simpson - kimS@gmail.com
OMG… You are not coming back, are you… I can read between the lines. Amber Marsden, I don't believe it… have you lost all sense of moral duty… you know you should be shut in your mouldy museum in grey London…which is my way of saying… whilst deep and violent green with envy… that you should go for it! Let me know if I have guessed aright? Let me know NOW!
All well here… I am officially in lerve with Mike and his lasagna. x

To: kimS@gmail.com
Cc:
Subject: hi
From: Amber Marsden - amber@hotmail.com
Things have accelerated out here… Grandy has just offered to invest in the hotel where we are staying… and the other one down on the coast. It's surreal! My life has sort of rocketed into free-fall but I have to say I am enjoying every moment. Painting a lot and to my amazement, Calinda has offered to hang them in the hotel and try to sell them. So much more to tell you but can't be done in an email. I really miss you and being able to talk things through. Tell Mike he is a lucky man… mind you, lasagna… yum yum! x Amber

      Amber was up early and running, the early morning air was cool on her face as she ran down the hotel drive and struck out in a different direction. She thought she'd jog along the side of the road, making use of the easy-going tarmac and then cross to the other side toward the blue hills that were always on the far horizon. Her mind was full of the long talk of yesterday. Nothing had been firmly settled but it was obvious that Calinda and Daniel had been as excited as she was at the prospect that Grandy had opened out before them. The plan for later in the day was to go down together and take another look at the Hotel de la Plage. It would be good to be near the sea again. Amber's mind wandered to Sam. He had her number but he hadn't contacted her. True, he had asked her to call him but still… she was just thinking it through when a motorbike came out of nowhere and roared past her. In the next moment it was gone, out of sight over the brow of the hill. Amber stopped running and leant forward onto her knees to get her breath back. The bike had been so close she had felt the heat and rush of air, now there was the lingering smell of diesel and cigarette smoke. She stood up and looked angrily up the empty road and then realised why she could smell cigarette smoke. Lying on the side of the dry grass verge was a burning cigarette stub. Amber ran over to it and stamped on it and then furiously ground it into the road. Any fool should realise how easy it would be to start a fire around here. Every blade of grass was as dry as tinder. She ran on at a slower pace and decided to cut back through the lavender fields to the hotel. Her mood had changed and now all she wanted was a cool shower.

Later over breakfast she told her grandfather about the motorbike incident.

'What a moron… a cigarette stub could start a dreadful fire. Do you think you should report it to the local police?"

'Well, I was too shaken to get the bike number… I know it was bright red and the rider wore jeans and a black leather jacket. He was wearing a shiny, black full face helmet. But I don't suppose that would mean much. I don't know. It all happened so fast.'

'Well, you had better stick to running in the fields and lanes and keep away from the highway. Of course there are a lot of tourists on motorbikes at this time of the year but I think when we pass through the village you should at least call in to the Mairie. You never know… it might be a local biker that they know. It's a criminal offence to throw a lighted cigarette away here, I'm sure of that.'

They were still thinking about it when Daniel came up to their table and Grandy asked him to join them.

'There's nothing I'd like more but if we want to get away to the coast later this morning I think I had better see to things here.'

'Amber was just telling me about a motorcyclist throwing away a lighted cigarette up on the road early this morning. She stubbed it out, of course, but we were wondering if we should report it?'

Daniel looked shocked and said, 'Definitely, if you want to come in to reception, Amber, I'll phone the local police and you can tell them anything you know.'

Amber went with Daniel, and with his help in some translation, she gave all the detail she could. The receptionist listened in and was as shocked as Daniel.

'Obviously it's a serious risk here.' Amber said as she ended the call.

'Oh my god, yes, you have no idea coming from the damp of England. Especially the lavender fields and pine forest around here… full of natural oils. We have very strict fire regulations for running the pottery kilns and there are fire hydrants all over the place. When you settle in I'll show you the routine, of course.'

There was a short silence at his words. Suddenly they both seemed to realise that Amber would be part of the hotel life now. They moved away from the reception and Daniel spoke first. 'I hope you are as excited about your grandfather's generous offer as we are, Amber? We've been up half the night talking and planning. Calinda is buzzing with ideas and I know she wants to talk them through with you. Ah, and there she is… looking as immaculate as ever, even after so little sleep. And Fleur, thank goodness she did sleep well.' Daniel hurried ahead and Amber watched, subduing a remnant tinge of envy, as Daniel enclosed Calinda and Fleur in a light embrace.

Amber looked over to the table where she had breakfasted with Grandy but saw he was not there and the table had already been cleared.

'I'm going to pack.' Amber called out, waving a hand to Calinda. 'What time shall we leave?

'Eleven OK?' Calinda called back, waving her long, elegant hand back in return.

'Fine, I'll be in the lobby at eleven.'

The journey down to the coast had gone well and they arrived at the Hotel de la Plage at lunch time. Grandy got out of Amber's car and stretched before ambling over to where Calinda had parked their estate car.

'I need to stretch my old bones. I thought I might leave you all to check in and I'll wander down the beach to that restaurant. Amber knows the place… and I'll get us a table.' He turned to Amber and raised his panama hat and she quickly snapped another photo of him on her phone. She checked the image in the screen and smiled as she saw that Grandy had turned the wave to shaking a fist at her for snatching a photo. Once again she thought there was not much that Grandy missed and then began to wonder if he had a hidden agenda, going straight to the restaurant. She slung her own bag on her shoulder and then grabbed Grandy's lightweight hold-all. He certainly knew how to travel light and yet look well-dressed. She smiled to herself and mentally added it to the growing list of things she was finding out about him. Amber followed Daniel and Calinda up the stone steps to the hotel entrance. Suddenly everything about the place seemed of importance. Amber rubbed the sole of her shoe in the dust and thought the steps might actually be marble. Some weeding and sweeping might be all they needed to look magnificent. She looked up and saw that Calinda, was looking down to where Amber's foot had cleared the dust and dirt.

'Rosa Aurora marble!' Calinda said in a low voice, then, standing between Daniel and Amber she said, just loud enough for them both to hear. 'This is so exciting!'

Less than an hour later they were all sitting at lunch in the beach restaurant.

'Tell me, Grandy, what have you been up to? Why did you shoot off to the restaurant and leave us to check in? Have you bought this place yet?

'My goodness, you're a suspicious little minx. Can't an old man need to stretch his legs after rocketing around Provence in your beetle?'

'Most old men, maybe, but I know you were up to something.'

'Well, I just want to keep a low profile at the Hotel de la Plage for a while longer. I'll come and go as discreetly as possible until I am ready to make an offer.'

'Well, that won't be difficult!' laughed Amber, the woman in reception practically threw the room keys at us and left us to find our own way.'

'Exactly,' laughed Daniel, 'definitely no offer to help with our luggage. Not even a smile of welcome.'

'Jolly good,' laughed Grandy, 'I won't need to make a consideration for buying their good will then.'

Calinda stood up and looked at the sleeping Fleur nestling in her arms and then, as though making an important decision, she turned to Amber.

'Amber, would you hold Fleur while Daniel and I take a swim?' There was a surprised silence and then Amber held out her arms and, trying to keep her voice normal, replied.

'Yes, of course, I'd love to.'

Grandy and Amber sat in silence for a moment, watching Calinda and Daniel walk down to the sea edge, hand in hand. Their figures were silhouetted against the bright light of the sun, Calinda tall and slim beside Daniel's muscled form.

'Well done, Amber. I think that's quite a step forward for Calinda to trust you like that. I've had a chat with Daniel and he told me how worried he was about Calinda's fears. Of course he understands that Calinda is suffering the agony of losing her sister but it is hard for him, too. Of course, he knew about the sister's disappearance before they married but until Fleur came on the scene it was never really an issue. It will be a good thing if she begins to trust you. It will certainly help Daniel, too. He comes from a large family himself so it is very different.'

'Yes, and he is a twin.'

Grandy looked at Amber in surprise, 'Is he? Is he now. I didn't know that!'

Before Grandy could ask her how she knew, Amber stood up and gently rocked Fleur who was stirring from sleep. 'Oh goodness, I hope Fleur doesn't start crying, Calinda will never trust me again. She's waking up Grandy, what shall I do?'

'Exactly what you are doing, Amber. Your natural instincts have kicked in! Don't start worrying as much as Calinda does, for goodness sake!'

Amber smiled and relaxed and looked down at Fleur who now had her eyes wide open and was absorbed in looking up at the blue and white awning as it flapped in the breeze.

'She's so sweet, Grandy. I want to have a baby one day.'

'Well, you said that as though you were a kid asking for a dolly. At least you added 'one day'. I'll take that as a good sign. Of course you will have babies, Amber... one day... but may I suggest you find the right father first?'

Amber laughed, 'You may suggest that, my dear old-fashioned Grandy, but ... oh look, Calinda and Daniel are coming back. Look at them!'

Amber and her grandfather watched as Daniel chased Calinda along the sand and how she ran like the wind, dodging his outstretched hands and turning to laugh at him. Suddenly she turned a cartwheel and then another and Daniel stopped running and stood on the sand clapping her as she turned from cartwheels to walking on her hands.

'What a girl!' Grandy said admiringly, 'This is how she will lose her fears and her resistance to being a famous named supermodel. Just some time to play in the sunshine. And now I shall order ice-creams for all you children!'

The ice-creams arrived just as Calinda and Daniel returned to the table. Daniel held out Calinda's robe and wrapped her in it, his arms resting around her.

'Did you see my gymnastic fantastic wife? She could get a job in a circus!'

They all laughed and Calinda reached out her arms to take Fleur from Amber.'

'Why don't you eat your ice-cream first… I'll hold Fleur a while longer while you dry off.'

Calinda looked at Amber in surprise and then dropped her arms to her sides and said,

'Oh thank you, Amber, that would be great.'

There was a companionable silence around the table as they all enjoyed the ice-cream. Then Grandy spoke, 'Well, my children, I shall regretfully be leaving you to play on your won tomorrow. I've booked a flight back from Marseille in the morning.'

They all stopped eating their ice-creams at the same moment, their spoons suspended in the air.

'My goodness, don't all look at me like that! Carry on eating or the ice-cream will be melting. You youngsters can have fun on the Cote d'Azur but I shall return to my sensible cottage on the Sussex downs.'

Amber was the first to answer, 'But Grandy, you can't go yet, my honeymoon's not over!'

They all burst out laughing at this ridiculous outburst from Amber. Little Fleur stirred in Amber's arms and gave a gurgle of what could have been laughter.

'Oh my, even a three month old baby can understand how ridiculous that sounds, Amber!' Grandy laughed, 'You will do very well without me and anyway, I have a feeling your holiday is nearly over. There is a lot to do for all of us but my work will be done in England and with my solicitors. I'm too old to live out of a suitcase any longer… but I'll be glad not to risk taking a taxi from here tomorrow if you would give me a lift, Amber.'

'Of course, if you really insist on going but I still think it's rotten of you.'

Calinda stood up and took Fleur from Amber. 'Well, Amber, I think you must have the most wonderful, rotten grandfather on the planet.'

The afternoon passed, as an afternoon does on a beach in the South of France. A gentle breeze blue in from the sea and the cloudless sky hung over them all. They talked, made plans for the future and relaxed, unaware of trouble that gathered like storm clouds, for now, out of sight.

To: amber@hotmail.com
Cc:
Subject: OK… I am in the picture now
From: Kim Simpson - kimS@gmail.com
Had very long convo with your Mum yesterday. We met for lunch at Fenwicks and talked about nothing but you. Well, OK, I did tell her about Mike moving in to our flat but honestly we talked practically non-stop for two hours about what you are up to over there in the sunny S of F. I have to say she is mighty miffed with your grandfather and thinks he is leading you well astray. Anyway, she said she was going to Skype you later so watch out. Your Mum wants you back in London and doing a proper job. Me? I think… much as I miss you… that you should grab the opp… you've always been a better artist than you realised and if you get any chance to paint then…that is what you should be doing. BTW you make no more mench of the dashing marine biologist… has he swum out of sight? I need to know everything and you are the meanest friend on earth not to tell me MORE/ALL … NOW.
x K

To: kimS@gmail.com
Cc:
Subject: hi
From: Amber Marsden - amber@hotmail.com
First: I am so pleased/shocked/delighted/jealous (a bit) that you are have found lerve and lasagna. That's a powerful combo…beware and don't do anything I did.
Next: Yes, I have had a long Skype sesh with Ma… it was really difficult… she kept pretending she thought I should stay out here and paint and then welling up and going all pink. Still, I toughed it out. I told her that I simply couldn't imagine going back to my old life and basically that I was going to give it a go in Provence. So now you know, too. Grandy has been up to all sorts of tricks and is going back to London

today. It will be strange here without him. Must go now as I am giving him a lift to Marseille airport.
We must have a proper talk about the flat and everything soon.
x Amber

Amber waited and waved until Grandy was finally out of sight in the queue through to departures. She turned away and walked slowly back to the car park. She felt the shock of loneliness mixed strangely with excitement. Now she was on her own and she could begin a new life here in the sunshine of Provence. Maybe, she would drive back and take some photos from that cliff road between Cassis and La Ciotat. Just as she was about to start the car, her phone rang. She snatched it up, immediately anxious, for some reason, that it was her grandfather. The name that came up on the small screen was Sam Robinson, not a text but an incoming call. Amber hesitated for a brief second and then answered.

'Hi Sam, how are you?'

'Fine, just fine, all the better for getting hold of you… did you mean to give me a wrong number? Efficient brush off, I know, but I was not to be deterred, Amber.'

'What do you mean? Oh, I'm so sorry, no of course I didn't meant to give you a wrong number. I'd never be so subtle… so how did you get hold of me?'

'Well, your grandfather just rang me on my cell phone. He was in departures at Marseilles airport. Luckily I had given him my card.'

Amber sighed, of course, it was Grandy at work again.

'He asked me to give you a message, Amber. Just to say 'over to you now, Amber' those were the very words. Does it mean anything to you? That's all he wanted me to tell you.'

'Thanks, yes, I get it. Just my grandfather being typically my grandfather. I've just left him at the airport.'

'Right, right... OK... well, I'm in Cassis right now... just going out on the boat. Do you want to come? It's a lovely day.'

'Well, it will take me a good half hour to get there and I was going to paint...'

'Bring your paints. I have some work to do but it will take an hour or so out on the water. I'm collating info on the coupling of the nitrogen and carbon cycles in planktonic and microbialer... sexy stuff, eh!' Sam laughed, 'and then we could have lunch?' Sam's voice was so eager and the day was heating to the point where the thought of diving into the sea was very, very hard to resist.

'Actually, that would be great. I could see you at the harbour at eleven... if I run late I'll ring you.'

'Great, that's made my day. So glad your grandfather happened on my card at just the right moment.'

'Yes,' agreed Amber, sighing again, 'he's always on the ball.'

As she drew up and parked in the harbour at Cassis, Amber could see Sam waiting by a pile of diving equipment on the end of the pontoon. As soon as he saw her he ran to meet her and held open her car door. As she stood up he gave her a light kiss on each cheek.

'That's one of the best things about living in France... all this cheek kissing!' Sam laughed and took Amber's bag from her. 'Do you have a swimsuit in here?'

'Oh yes, I've learnt there's usually a chance to swim wherever I go round here. But I must say your particular corner of the Med is the best ever.'

'Yeh, beats a swimming pool any day. OK, let's get out there!'

Soon the cruiser was pulling slowly out of the harbour. The sea was as smooth as a millpond, blue and calm. Sam had pulled a dark blue canvas awning over the white leather padded deck area and Amber stretched out in the shade, enjoying the luxury and lulled by the slight movement of the sea and the low noise of the motor. Sam busied himself with the instrument panel and was writing in a detailed log book. Amber thought about getting out her paints and then thought about what she might paint and then… she fell into a light sleep.

She awoke with a start and realised she could smell food and at the same moment realised she was very hungry. Sam wasn't at his place at the helm and the engine noise had died. She moved carefully along the deck and peered down into the cabin and saw Sam was cooking. He looked up at her with a wide smile.

'Sleeping beauty awakes! I've cooked up a pasta sauce and it's ready to go… but shall we have a quick dip first?' He wiped his hands down his shorts and turned off the gas.

'That would be lovely !' Amber grabbed her bag and moved down the small staircase just as Sam moved to come up the stairs. For a moment they collided and then moved apart. Amber was very aware of the impact, her stomach fluttering at the brush of his skin against hers. Sam leapt up the top two steps and called back, 'I'll lower the diving deck while you change.'

'Thanks, won't be a minute.' Amber smiled to herself as she suddenly wondered what Kim would make of Sam's impeccable manners. She could imagine telling Kim about the moment on the stairs and how they would giggle but… but then, the truth was she liked this slow dance of getting to know a man.

They swam together, side by side in the deep water. It seemed to be Sam's natural habitat, he dived and surfaced effortlessly, enjoying moving in the water. Amber floated on her back for a while, looking up at the cloudless, azure sky. Sam swum under her and then surfaced, his dark lashes studded with drops of sea water. 'You're not going to fall asleep again, are you? Come on, time for my amazing lunch on board the Sophocles. Race you back?'

Amber flipped in the water and swam strongly toward the boat, she could feel Sam thrashing through the water beside her and pulling ahead. 'Ouch, think I've been stung by a jelly fish.' Amber shouted. Sam immediately stopped swimming and trod water, looking at her anxiously. 'Here, on my foot! Can you see a sting?' Sam dived under and immediately Amber struck out for the boat and reached it just a moment ahead of Sam.

'Amber, you are a rotten cheat! I totally believed you...' His look of indignant outrage caused Amber to burst into helpless laughter.

'Oh my, you should see your face ! You should never trust a London girl.'

Sam smiled back at her and pulled himself up on the deck. He held out his hand to Amber, 'You're a bad girl, here, take my hand.' Amber was still laughing so much that she grabbed his hand weakly and let him pull her up. Just as she was about to step onto the deck he let her go and she fell back in to the water. She came up spluttering and still laughing.

'Well, I guess I asked for that!' Amber pulled herself up quickly onto the deck in case he pushed her in again.

'And you thought we Harvard boys were so well-mannered? Now, shall I serve lunch, are we quits?'

'Definitely! Actually I am famished.'

'I just love the way you say 'actually', I've never heard anyone more English than you, Amber... actually.'

'Actually? Actually... do you know you just can't say it, can you?'

Sam laughed at her and then went down into the galley to serve lunch. He dished out two large helpings of tagliatelle, topped with his tomato and fish sauce.

'Mmm, mmm!' Amber twirled a large forkful into her mouth and nodded, 'Actually, yes, actually and quite possibly the best pasta I have ever eaten. And I have actually eaten a lot of pasta. My compliments to the chef !' Amber raised her glass and Sam clinked his against it.

'Sorry, it's only water, but it's one of my strict on board rules... no alcohol!'

'I know, apart from the medicinal cognac that my grandfather was served. He really enjoyed his day on the water.'

'It was great having him on board. I wish my own grandfather was half as easy to get on with.'

'You seem to have trouble getting on with your family life altogether... why is that, Sam?'

'Oh, you may wish you had never asked. Can you begin to imagine life in an extreme right family? Have you heard of the Tea Party? My father believes in everything I detest... he has never forgiven me for refusing to go into the family oil business. He's on top of the world fracking around whilst I swim below the surface of the sea trying to find out how to conserve life. I mean, how far apart can a man and his son get?' Sam angrily picked up the cheese grater and began to grind cheese all over his pasta. Amber watched for a moment and then put her hand over his. He looked up at her in surprise and then grinned. 'You're right, that's enough cheese, isn't it? Enough lousy politics too. Look around, the day is much too beautiful.'

Amber took her hand away from his and turned to scan the horizon. The blue sea was now almost turquoise in the mid-day sun. She turned back to the table and realised Sam was looking at her. He reached out and smoothed back a tendril of her hair that had blown over her forehead.

'How could such a beautiful, kind girl come along just when I was settling into my work. It's just not fair or reasonable.' He smiled at her but their was a hint of sadness in his words.

'And how could such a cool Harvard guy break into my new resolution to devote my days to painting? That's not fair either... actually.' Amber smiled back and began to serve the salad. 'Do you think it would be best if we finished this lovely lunch and then you had better return to your research and I'll get my paints out.'

Sam nodded, 'I guess so.'

And that is exactly what they did all afternoon. Amber sat in the shade of the awning and made several watercolours of the deep inlets of sea between the white rocks. The colours were all so different from her work in the lavender fields. She worked hard until she was satisfied with her palette of colours and then began to produce sketch after sketch. She was so absorbed in her work that for a while she didn't notice that Sam was standing behind her, dripping wet, and looking over her shoulder at her sketch pad.

'Oh my god, you're good, aren't you! I imagined something far more … I don't know… delicate, I suppose. I thought … you know, English water colourist… but these paintings are so dramatic, so dynamic. They're really impressive, Amber. No wonder you want to spend your time painting. You really should!'

'Well, thank you, kind sir!' Amber laughed and began to clean her brushes. 'But you have really been working. Shall I go down and find some drinks?'

'That would be great… I've had enough for one day. You can't believe how detailed the work is… but still, I have enough statistics to keep Matt busy tomorrow. I do all the donkey work but he is brilliant at analysis. Anyway, you stay right where you are… I have some apple juice in the fridge, I'll get it.' Sam jumped down the steps into the galley and returned a moment later with a large bottle of juice and two glasses. 'I found a packet of chocolate cookies, too. We're in luck!' He sat down beside her on the deck and carefully poured two glasses. 'I drink to your talent, Amber, may you paint every day and preferably on my boat!'

'Thank you, it's certainly heavenly out here, so peaceful. I've never really been anywhere like it.'

'I know, it is a special place in the world, isn't it? I am so determined to help with its preservation. Now it is designated a national park it is protected but there are always problems linked with tourism.'

'I suppose so, I must be part of that too.' Amber was quiet for a moment, thinking of the plans she was embarking on with Calinda and Daniel… how another successful hotel would just bring more and more tourists to the area.

'You look miles away, Amber, are you thinking about home in England?'

Amber looked at him in astonishment, 'Good heavens, no, not at all.' Then suddenly she added, 'Actually, I try not to think about England.'

'Are you going to tell me why? Actually?' he smiled at her but his eyes were serious as he added, 'I have a feeling we both have some issues hanging in the air around us.'

'True enough, well, you told me about your break up and so you may as well know that I'm in the same boat!' They both laughed at her choice of words.

'I guess we're both what the magazines would call 'on the rebound' then.' Sam said quietly, 'That's supposed to be a dangerous state, isn't it?'

'Definitely, we're vulnerable, easily led astray… err… susceptible to the slightest risk of being hurt again.'

'Yeh, terrified of commitment and determined not to get involved.' Sam nodded in agreement.

'Absolutely.' Amber was looking out to the horizon when she felt Sam's arm around her as he whispered in her ear. 'So, I would be mad to kiss you and you would be foolish to let me, isn't that right?'

'Quite right!' Amber said softly as leant back against him and turned her head towards him.

'But, if I were to say that I just couldn't help myself?' Now they were face to face and Amber looked into his grey eyes, feeling the tension of the moment between them, knowing they would kiss. Then she closed her eyes and felt his lips brush her forehead and then her mouth. First their kisses were light, tender and soft, then as their mouths opened and Sam's hands ran over Amber's body, they began to devour each other. Soon, Sam was breathing hard and Amber pulled him close to her as they fell back onto the white, leather deck. There was no time now for words or friendly smiles as the tempo of their emotion rose. At first they moved together to the slow rhythm of the rise and fall of the waves and then faster, their bodies entangled in wild passion.

I feel like I am bouncing back

To: amber@hotmail.com
Cc:
Subject: Back in Sussex
From: William Marsden - wmarsden@talktalk.net

Dear Amber, I know you will be smiling at those first two words and that emails are not like letters… but I am just your old-fashioned Grandy so please imagine that this is penned in dark blue ink on expensive light blue paper. Most of all, it is a letter of thanks to my sweet grand-daughter who gave me a holiday of a lifetime just when I was settling down into a very boring old age. I feel rejuvenated and all thanks to our time together. Tomorrow I shall begin work on our new projects but this evening I shall just put my feet up and read a good book. I hope you carry on with your painting and enjoy messing around (in a boat or otherwise) in the beautiful world that is Provence. Best love, your old Grandy.

To: wmarsden@talktalk.net
Cc:
Subject: hi Grandy
From: Amber Marsden - amber@hotmail.commail.com

Sorry not to reply earlier but as you may have guessed or even planned… I was messing around on a boat. Tomorrow I definitely start serious painting but right now I am sitting in the garden of the Hotel de la Plage with Sam and drinking a surprisingly good cocktail. We seem to have found something they do very well here. Calinda, Daniel and Fleur are joining us soon and we are going to eat at our beach restaurant again. Thank you so much for all you have done and are still doing for me. I'll Skype you tomorrow when I'm back at the Hotel Lavande. Right now I am sipping my Mimosa and nibbling olives as the huge red sun sinks into the dark sea. x your loving and favourite, ok one and only grand-daughter, Amber

'Sorry about that... I just wanted to send a quick reply to Grandy.' Amber snapped her phone off and slipped it back into her bag. 'I know it's really rude to be tapping into my phone when we're sitting here together.'

'Don't worry, of course you should answer your grandfather. Is he back home yet?'

'Yes, safe and sound and in his cottage in Sussex. Probably planning his next move! He's a great fixer.' Amber looked across the table at Sam and then out to sea. Maybe soon she would tell him about the plans they had for the Hotel de la Plage, but not right now. As for Grandy's idea and hopes of finding Calinda's sister, that would definitely remain a secret. Amber still wanted time to enjoy this holiday that was to have been her honeymoon. Her life had been a roller-coaster ride since that dreadful day at the church.

'You're miles away from me! A dollar for your thoughts?' Sam took her hand in his and Amber turned to look at him. The brightness of the sun still shone in her eyes and she blinked rapidly.

'You're not crying, are you?' Sam stood up and came round the table to put his arm around her.

Amber leaned against him for a moment and then laughed, 'No, no, just the brightness of the setting sun made tears come to my eyes. Or maybe it was just the beauty of it all and my luck at being here.'

Sam gave her a light kiss on the top of her head and sat down again.

'You realise I am on red alert for signs of any vulnerability! Now, what was it? Fear of commitment? Rebound symptoms?'

They sipped their cocktails and Amber smiled at Sam, 'I may be on the rebound but I feel like I am bouncing back, actually!'

'Me too, actually! Bouncing high and fine, actually! "*If you can bounce high, bounce for her too,*' Sam spoke now in a deep American voice, with a serious expression. Did you know I could quote from American literature? *"Till she cry, lover, gold-hatted, high-bouncing lover, I must have you!"* With his last words, Sam placed his hand on his heart and fluttered his long, dark lashes at Amber.

'I had no idea you were so poetic.' Amber laughed

'Not just poetic but so damned well-educated. Not just the Great Gatsby but I also read Fitzgerald's first novel, *This Side of Paradise*, dear old Scottie was quite a wheeze… did you know he made up the author of the quote, Thomas Parks d'Invillers? You didn't know that? What do they teach you over in Blighty? Just Shakespeare? Young lady your education has been sadly neglected.'

'I know, I'm just a grammar school girl! I am so very impressed.' Amber wiped tears of laughter from her eyes, 'Somehow the poetic look just doesn't suit you though.'

'Ah, you've sassed me! You're so right. I was force-fed literature and could never wait to get out the class room.'

'Oh, I loved English lit.! It was my favourite subject after art. We obviously have nothing in common!'

'Nothing,' agreed Sam, solemnly, 'Isn't that just so great!'

They were both still laughing when Calinda found them on the terrace. Sam jumped to his feet and held a chair for Calinda. Amber stood up too and had a peep at the sleeping Fleur.

'Sam, may I introduce you to Calinda and baby Fleur? Calinda this is Sam Robinson.'

Calinda smiled graciously and held out a long and elegant hand, '*Enchantée*, I have heard all about you from Amber.'

'*Enchanté, le mannequin de mode le plus célèbre…* you hardly need introduction, the pleasure is all mine but I hope you didn't believe everything Amber said about me?'

'My, an Amercian who speaks good French and knows about fashion… where did you find him, Amber?'

'She fished me out of the deep blue sea. I speak French all day at work and I do have three sisters who are obsessed with fashion… so! Anyway, Calinda can I get you a drink? We're on our second glasses of Mimosa but I am guessing you aren't drinking alcohol at the moment. Not with your little Fleur in arms?'

'Absolutely… I'd love the orange juice without the champagne, *merci*.'

Sam went off to the bar and Calinda settled in her seat and then gave a little giggle.

'Really, Amber, he is a model of perfect manners. *Très beau, très bobo!*'

'Boho? Surely not!'

'*Non, non*' Calinda giggled again, '*Bo Bo not boho*!'

'*Bobo?* Oh god, I wish I spoke better French, what does that mean, *bobo?*'

'I don't know, *bon chic, bon genre…* you know, preppy or in London you'd say Sloane Ranger. Exuding old money and all that… you're on the edge of being *bobo* yourself!' Calinda laughed at Amber but before they could continue their girly chat they saw Daniel and Sam both coming out from the bar together, carrying a tray of drinks.

'This hotel is kinda self service! I met Daniel in the bar and both being under the age of eighty it seemed likely that we would be with you two? How did you decide to stay here? The place is falling apart.'

'Oh, we like the old world charm,' Amber said quickly, 'and the location is great.' She glanced at Calinda who gave a small nod. It seemed better to keep their business to themselves.

'We enjoy a quiet place anyway. No rowdy parties at night. Actually, I like the place.' Daniel smiled into his drink and glanced across to Amber. He obviously agreed it was better to keep silent about their hopes of buying the hotel.

'Well, I'll drink to a quiet place any day and the garden running down to the beach is lovely … actually! I can tell you've picked up the word from Amber, Daniel. It beats me how you can say it better than I can, actually… no, that's not it, actu-ally. It's no good at all. I shall have to cut the word out of my vocabulary altogether.'

'Actually,' said Amber, laughing, 'I was just wondering about dinner. 'If I drink another Mimosa I shall have to be carried away.'

'Hmm, tempting as that sounds, maybe we should walk along the beach and find a table.'

'I think we should go to our favourite... if we can still get a table.' Calinda stood up and looked at Daniel. He downed his drink and stood up. 'Shall I go ahead and take a look?'

'That's a good idea.' Calinda said with a beautiful smile.

'I'll walk along with you and the girls can carry on giggling about us.' Said Sam, he gave Amber a light kiss on the top of her head and strolled off with Daniel.

'He seems a nice guy.' Said Calinda, sipping her orange juice. 'Are you going out with him then?

'I'm not sure just what I'm doing with him, actually!' Both girls laughed at her last word, spoken in a mock American accent, and began to walk along the path by the beach. They found Daniel and Sam at the table that seemed to almost belong to them now. They were deep in conversation and Amber was surprised to hear Sam speaking so fluently in French. As soon as he saw them he stood up and held out a chair for Calinda and Fleur. He changed to English, saying, 'Mothers and children first, Calinda, where do you prefer to sit?'

'I'd love to sit facing the sea. It's a while since I have watched the sun set over the Mediterranean. Such a beautiful evening.'

'It sure is, now Mademoiselle Amber, which seat for you?' Sam smiled at her and put his arm around her for a brief moment as Amber sat down. 'Have you had enough of looking out to sea for one day? You were painting it all afternoon.'

'Oh no, I could never have enough of the Mediterranean, anyway, I wasn't looking at it *all* afternoon.' Amber glanced up at Sam with a meaning look and to her amusement his usual calm manner seemed slightly ruffled. She changed the subject quickly, 'I've just been thinking about my

French. I even took A level at school but I envy you your fluency.'

'He's certainly speaks French better than any American I've ever met!' said Daniel, 'And he has been telling me so much I didn't know about the sea and what lies beneath. Fascinating!'

'Oh, I can certainly bore for America or France in either language if you get me started on talking marine biology. Anyway, Amber, I have been working here over a year now and with French nationals. Give me a break, I would have to be pretty stupid not to speak reasonable French.'

'How long do you intend to stay… do you have a timed contract at Sophia Antipolis?' asked Calinda.

'I'm already past my sell-by date on that… I should have gone back in April but Matt and I managed to extend our contracts. The work is kind of endless but we haven't decided yet when we shall leave. Now, does anyone want another aperitif or shall we order?'

'No more to drink for me, thank you… the Mimosas are deceptively strong. I'd like to eat… I'm ravenous actually!'

'And ravishing, actu-ally!' Sam said in an English accent, 'Let's eat!'

The meal was long and excellent and as a new moon rose high in the sky, Amber looked around and felt a new relaxed happiness. Small stars were beginning to pierce the dark midnight blue sky and the air was still and warm. They had all teased Sam about his passion for marine biology and how his conversation relentlessly returned to it. Amber looked at him across the table as yet again he was attempting to explain the need for conserving marine life. His hands were spread wide and his face alight with fervour as he talked. He was a man with a mission, Amber thought to herself, and nothing wrong with that. As though he had read her thoughts, he looked back at her.

'OK, more than enough about me and the marine world, I know, I am often warned that I become socially inept when I am allowed to air my views. Shall we move on somewhere else for coffee? Maybe if I'm not on the edge of the sea I'll manage to talk about something else?'

They all laughed and tried to reassure him that he had not bored them. Daniel then said,

'Calinda and I will be returning to the hotel and the peace and quiet of the 1920's but you and Amber should carry on. Why don't you go back to that club, Le Bateau Noir, in Cassis? Where you met… Amber told me about the jazz scene. My brother goes there whenever he's in these parts.'

Daniel looked at Amber and gave a wide smile. Amber blushed, remembering how she had lashed out at Daniel that day in the lavender fields. She smiled back, grateful that he didn't bring the matter up now. It would have been hard to explain to Calinda. But Sam was talking,

'How lucky you are to have a brother. I have three crazy sisters who run me ragged. I always wanted a brother. If you and Calinda would like a night out I'm sure Amber and I could manage to babysit with Fleur at the hotel. You might bump into your brother if you go along this evening.'

'That's very kind of you,' Calinda said in a determined voice, 'But we'd rather go back with Fleur.'

'Well, if you're sure, but I do have very high qualifications as a sitter. My oldest sister has three fantastic kids and I've looked after them all at various times. Do you have any brothers and sisters, Calinda?'

There was an awkward silence and then Daniel spoke quickly and changed the subject,

'Calinda's right, well, of course she always is… we'll go back to the hotel, but thanks for the offer… maybe some other time. Anyway, my brother won't be there, I think he's in New York right now or San Francisco. We don't keep in touch that regularly but being twins we have some sort of symbiotic thing going on.'

'Great Scott… you're a twin! I've been working on symbiosis, particularly the commensalism of certain barnacles attaching themselves to whales to get a free ride home and to food-rich water… unlike the mutualism of the tick-bird on the back of a rhino…it's all about…' Sam looked up in surprise and then laughed as he saw them all looking at him and pretending to yawn.

'Sorry, OK, OK… I'll stop but it is really interesting, act-u-ally!'

17 *the silvery olive trees shimmered in the heat*

To: amber@hotmail.com
Cc:
Subject: sorry but..
From: Kim Simpson - kimS@gmail.com

Sorry not to have written before… though why I am, I dunno, as you have not written to me… anyway I thought I'd wait as yesterday Mike and I went down to Sussex for the weekend. Yes, I took him to meet the parents, omg, that's almost a first… all went well, in fact, they seemed to like him more than me and spent all Friday evening telling Mike all my faults and childhood sins. Great, eh? Just managed to stop them getting out the family photo album. Anyway, Saturday we were invited to tea at your Grandy's…oh, how I love his cottage and the whole package of Aga wisdom, cream tea in the conservatory etc etc (am I making you jealous… hope so). He has told me all about your plans to stay in Provence. OK so I am the jealous one now. Mike said he would be pleased to take over your lease/rent thing on the Bloomsbury squalor that was our flat. You won't be surprised to know that without you being here it has become a complete wreck. Anyway, if you have a moment to write between roaming the lavender and diving the coral etc do write to me, your best friend ever ever,
x K

To: kimS@gmail.com
Cc:
Subject: I know, I know, guilty as charged…
From: Amber Marsden -amber@hotmail.commail.com
I haven't written for a while but it is truly hard to find time… stretched out on white leather mattress/deck with Sam… do I need to say more? I have promised myself I will bite the bullet of reality at the end of June… when my honeymoon is over ha not very ha. Just need to tell you that I am SO glad Rob walked.
More soon as…? your devoted and absent friend, x Amber

Amber drove slowly, concentrating on the winding road between the olive groves. In another hour she would be back at the Hotel Lavande and Sam would already be at work in his lab at Sophia Antipolis. She found herself thinking about him and smiling. Was this new love? There was definitely a good friendship that had sparked into hot passion. But what was love all about? Amber sighed and pulled into a shady lay-by with a good view across the olive groves to where the red rocks rose up to the blue sky. She turned off the engine and as the sound died she listened to the call of the cicadas. The air was still and so hot that the earth between the silvery olive trees shimmered in the heat. She stretched and went to the car boot to find her painting bag. Love and what it was all about would have to wait. Now she would paint. She set up her easel in the deep shade of an ancient olive tree and took a long swig from her bottle of water. Sam had insisted she took his large vacuum and she was glad of the refreshing icy cold water. She laid out her palette and brushes and then stretched again, her hands high above her head. Her muscles were aching pleasantly from the love-making of the night before. After dancing until the small hours at the Le Bateau Noir club in Cassis, they had returned to the Hotel de la Plage. The large old bed had creaked and groaned under their love-making. They had laughed and loved again out on the balcony under the pale light of the new moon. Amber smiled at the memory and at herself as the muscle ached turned to the beginning of new desire. She thought of Sam's long, athletic body and his dark-lashed grey eyes looking down at her… then shaking her head impatiently, she picked up her paint-brush and laid the first strong line of the horizon across the blank page.

Nearly two hours passed before she realised she had come to the end of another sketch pad. She looked impatiently in her bag but she had run out of paper. She surveyed the sheets spread at on the dry earth around her. Her own work almost surprised her. Calinda was right, there was an urgency to the style, the way the colour slashed across the paper. She nodded in quiet satisfaction and began to collect them up. She was also surprised at the pleasure she found in the finished pages. Normally there would be several that she would tear up. She flicked through them again and smiled. She might not be sure about finding new love but she had certainly found a new way to paint.

That evening, eating supper with Calinda and Daniel, Amber began to ask their thoughts on the new project down on the coast.

'What do you think about the Hotel de la Plage? I know you have had your eye on in for a while, now, but what did you think after our stay there?'

'I am more excited than ever,' said Calinda, glancing at Daniel, she added, 'we have talked of nothing else and we are both very keen to go ahead. We've had email from William and he has made all his searches now. Apparently there is a heavy mortgage on the property and the owners are near to going bankrupt. I think they will look at an offer as salvation.'

'So it's going ahead?' Amber said excitedly.

'Yes, as far as Calinda and I are concerned it is a win win situation with your grandfather investing in us and only asking for your share of 33.3%. How do you feel about it, Amber?' Daniel looked at her seriously as he sipped his wine. 'It is a huge jump into the unknown for you. We were planning a loft conversion, obviously the view is mind-blowing and you would have room for a large studio as well as living accommodation. We would take over the ground floor annexe and then the main block of the hotel would offer about twenty ensuite rooms. That's our first thought, anyway. Obviously open to your input.'

'Sounds great to me. Funnily enough, just today I began to feel more confident about my own work. I thought I could give it a year and see how it went… then, if I didn't make a go of that I'd… well, I'd think of something. One thing I have had on my mind, having been with Sam the last few days… I mean, I know we tease him dreadfully about his under-sea work but actually, act-u-ally as he would say, it is so important. I thought there might be something in having a small hotel like ours as a special place. Maybe devoted to ecological tourism… I don't know as I am only just thinking aloud… but offering tourists the chance to follow the undersea paths and make their own contribution to saving the… well, whatever it is needs saving… under the sea! Sorry to be so vague!'

'Not vague at all, I get it completely.' Daniel said quickly, 'Sam is a tremendous enthusiast, of course, but it's all so true. Yes, I can really imagine the theme for the hotel set on the edge of the Mediterranean and the superb Calanques cliffs, yes, absolutely.'

Calinda was slower to react but then she said, 'Fantastic, Amber, what an idea! We shall have to do some research… We could have a thalassotherapy sea water spa… endless possibilities! I can well imagine the ideal clientele. Tomorrow, for instance, we have a couple coming from Tuscany. He's an English architect from Bath and she works with property in Tuscany. They commissioned Daniel to make them a large tiled fountain for their own villa. They have been staying at our friend's Bastide near Aix en Provence. It's a boutique hotel devoted to the arts and we often have guests referred to us and vice versa. I hope maybe Michelle and Marc may come over, too and Kelly and Leon, the other directors… I'd like you to meet them.'

'Interesting! Imagine a ceramic work going all the way to Tuscany. I didn't know you worked on individual large pieces, Daniel. Was that the leafy thing I saw you making in the courtyard?'

'Yes, very leafy! The vine leaves are placed around the tile frame. I don't know whether it would be cheeky to ask you, I mean, I know you work on your own stuff… but I was wondering if you would possibly decorate the centre piece.'

'I'd love to try!' I've worked on ceramic but only restoring, of course.'

'Come and see it tomorrow, I'll show you the idea that Alexander, our architect client, had in mind.'

'I will, I'll come down straight after breakfast. Thank you so much for a lovely meal. The melon is so refreshing in this heat.'

'It's certainly hot tonight,' Calinda stood up and carried Fleur through to their bedroom.

'Did you go to the jazz club with Sam last night?' Daniel asked.

'Oh my, yes indeed! We stayed really late. The music was great and Sam dances better than he thinks he does. Matt and his girlfriend, Yvette turned up too and we had a great evening.'

'No sign of my brother this time then!' Daniel laughed and patted Amber on the shoulder, 'Don't worry, Amber, I have quite forgiven you for slapping me around in the lavender field.' They both laughed and began to clear the table. Calinda came back and helped them and then said, 'Amber, if you're not too tired, I was wondering if you would keep an eye on Fleur while Daniel and I had a walk around the lavender fields?'

Amber tried not to look surprised and said quickly, 'Of course, I'd love to… is she asleep?'

'Oh yes, she never wakes after nine at night. She's such a good sleeper. Anyway, I'll take my mobile… do you have yours?'

Amber patted her pocket, 'Yes, absolutely, and I have your number in my address book. No problem, off you go both of you!'

Daniel stood up quickly and, with a quick glance at Amber, he accompanied Calinda to the lift.

Amber stood still for a moment and looked around. The large apartment suddenly seemed very empty and quiet. She tip-toed into the bedroom that opened off the living space. Fleur was sound asleep, her small mouth slightly open as she breathed gently. Amber looked down at her in wonder. Suddenly she realised she knew absolutely nothing about babies, nothing at all. She crept over to a wicker armchair that was placed near the cot and sat down. The chair creaked and she glanced quickly over to Fleur but she was still sound asleep. Amber had thought to clear up the dinner dishes and the kitchen but she decided the best course of action would be to stay on guard. Of course, she knew it was ridiculous, but on the other hand she could think of nothing better to do. When Calinda and Daniel returned less than an hour later, she was still sitting in the chair and watching Fleur.

'Thank you so much, Amber. I knew you would understand that this is a first for me.' Calinda gave Amber a quick kiss on her cheek. 'Thank you for taking care of Fleur.'

'Oh, it was nothing, she was as good as gold. Next time, maybe she will wake up and we can play.' Amber spoke more confidently than she felt and she was amused to notice that Fleur still hadn't woken even with their voices in the room. Maybe this baby-sitting was easier than she thought. 'Sorry, I was going to wash up and clear but I sat here and… well, it just seemed so peaceful and you were back so quickly.'

'Oh, no, you did very well. Anyway, you'll find one big advantage of living in a hotel is that there are always staff around. We both work hard and enjoy cooking but someone will come in tomorrow morning and clean up everything. One of the perks!'

'Great, then if you don't mind, I'll go to my room now. It was a great evening but I'm tired out.'

'Of course! Dani!' Calinda called out and still Fleur did not stir, 'Dani, Amber is going.' They walked to the lift and Daniel came in from the balcony.
'Thanks for the baby-sitting, Amber. It was very strange to take a walk with my wife without a baby bump with us. Strange but good, too. We used to walk a lot together once.'

'Well, any time!' Amber answered casually but she guessed Daniel was grateful for this small breakthrough. 'Thank you for another great supper. See you tomorrow, *à demain!* I must speak French more, that is my end of day resolution! *Bonsoir!*'

'Bonsoir, Amber, et merci encore!'

As the lift slowly descended to the first floor, Amber thought back through the day. It seemed to have been one of those days that seemed more like a week. Just this morning she had kissed goodbye to Sam and set off to the hills. This evening had been a success in many ways. Their shared ideas for the future of the Hotel de la Plage and most of all that Calinda had trusted Amber to watch over Fleur and have a little time with Daniel. Amber thought about her grandfather working away in England at tracing Calinda's sister. It seemed impossible to believe that he could be successful after all this time. As she made her way to her room, alone but not lonely, she allowed herself a moment to enjoy thinking about her paintings.

To: amber@hotmail.com
Cc:
Subject: Still in Sussex
From: William Marsden - wmarsden@talktalk.net

Well, Provence already seems a long way away but I am busy here in Sussex, so, not too much time to miss all those clear blue skies. Kim brought her new man, Mike, to meet me last weekend. It seems very serious indeed! I have never seen Kim so ... well, for want of a better word... devoted. Of course I told them all about our exploits in Provence, everything except my plan to try to trace Calinda's sister. Not a great deal to report although I do have a glimmer of hope. The detective has now succeeded in gaining access to the prisoner I told you about. He has been removed from prison and is in a secure wing of a hospital. Already he has begun to talk to Giles, the detective I employed. It may take several sessions and I have given Giles carte blanche to proceed however he thinks best. There is absolutely no point in telling Calinda anything yet, I am sure you agree. I have a few other irons in the fire too. It seems likely that the gang were kidnapping children and placing them in wealthy families all over the world. This may be the problem but, as I said, I am working on it. Apart from that I have enjoyed thinking about your ideas for the Hotel de la Plage. Calinda sent me a copy of the draft plans. I think a loft conversion would suit you very well for a studio and apartment.

Well, I know this is long for an email so I'll end now with all my usual grandfatherly love and affection. I trust you are enjoying yourself... between lavender and the deep blue sea. What's not to like? x Grandy

To: wmarsden@talktalk.net
Cc:
Subject: hi Grandy

From: Amber Marsden - amber@hotmail.commail.com

Dear Grandy, I am trying not to be excited at the progress you are making with tracking down Calinda's sister. Only last night I was lying awake thinking how hopeless it could be. Now, there does seem a ray of hope but of course I won't say a word here. I spent the evening with Calinda and Daniel... another fantastic supper on their roof terrace and... guess what... Calinda actually asked me to watch over Fleur whilst she went for a walk with Daniel. Admittedly it was under an hour and Fleur was sound asleep but at least it is a start. Daniel looked as surprised as I was when Calinda suddenly suggested it!

I'm glad you've seen Kim and met Mike... yes, it does sound as though it may be something more permanent for Kim...she has asked me if Mike can take over my share of the rent on the flat.

Must go now as last night Daniel asked me if I could help with some ceramic decoration. He's building a large fountain for some clients who live in Tuscany of something. Anyway they are calling in today and I shall meet them and tell you more tomorrow. Every day something new seems to fall in my lap here in Provence. I have been so lucky and I am still very grateful to you for somehow making it all happen... but then that's what you're so good at, isn't it, Grandy?! Yes, btw, Sam did call me as soon as you rang him from Marseille airport.... bye for now, best love, as ever, from yr fave grand-daughter x

    Amber sent the message to her grandfather. There was so much more she could tell him but it was nearly nine o'clock and she knew Daniel would be waiting in the courtyard. She quickly pulled her long hair back into a band and checked her reflection in the mirror. Her face was now lightly tanned and her light brown hair streaked with blonde. No need for make-up when she would be working in the ceramic studio, so, with a quick nod at herself she ran out of the bedroom. She went quickly through the reception and out into the brilliant sunshine. She could see Daniel standing by the well, looking up at the sky. Amber called out,

'Sorry, have you been waiting long?'

Daniel turned and smiled at her, 'Possibly all my life? You must be Amber, Daniel has told me all about you! My name is Luc, I'm Daniel's brother. Twin brother obviously!' He held out his hand and Amber, reeling with shock, took it like an automaton but remained speechless.

'Don't worry, our likeness to each other often has this effect on people. We once or twice used it to advantage but now we're supposed to be grown-ups and I like to tell people straightaway in case it causes embarrassment or trouble. It has been known!' He laughed, tilting his head back and Amber stared at his strong throat, his broad shoulders, it was Daniel and yet not quite Daniel. She struggled to speak,

'Sorry, I am being so rude, just staring at you. I've already been in trouble confusing you and Daniel before. Your warning comes too late!' Amber realised she was still holding his hand and she dropped it and took a step back in embarrassment.

'How can that be? We've never met… I know I would have remembered.'

Amber suddenly realised the difference between them. Here was Luc standing before her and blatantly flirting. Daniel never flirted and his face was more serious. But when they smiled or laughed she doubted she would know the difference. But Luc was still talking, 'How intriguing… how did you manage to confuse me with Daniel… I'd love to know what happened…'

Before Amber could begin to try to explain they were joined by Daniel himself. He stood next to his brother and put his arm round his shoulder.

'I should have warned you, Amber, I thought Luc might turn up today but I was so busy getting the fountain ready, I quite forgot. Anyway, now you have seen us together… can you tell us apart.'

Amber looked at them both for a moment. Same height, same dark colouring, same strong black eyebrows, same muscular build... well, they were identical twins... but then she replied,

'Well, Daniel has a mole over his right eyebrow and his hands are stronger, I should say... or at least more workmanlike.'

Luc clapped, 'Bravo, Amber... obviously you have the keen eye of an artist. It usually takes a while before anyone notices the mole.'

'When we were at school Luc used to draw a mole over his eyebrow to get me in trouble,' Daniel laughed and then looked down at his hands, 'And of course you're right, my hands are workman's hands... Luc's are much more delicate. He plays for his living.'

Luc slapped his brother on the back and said, 'Oh you like to think that, don't you!' He turned to Amber, 'I work just as hard as Daniel but instead of messing around with clay, I play the flute.'

'The flute... really? How interesting.' Amber looked again at Luc's hands and then at his face. For a second she had a wild vision of Luc as a mythical satyr, wandering through lush valleys and across streams playing a magical reed flute. Once again she realised that the conversation was continuing without her paying attention.

'Amber is becoming well-known for her ability to dream away from the conversation at hand.' Daniel laughed and patted Amber affectionately on the head. 'Wake up dreamer, where did you go this time?'

'I was just imagining a painting...a mythical scene, maybe somewhere in ancient Greece...' Amber's words trailed away before she could add that she had imagined Luc naked apart from a wreath of laurel leaves. 'Sorry, ridiculous, I know.'

'Not at all,' said Luc, his handsome face suddenly serious, 'Inspiration is never to be dismissed. If you go and paint now it may be the best painting you have ever done. I am like that with my music. I work in an orchestra but sometimes, at any moment, a strain of music flies into my head and I have to write it down. I used to think I would remember it, but later but I have learnt that it is never the same.'

Amber looked at Luc and recognised the truth in his words.

'You're probably quite right, but I have worked ever since I left uni for a museum in London. There was no time for inspiration, just hard and careful work.'

'But now you are in Provence, taking time off?'

'Yes, my life has changed drastically in the last few weeks so I am just catching up. Anyway, Daniel, you were going to show me your fountain. Don't worry, I really don't need to rush off and paint a mythical scene, not my style at all!'

'Well, funny you should say that because the centre piece of the fountain is pictorial and Alexander, the client I told you about, has the idea of a pastoral scene with a traditional wine harvest. Not sure there were any nymphs or shepherds involved... more jolly harvesters or something like that... I'll show you the file of his ideas.'

'I'll leave you to it, then,' said Luc, 'Unless you'd like me to pose as a flute-playing shepherd, I'll go and eat breakfast?'

'I think we can do without you modelling, thanks Luc. We'll join you for a coffee in an hour or so, Calinda will be down by then.'

Amber and Daniel walked off together in the direction of the pottery studios. As they reached the far corner of the courtyard, Amber could not resist turning to catch a last glimpse of Luc. He was still standing by the well and watching them leave. In fact, she was fairly sure he was watching her. She dismissed the thought that he looked like a Greek god statue and quickly raised a hand in farewell, then followed Daniel into the cool of the barn. Daniel laid a large portfolio onto the table and began to spread out the drawings. 'Alexander is an architect so these are more plans than drawings. I've followed his dimensions exactly... if you come through to the pottery studio you can see the construction.'

Amber followed Daniel into the adjoining room and

then stopped in surprise. 'Oh my goodness, it's a huge piece of work now you have it all together. It's incredible, Daniel, fantastic work!' Amber moved closer and studied the mosaic and tiled structure that formed a tall arch with a low walled surround.

'We've built a wooden support to represent the actual niche where it will fit at the Villa Sognidoro in Tuscany. It's been a long time in the process and really, I'm glad it's nearly finished. As you can see, the centre piece is tiled in this milky cream colour and that's where we want the pictorial work. If you come back to the drawing board, I'll show you Alexander's ideas.'

They spent nearly an hour looking through the rest of the file and then folded it away and looked at each other. Daniel nodded with satisfaction,

'I don't know what guardian angel sent you to stay at the Hotel Lavande, Amber, but Calinda and I just feel so lucky to have you here… and now, the way you pick up on the artistic side of our work… well, it's just amazing!'

'Well, nice of you to say so, of course, Daniel, but really, I'm the lucky one. You and Calinda have turned my life around. I shall enjoy working on the ceramic scene. I think the traditional wine harvest will work well.' They continued talking about the work as they walked back across the courtyard. Amber almost expected to see Luc still there, standing by the well, a marble statue of a perfect Greek hero. As it was they found him on the side of the swimming pool, standing ready to dive. Amber drew in her breath sharply, if there was anything more perfect than a marble god then it was surely this very alive man.

'There's Luc!' Daniel said to Amber and, running swiftly ahead he came up behind Luc and pushed him into the water. Luc spun in the air and still managed to execute a perfect dive. He surfaced and shook his fist at Daniel.

'You just wait!' Then he laughed and Amber stood mesmerised, watching the water running off his dark hair and over his broad shoulders. She attempted to pull herself together and went over to the shade of an umbrella where Calinda was sitting with Fleur.

'Hi, Amber, how did it go at the studio?'

Amber tore her eyes away from watching Luc as he ploughed through the water, up and down the pool in a lazy crawl.

'Hi, Calinda, hi Fleur! Oh look, she smiled at me!'

Calinda and Amber looked at Fleur in delight as she gurgled and smiled up at Amber.

'She really has taken to you, Amber… well, we all have! It's been so great having you to stay with us. You must come up to the apartment later, we'll be eating up there again as Luc is here for a few days. If you come around six you could see Fleur's latest trick… at bath-time, when I lay her on a towel on the floor, on her tummy, she is beginning to hold her neck up and look around and yesterday she completely rolled over!'

'Wow,' Amber looked down at Fleur in surprise. It really hadn't occurred to her that a baby couldn't roll over anyway, but she decided not to show her ignorance to Calinda. 'I'd love to but I've arranged to meet Sam at a restaurant between here and the coast. Sorry!' Amber looked across the pool at Luc who was just pulling himself out of the water. His back was so muscled that it was hard to believe he was a flute player. Amber realised that indeed she was very sorry not to be free to eat with them all tonight. Then she thought about Sam, his beautiful grey eyes, his slow Amercan drawl, his lean tanned body diving and turning in the water and… yes, the fun they had together. She sighed and looked back at Fleur. How simple life must be at three months old, she thought and then said to Calinda,

'Don't you find it sort of strange, you know, the incredible likeness between Daniel and Luc?'

Calinda laughed, 'Not really, I mean they are so different in so many ways. I suppose the first time I met Luc it was a shock but Daniel had told me he had a twin brother. We went to hear him play in a concert at Nice. Did you know he is a flautist?'

'Yes, he told me earlier when we met. So, does he play in an orchestra?'

'Oh goodness, yes. He is world famous now. He has made several best-selling recordings too.'

'I didn't realise. How exciting!'

'Yes, he travels all over the world. So different from my Daniel who loves nothing better than being at home. They are both creative in their own way, of course. But Daniel has a far more practical approach and skill. Luc is so musical it's almost too easy for him. His work doesn't really seem like work at all.'

'I suppose so, but there must be so much practicing to play at world standard. I should think it is hard work in its way.'

Calinda shrugged, 'Maybe, but Daniel is the real worker. Anyway, let's have lunch now. I've ordered some salad and panini at the bar. Daniel will be starving and I am sure you must be, too. As for Luc, he's always hungry for food and everything else.' They wandered over to the poolside bar and found Daniel and Luc already there.

'Here come the most beautiful girls in Provence!' Luc greeted them and kissed Calinda on both cheeks and then gave Fleur a small kiss on her forehead.

'Only in Provence? How rude you are, Luc… but then you have never had the good manners of your brother.' Calinda laughed and sat down at the bar. 'I thought we'd eat early as Alexander and Zoe Knight have already sent a message to say they have left La Bastide.' She turned to Amber, 'Will you be around in an hour or so… I'd like you to meet them?'

'Oh yes, I don't need to leave until six-ish. I'd love to meet them, especially to have a talk about the fountain scene.'

'Are you leaving today?' Luc turned to Amber and asked.

'No, I'm not leaving, just out for dinner tonight.'

'And I have to leave in the morning. That's a shame. I'd like to have got to know you, Amber. I've heard so much about you from Calinda and Daniel… all your future plans. *Quelle dommage!*'

It was the first time that Amber had heard Luc speak in French and it came as something of a shock.

'Goodness,' she said without thinking, 'I had quite forgotten you are actually French! Your English is so perfect.'

'Well, thankee kindly, ma'am. I usually get told I have an American accent.' Luc replied in an exaggerated American voice.

'Maybe just slightly with some words.' Amber replied, at the same time thinking of Sam and his soft voice. The two men were so very different, although they both joked, it seemed to Amber that Luc had a more moody side to him, something perhaps more passionate and involved with his artistic temperament. She wondered idly how Luc would look when playing his flute. Would his face remain dark and serious or would it light up with laughter.

'Amber's dreaming again!' Daniel laughed and Amber smiled. Sam and Luc were both fascinating to dream about but it was Daniel that seemed to understand her. As though reading her thoughts she was surprised to hear Daniel's next words.

'Why don't you play something to us, Luc. There's just time before the Knights arrive.'

'I shall play something for my niece, Fleur!' Luc's face lit up with pleasure, 'I wrote a new little piece especially for her... I'll get my flute.' He left the bar and Amber could not resist watching him as he jogged round the pool until he disappeared into the hotel.

'How sweet of him! That's quite something. A special piece of music for Fleur, do you hear that, Fleur. *Ton oncle Luc a composé un petit chanson pour toi!*'

'Do you speak to Fleur in English and French, Calinda?'

'Oh yes, I believe in that and... ah here is Luc with his magic flute!'

Amber looked round and saw Luc approaching the bar carrying a small, black leather musical instrument case. He laid it carefully on the bar and opened it. Amber drew near and looked at the beautiful silver flute lying in the dark blue velvet. 'Why, it's so beautiful!'

Luc looked up at her and gave her the full benefit of a wide and dazzling smile. 'Beautiful!' he agreed with a glint of wicked laughter in his dark eyes. Amber held his gaze for a long moment and felt a small ache of desire. Was this the beginning of something new? How much more could happen to her on this strangest of honeymoons?

Amber looked at her phone and saw she had three messages, then she looked at the time. Definitely running late to meet Sam by six and she still had to shower. She quickly flicked through the list and then saw there was a voice message from Sam. She called him back and he answered immediately.

'Amber, I'm so pleased you have called back at last. Did you get my message earlier? I am so sorry.'

'No, I'm sorry, I haven't checked my phone all afternoon… I was down at the pool and I'd left my phone in my room. What's up? You sound so stressed.'

'I'm on the train to Paris. I have to fly to New York tonight. My father's had a heart attack.'

'Oh Sam, I'm so sorry.'

'No, I'm sorry to break our date. I was looking forward to it but… well, obviously I have to go home right away.'

'Absolutely, don't worry at all about it. Of course you must go! I hope you'll find things are better when you get there. It must be dreadful for you.'

'Well, as you know I have had a long-standing row with my father so I feel kinda bad. Anyway, my Ma really wants me there and my sisters too. I'll call you as soon as I can. We're approaching Paris now so may get cut off in the tunnel.'

'Don't worry about anything this end…is there anything I can do to help.'

'Thanks Amber, but Max is holding the fort in Sophia Antipolis. But I'll let you know if there is anything, thanks.'

'I'm so sorry, Sam. Look after yourself, too. Go well!'

'Thanks Amber, I …' and then the line went dead. Amber looked at the phone for a moment and wondered about trying to call him again but decided against it. Sam would need to get to the airport and cope with everything ahead of him. They had said all they needed, although she had a strange feeling that he had been about to say 'I love you'. Well, he was in a highly emotional state and it was not the time to be thinking about a new love affair. Apart from which he could have been going to say anything at all. She threw the phone on the bed and considered what to do next. Suddenly there was no hurry. The evening lay ahead of her. She could begin some studies for the ceramic decoration or she could call Calinda and ask if it was too late to go to see Fleur do her new roll-over trick. Amber pulled her sketch pad out of her bag and took it to the table on the balcony of her room. She looked out across the hotel gardens and could just see a turquoise corner of the pool. Her thoughts returned to the afternoon. Calinda had been right… it was a magic flute. Luc had carefully joined the sections of the silver flute together and, after a few warm up notes, he had filled the air with sweet and soothing sound. The refrain had a haunting melody and Fleur watched Luc in delight as he played for her. Slowly a small crowd of hotel guests and staff formed a circle around Luc as he played on, the music changing to a clever medley of music that was for moments familiar and then changed again to something completely new. He approached Amber and then circled around her, still playing, looking at her over the flute, his eyes smiling under his dark eyebrows. Finally, he ended up beside Fleur again, playing the first refrain once more and then ended and bowed low. There was a moment of silence, even the birds seemed to have stopped their song and then a quiet ripple of applause started. Luc turned, gave a small bow to the audience and then held up his hands, asking them to stop. He quickly took the flute apart, shook it lightly and replaced it carefully in it case.

Amber sighed with pleasure as she sat now on the balcony, still recalling the dulcet tones of the flute. There had been no time to talk to Luc and begin to tell him how the music had affected her because, as soon as the music ended, a tall grey-haired man and a young woman, very pregnant, had moved forward from the group of guests and Daniel had introduced them as Alexander and Zoe Knight. Calinda and Zoe had soon gone up to the loft apartment and Amber had spent the rest of the afternoon discussing the fountain with Daniel and Alexander Knight. She knew exactly how she would paint the wine harvest scene. Alexander had made some interesting research into the history of his villa and had brought some original 18th century etchings of grape pickers and Tuscan vineyards. Now she looked down at the blank page of her sketch pad. She selected a soft leaded sepia crayon and then… she closed the pad again and placed the crayon back in her wooden pencil box. She went back into the room and called Calinda.

An hour later she was in the kitchen of the loft apartment helping Daniel to slice tomatoes. Fleur had been bathed and successfully demonstrated her new ability to roll over. Now Calinda had disappeared to change and dinner was to be prepared. When Amber had called Calinda she had been surprised to be told there was quite a dinner party planned for the evening. Zoe and Alexander Knight, Luc and now another couple from La Bastide.

'It's quite unusual for Kelly and Leon to get away for an evening here with us. They run the Bastide with their friend, Michelle. It is quite an undertaking… a huge and historic fortified Bastide that they have now converted into a very exclusive boutique hotel. Their guests are all the mega-rich who are on the European art trail. They come up from the cruise ships that dock at Marseilles… whizz around Provence for a few days then dash back on board.'

'Do they stay here, too?' Amber asked as she continued laying out the thin slices of large tomatoes on a serving plate.

'Oh no, we're not their style at all. They want to look at art, not create it.'

'But I'm sure they'd love your pottery.'

'Yes, but we have that covered. Michelle buys from us and they hold a good stock in the hotel shop. You must go over there some time… it's quite a place.'

Before she could reply, there was a buzz from the elevator and Daniel went into the hall, wiping his hands on his apron. 'That will be them now! Leave the rest of the tomatoes, Amber, you've done a magnificent job.'

Amber went into the hall and the lift doors opened to reveal Luc, carrying his flute case. He gave a wide smile and kissed Amber on both cheeks, 'Ah, you decided to stay for dinner. Great!' Amber managed to smile back but the warmth of his lips brushing her cheeks had made her feel on fire. This flute player was not only magical but had some strong magnetic attraction. For a moment she wondered if he had felt her response as he took a deep breath before continuing. 'As you can see, Dani, I have brought my work with me as you requested. I don't usually perform at dinner parties, you know. Unless I am extremely well paid, of course!'

'Just get in there and pour Amber a drink, you are such a dreadful show off, Luc, and always have been. Amber deserves a drink she has been working as *sous chef* in the kitchen. If you had been earlier you could have helped.'
'Then, I'm glad I am just fashionably late although I wouldn't have minded being *sous le sous chef!*' He moved on into the apartment and then saw the long table out on the terrace laid for eight people. 'Who else is coming to hear me play tonight, then?'

'Alex and Zoe, the clients you met earlier and now Kelly and Leon from la Bastide de Rosefont.. you met them last time you were here.'

'Yes, I remember, he's an interesting guy, he studied forensics and worked as a private eye before he married Kim and joined the team at the Bastide.' he turned to Amber, 'You'll like them, they're both fun and clever at the same time. Not quite so much fun or quite so clever as myself, of course, but...' He laughed, throwing his head back to duck the mock punch that Daniel was aiming at him. 'OK, I promise to stop showing off now. It's all Amber's fault anyway. I am nervous of her beauty and trying my best to impress her. You know how shy I am really!'

Amber laughed and began to blush at the compliment even though it was made as a joke. She quickly took the cold glass of wine that Luc offered her and sat out on the terrace in the fresh evening air. Luc was about to sit beside her when the lift doors buzzed again and the rest of the party arrived all at once.

Amber stood back whilst everyone seemed to be talking and exchanging kisses. Calinda came over to Amber and put her arm lightly around Amber to push her forward.

'*Maintenant, tout le monde*, everybody... I want you all to welcome Amber to Provence. She is our very special guest of honour.'

Several hours later they were still finishing the long dinner that Daniel had served. The candles were burning low when Daniel spoke into Luc's ear. Luc stood up and left the terrace, returning with his flute. There was a round of applause as Luc opened the case and joined up the parts of the flute. Then silence fell around the table as he played the first tuning notes. Fleur raised her head and looked around at Luc from where she was sitting with Daniel.

'Ah, Fleur hears her famous uncle, *attends Fleur, ton oncle prepare a commencer son magique!*' Amber looked at Daniel and saw the brotherly pride on his handsome face. He held up Fleur so she could get a better view and Luc moved toward her, saying,

'*Voilá*, my star fan. So, I shall play for you first and for your soon to be born little friend, you can share the song I have written for you. *Mes amis, je vous offre Le Chanson de Fleur.*' Fleur wriggled with delight and then held still, entranced as the first notes flew into the air, clear and sweet. Now the refrain was familiar and Amber found herself almost singing with the notes. When the music seemed to be ending, everyone ready to applaud, Luc merged the melody into the familiar sound of Prokofiev's Peter and the Wolf. He walked around the table, ducking and diving between the guests and ended up in front of Amber. She watched as he stood outlined against the dark night sky, the silver flute catching the moonlight. Had ever there been a more romantic moment than this? Amber almost shivered as the music ended and the last note died into the silence. Then everyone was clapping and congratulating Luc. Amber remained silent apart from lightly clapping her hands. Luc leaned over her and then looked back at the others as he said,

'*Merci beaucoup, mesdames et messieurs*, as you have probably guessed, I am playing to impress our beautiful new friend, Amber. But she remains calm and aloof. Is that the right word? Aloof? Only a girl as beautiful as Amber can truly be so… yes, aloof! *Si distante!*'

There was quiet laughter at his words and Amber smiled and then joined in the laughter at her own expense.

'You could not be more wrong, Luc. The fact is that I am so moved emotionally by your music that I cannot speak… and don't forget, I am English and have my reputation of sang-froid to maintain. So, yes, I remain aloof in case I should fall at your feet in a pool of tears.'

There was more applause at Amber's defiant reply and Daniel said, 'Aha, Luc, I think you have finally met your match in Amber. She will outplay you with clever words and, I have met her grandfather, there is definitely a strain of wicked humour in the family. Beware!'

Luc laughed and took his place again at the table, laying the flute carefully beside him on the white tablecloth. Amber looked at it and carefully reached out a finger to touch the silver keys. 'It really is a beautiful instrument. The craftsmanship in making something like this… it's magnificent.'

'You're right. I am very proud of this flute. It was made especially for me. I studied the piano, too, when I was at music college but I am always glad I decided to play the flute. It is so easy to take around with me, wherever I go.'

'So you travel all the time?' Amber asked.
'Well, I am the first flautist for the orchestra of Nice and as such I am attached to the conservatoire, too. I travel away for concerts but I also give master classes in Nice and Monaco. I suppose I spend over half the year there at the moment.'

'That must be hard work.'

'It is… not that Daniel or Calinda would agree with you… they regard it as playing. Of course, it's nothing like the gruelling work that they have done here. I mean, Dani practically rebuilt this place with his own hands… and then there is the lavender farm.' He turned to Leon, 'Leon, tell Amber what a state this place was in when Calinda and Amber bought it!'

'Oh, you just wouldn't recognise it. Where to begin?' He shrugged and then laughed, 'They bought it from an alcoholic wretch who had inherited it from his alcoholic mother… when I was first working at the Bastide I bumped into him in a very unpleasant way. He actually drove his van at Michelle, just after she inherited the Bastide. He's crazy even on the rare occasions when he's not out of his mind on booze or drugs. Last I heard he was in prison in Marseille and the best place for him.'

Amber was surprised at how angry Leon sounded. 'He must be quite a nasty character for you to take against him like that.' She said, 'The rest of the evening you seem to have been so easy-going and relaxed.'

Leon smiled, 'You're right, it takes a lot to rile me but this guy was seriously dangerous. Kelly will agree with me. Kelly I was telling Amber about our old enemy, Pascal Mazin.'

'Oh god, don't spoil a magic evening, my sweet Leon!' Kim leaned over and gave Leon a kiss. 'You know it is all over now! Don't worry, Amber, the wretched little guy is banged up in the hell-hole of Marseille prison. My dashing hero, Leon, sorted that out. One day I'll tell you the whole gory story but right now, the moon is shining bright and we need more wine and more music. Please, Luc, just one encore?'

Amber looked at Kelly who was now practically sitting on Leon's lap with her arms around him. Leon was gently stroking her arm as he carried on talking to Luc. Then, she looked around the table at all the new friends she had found. It was a stunning night, full of good conversation, fine wines, good food… even a world class live musical performance… but, best of all, she was thinking how good it was to find that marriages could be so very happy. Although she had hardly had a chance to get to know Zoe, it would be apparent to a complete stranger that she was as in love with Alexander as he was with her. Her pale face was alight with the beauty of her pregnancy and Alexander was constantly looking at her and making sure she was comfortable. He was an unusual looking man, his dark grey hair at first making him looking older than perhaps he was… there was something about him… under his easy smiles that spoke of sadness, or perhaps just experience. Amber had enjoyed their discussion for the drawing for the ceramic fountain. He had strong opinions backed with sound knowledge and she looked forward to showing him her preliminary sketches. For a moment she was lost in thought as she envisioned how she would paint the wine harvest scene, the women grape pickers in long dresses with baskets on their head, the men throwing the grapes in great piles in the horse drawn carts. She mused on for a moment more and then looked back at her new friends, Calinda and Daniel. Now there was a perfect example of a happy marriage, she was sure of that and the more she knew them the more she found it to be true. It was a strong friendship, a good working relationship and there always seemed to be a hint of romantic love in the air. Finally she looked at Luc as he stood up again and prepared to play for them all. An interesting man, full of vigour and confidence. She wondered if there was a serious side hidden under all his joking and teasing. Then he began to play and she tilted her head back and looked up to the stars as the music flowed over her. She let her dreams fill her head until reality and present problems began to seep into her consciousness. Had Sam arrived safely in New York and how was he coping with his father's illness? How far had Grandy progressed with his search for Calinda's sister? Would she be able to make her life here in Provence? Then she realised that there was applause all around her and the music had ended. She clapped quietly and then looked across at Fleur who had fallen asleep in Daniel's arms. This time, when the music died away, the applause was even more enthusiastic than before but Amber noticed that Fleur slept on, oblivious to the noise around her.

Luc gave a small bow and held up his hands in protest at the cries of '*encore, encore*'.

'*Mes amis,* thank you for your applause but that is definitely the end, *le fin!* How can you expect me to work on such a night as this?'

'Work?' Daniel clapped his brother affectionately on the back as he sat beside him. 'Do you hear that? He calls playing his magic flute... work! Of course, he does not know the meaning of the word and never has... always my spoiled little brother!'

Luc laughed and shook his head but before he could reply, Calinda spoke up.

'*Suffis,* Dani, enough teasing your brother. It's a hard task being famous and I know it only too well. Until very recently I have tried to hide myself away. I suffered the best years of my twenties being hounded by the media. Luc has been very generous playing for us so beautifully tonight, but enough is enough, now he should be allowed time off. It may seem like play to us but it really is his work.'

'Why thank you, my beautiful sis-in-law! How sweet of you to stand up for me. What do you mean... until very recently... have you decided not to hide away from your adoring public any longer? Are you going to return to modelling?'

'Oh goodness, no, but it was Amber's grandfather who made me think about it. He said that the name I had built was an asset and that we should use it to the full. So, look out for my new marketing campaign. '*Calinda*' is about to have a face lift! First we are thinking of a range of porcelain to be designed by our very own in-house artist, Amber Marsden.'

'That's a fantastic idea, Calinda!' Kim sat forward enthusiastically. 'We would certainly use it in our hotel. It would be so chic! Hundreds of other ideas are already filling my head. You know I used to work in Chelsea with Michelle, before the Bastide took over our lives. Your name was huge in London and all over the fashion world. Your perfume has kept the name going... yes, it's a great idea. Amber, your grandfather must be a very clever guy!'

'Oh, he is indeed!' Amber smiled and thought how Grandy would enjoy hearing about this. She would email him later. 'My grandfather is very good at a number of things actually!'

'I hope to meet him one day. Calinda and Daniel have told me about him and the advice and help he has given them.' Luc looked at Amber as he spoke and she answered quickly.

'I'm sure he'll be back in Provence soon. He had a great time here.' Then she remained silent thinking about how Grandy had enjoyed his time on the water in Sam's boat… then she though about what he was doing now… searching for Calinda's sister. There was so much that made it difficult to say more. She was well aware that Luc was flirting with her and trying to enter into this new life of hers. She sighed and sipped her coffee. Not the end of June yet and she was still on her non-honeymoon. The stars were shining down, the air was warm and the conversation had returned to a general discussion of music. All to be enjoyed… all thoughts and problems could be resolved in the future.

pain that could only be diagnosed as jealousy

To: amber@hotmail.com
Cc:
Subject: Still in Sussex
From: William Marsden - wmarsden@talktalk.net

I have news. Giles has now definite information. I will keep this brief and phone you soon as there is still a lot to arrange. The imprisoned kidnapper is Catholic and terrified of dying with his sins. He is confessing to Giles. Whether he thinks Giles is a priest or understands that he is a detective I do NOT know… or want to. It appears that the kidnapping in the village of Nabeul is the only time that this man was involved. Or so he says. He remembers the whole incident and was horrified at the time. The child was taken first to Morocco and then on a boat to Spain. He repeatedly swears that he looked after the child and no harm came to her. Also repeats that he had children himself and needed the ransom money very badly. Anyway, he knew it was very wrong and now repents. He took the child to a convent in Malaga. That is where his story ends. I have instructed Giles to go straight to Malaga and begin a search. I think this is good progress but still there is a long path of uncertainty ahead. I just wanted to update you. Nothing to Calinda yet, of course. Speak soon, my dear. Hope you are still enjoying everything that Provence offers… which is so much! Grandy x

To: wmarsden@talktalk.net
Cc:
Subject: hi Grandy
From: Amber Marsden - amber@hotmail.commail.com
How amazing and sort of terrifying too. I await your next news but I do think it is terrific progress.
Everything is beautiful in Provence, indeed. Poor Sam has had to rush back to NY as his father has had a heart attack. I haven't heard from him since he left. I have just woken up and

it's another blue sky day. Last night there was a dinner party in the loft apartment here… Calinda and Daniel invited their clients from Tuscany and another couple from a hotel/Bastide near here and Daniel's twin brother turned up too. Amazingly alike except that he is a flute player and very extrovert/arty type. It was a great evening. Your name was brought up by Calinda and she praised you for making her realise she should flaunt her name not deny the celebrity thing. Everyone now wants to meet you!

I'm going for my run now before it gets too hot and today I have two new projects to think about 1/ painting a pastoral scene for the fountain destined for the Tuscan villa 2/designing a motif for *Calinda* porcelain (explain later)… and then, there is my own painting … I am such a busy bee here amongst the lavender fields. Love you, Amber x

      Amber ran slowly along the path that led away from the forest and toward the road. She still wanted to see the other side of the main road and get nearer to the hazy line of blue hills that were always on the horizon. Glancing quickly from left to right she saw the grey tarmac of the road completely empty in both directions and she ran quickly across, the heat rising from the surface of the road. On the other side there were a few pine trees offering some shade and she headed in their direction and then on into a sloping olive grove. Here there was a light breeze and she ran faster between the long lines of trees. The ground began to rise but she maintained her pace, breathing easily and still focussing on the tantalising blue hills in the distance. Then, to her surprise she saw another figure running ahead. In an instant she was sure it was Luc… but then could it be Daniel? She had never known Daniel to run… his exercise was taken in more practical and manual labour, working in the lavender fields or the pottery studio. It had to be Luc but he was too far ahead to be sure. Amber thought for a moment of turning around and heading back to the hotel. She certainly didn't want Luc, if indeed it was Luc, to think she was chasing him. Before she could decide, the figure ahead had stopped and was leaning onto his knees, catching his breath. Then he saw Amber and raised a hand in greeting and began to jog toward her. Amber ran on too, the ground between them disappearing so quickly that before she had time to think, they were jogging on the spot looking at each other, face to face. Amber, smiled as she saw there was no defining mole above Luc's dark eyebrow.

'*Bonjour*, Amber! I had no idea you were a runner! Shall we jog back or are you going onward?' His dark eyes smiled as they travelled from her face and down over her body. Amber was very aware of her thin t-shirt and the sweat running between her breasts. She brushed back her hair and replied,

'I want at least to go to the end of this olive grove. I've been looking at those hills in the distance for days now and I wanted to get nearer…' Then she suddenly stopped jogging and stood quite still, listening, 'Wait, that's a motorbike!' She turned and ran at full speed back toward the road. She was aware that Luc was following close behind her and saying something but she ran on faster. She reached the road just in time to see a motorbike disappearing over the brow of the hill. She stopped on the spot and stamped her foot.

'Damn, damn! I've missed him.'

Luc drew up beside her, panting heavily.   'Amber, you are a woman of mystery! Did you have an assignation with the biker?'

Amber managed to laugh and, as they jogged slowly back to the hotel, she told Luc about the day she had seen the biker throw his lighted cigarette into the dry grass.

Daniel was by the pool when they returned,
'I'm sure it was the same man, all in black leathers,black helmet and the red bike… but he was gone before I could get the bike number. I'm so angry.'

'Maybe he passes that way every day, early. I shall walk up there myself tomorrow…' Daniel looked at his watch, 'must have been about seven thirty.'

'No, I'll go… I usually run about that time.' said Amber.

'You should be careful then… I wish I was going to be there to run with you tomorrow.' Luc looked at Amber and she became aware once more of her thin running clothes and the sweat pouring down her body.

'Are you off again then?' Amber asked, feeling her heart sink without reason. 'Do you have another concert?' Suddenly she didn't want him to go, to disappear off again and then she remembered the singer at Le Bateau Noir club in Cassis. Of course, he would be going back to her. Amber felt a small pang of pain that could only be diagnosed as jealousy. She recalled Luc's hand on the back of the girl… sliding downward… but he was replying,

'I have a two week tour in Holland. But I'll be back as soon as I can? Let's take a shower and have a swim.' Then he took Amber's hand and led her toward the end of the pool. She followed like a robot and then suddenly shook her hand away.

'No, no… I'm going to shower in my room and then I'll swim later. I have so much work to do today.'

Luc looked at her in surprise or was it disappointment?

'I'll have to say *au revoir* then… but I'll be back, you can count on it, Amber. I'll be back the minute my tour is over. I'll be back.' With his last words he quickly ducked his head and kissed her full on the lips.

Amber reeled back and looked up at him. His eyes were dark and shining with passion. There was no laughter just an intensity of… Amber couldn't decide what the emotion was that shone behind his obvious desire… was it determination? She nodded quickly and without another word she turned her back on him and ran along the side of the pool and into the hotel.

When she reached her room she stripped off her t-shirt and running shorts and stood for a long while under the cool shower. As the water ran over her body she felt such a longing for Luc's kiss to have been more, so much more. Finally, wrapping a towel around herself she walked out onto the balcony and let the warm air dry her skin. This man disturbed her in a way that Sam had never done. She was terrified of the emotion that ran through her, making her heart beat fast. This was not to happen. This is how she could be hurt again. She closed her eyes and saw herself standing at the church door, her father beside her. The misery and shame of being deserted swamped over her and she gulped a deep breath of air to stop herself from crying aloud. She gripped the balcony rail and forced herself to open her eyes and look toward the blue horizon. The calm beauty of Provence would be her cure and new work would be her salvation. With a deep intake of breath she pulled back her shoulders and went back into her room to prepare for the days ahead.

back where you belong

To: amber@hotmail.com
Cc:
Subject: more news
From: Kim Simpson - kimS@gmail.com
Good to speak last night… so much quicker than our texts and emails. Sorry to hear that Sam has had to go back to the States… so what was all that about a flutist… is that really what he does. Sounds like a joke or at least a euphemism… don't know why. I forgot to tell you that I have managed to squeeze a pay rise out of my miserable boss and now have an assistant… get me!
x K

To: kimS@gmail.com
Cc:
Subject: Good to talk
From: Amber Marsden - amber@hotmail.commail.com
Hi… yes it was great to Skype at last. Don't know why we didn't get round to it before. Well, I know why you didn't as obviously you are spending every spare minute with Mike. I just caught a glimpse of him in the background. It was weird to see our flat again. Thanks for the offer of packing up my gear. Shall I ask Mum to help or would that be worse? Let me know… I am so gratefully, seriously. Congrats… pay rise and an assistant…give her/him my deepest sympathies ha ha. I have begun preliminary work on the scene for the fountain and Calinda likes my ideas…so far anyway, for a spriggy sort of lavender design for the planned porcelain. I'll send you a photo soon as… Once I get this first work over I shall begin my own work again…can you believe that one of my drawings has already sold to a hotel client here… one I didn't like very much either! Get me! Aren't we both so clever nowadays… very ha ha… nothing more to tell about the magic flute player yet and no news from Sam either…so… it is all work and no play for me now x Amber

Amber sent the message to Kim and her thoughts flew with it, back to her life in England. Right now, nine in the morning in Bloomsbury her old boss would be opening up the small studio at the back of the museum. Amber could almost smell the distinctive mix of oil paint, linseed oil, varnish and… well, it always seemed like the smell of history. She walked out onto her balcony and looked across to the hills, today almost invisible in the early haze of heat that rose from the dry fields. There had been no sign of the motor biker when she had taken her early run. Amber sighed and picked up her drawing pad to look back through the preliminary sketches for the fountain. Zoe and Alex would be leaving later today and she wanted to be quite sure they agreed with her ideas. Just as she was deciding the last drawing would be the best to show to them as the final art work she heard her phone bleep a message. At last, a message from Sam. Amber read it hurriedly and then, before she could tap a reply the phone rang. Again it was Sam. Amber answered hurriedly,

'Oh Sam, I am so sorry to hear your sad news… I have only just had your message.'

The line was not good but Amber could hear a different, sad tone to his usual upbeat voice as he replied.

'I thought I'd ring, hope I haven't woken you, Amber. It's difficult to find the right time to do anything here at the moment. It's chaos.'

'I am so sorry, Sam. It must be awful. How are your mother and your sisters… and you?'

'Oh, we're all being very stoic and bottling it all up, of course. Ma seems well enough and already busy planning the funeral. I guess the shock may hit her later. It may not have been an altogether happy marriage but it was a long one. She was only twenty-one when she married him.'

'She must be glad to have you there.'

'Yeh, she likes to pretend she leans on me but in fact, she's as tough as old boots. I am glad I came back in time to talk with my father before he had the second fatal heart attack. Not exactly a peace talk but at least we conversed and he did say he was trying to understand my views on conservation. I realise he was a very intelligent guy. That was good.' There was a break in Sam's voice and then he seemed to pull himself together to carry on talking. Amber remained quiet, giving him time as she realised he wanted to tell her more. 'Yeh, so, it's been a hard time and now, Amber, this has to be said. I have to tell you that I am back with Marianne, my fiancée. I had to tell you and I expect you'll think I'm a cad and… '

Amber interrupted, 'Sam, stop right there, of course I don't think that or anything near it. You're back where you belong. Be honest. I can well imagine the stress and tension of your world around you at the moment and if Marianne is there for you…then…' Now it was Sam that interrupted. 'But Amber, I don't want you to think that what we had wasn't so special. The short time we were together was possibly the happiest time of my life. Here, everything is so formal, I don't know how to explain it… but it seems my life is drawn out for me here. There is so much to take on now.'

'What about your work, your research at Sophia Antipolis.'

'That too, it already seems like a dream. Matt is taking it on… and Yvette… then they'll find someone else for my side of the work. Most of the time I am too busy here to think about it but when I do… and I think about you… well, yes, it does seem dreamlike.'

'Listen, Sam, you have enough worries without adding me to them. I absolutely understand and you have all my sympathy. Please don't worry about me. I have new work here and plenty to do. What we had was perfect and just when we both needed it. I shall always look back on our time together with great fondness, I'm smiling now… but we both knew we were on the rebound, remember!'

'Amber, you're so sweet not to yell at me. Although it makes me feel more of a heel than ever. I'm not even sure that Marianne is the right wife for me… she has been so kind, of course… but in a way, I feel more on the rebound from falling in love with you. It's hard to explain… I guess my emotions are all in a mess right now. I'll write to you if I may?'

'Of course, that's a good idea, and I'll write back. Look after yourself, Sam. You're a good man and you deserve a good life. That sounds like something out of a girl's magazine but it's true.'

'You too, Amber, look out for yourself, you're too beautiful not to be chased by every red-blooded man on the planet. Look out for yourself!'

Amber closed the phone and looked down at it for a moment, feeling the loss of the connection with Sam. Poor Sam. What a shock he must have had and what hell it must be trying to cope with everything. His father's business affairs alone would be a huge task to take on. She tried to imagine his world and failed. He was the other side of the globe, in his rich American world and, as she had said to him directly, probably where he belonged. She gave a small smile as she heard his voice saying, 'I'll write to you, if I may?' Who asked permission to write a letter nowadays? There was something charming about his old world manners but also something that just wasn't part of Amber's life. Still, she admitted to herself, she hoped he would write and she would be happy to respond. She returned to looking through the sketches in her drawing book. But her thoughts wandered… should she be feeling abandoned and deserted again? Amber closed the book sharply and stood up, suddenly ready to get on with the day. That had been the best thing about her short affair with Sam. She would miss that… there was no great feeling of… Amber stopped short and stood still for a moment… how could she define what she had felt for Sam? Attraction, certainly, passion… fun, friendship… so why wasn't she sad at losing him to Marianne? Where was the stab of jealousy she should be suffering? Amber shrugged away her thoughts and left the bedroom and took the lift. As it dropped down to the ground floor she felt a flutter in the pit of her stomach. Why did she not feel sad about losing Sam? Answer, loud and clear, now she would feel free to think about Luc?

When the lift doors opened she found Zoe waiting in the lobby, talking to the receptionist. Amber quickly closed her mind to thoughts of Luc, the magic flutist, and went across to meet Zoe.

'Hi, Amber, that's lucky! I was just asking reception to buzz you to see if you were in your room. Alex and I were wondering if you could join us for a coffee as we've decided to get away before lunch now.' Zoe stood, smiling at Amber with her hand resting lightly on her bump. 'Now I don't have morning sickness I'm getting back to my normal energetic self.'

'When is your baby due?' Amber asked, looking at Zoe and thinking how she glowed with health.

'Oh, another four months yet. Already, I can't wait. I'm so excited!' Zoe giggled and the two girls began to walk together toward the terrace.

'Your first baby?' asked Amber.

'Yes, but we already have a four year old daughter, Delphi, from Alex's first marriage. He was a widower when I met him in Tuscany. That's partly why we want to get off early as we miss her so much. She's been down on the coast in Menton with Alex's parents. Of course, she's been having a great time but we can't wait to get back with her again.'

'Will you go back to England to have your baby?'

'Goodness no, our real home is in Italy now. Delphi is at nursery school in Siena and the local hospital is fine. No, we only go back to Bath, where Alex still has a house and his architect's office, when we can't avoid it any longer.' Zoe giggled again, 'I dreamt of living in Italy when I was a teenager... then I studied Italian at uni, then found a job teaching English in Siena, then changed to working for an estate agent. That's how I met Alex, he was house-hunting and I showed him the Villa Sognidoro. In my wildest dreams I never thought I would end up living there...and with Alex and Delphi. I've been so lucky.'

The conversation ended as they joined Alex sitting at a table on the terrace. He stood up as they arrived and put his arm round Zoe.

'Come and sit in the shade, my love. Now, you're not feeling sick I can tell that I have a full time job ahead telling you to take it easy.'

'Well, you can try but I doubt you'll succeed. I feel great this morning. Anyway, let's get down to work. I'm sure Amber is eager to get started and I have already been holding her up with my gossip.'

'Goodness, does that mean you have been talking about me?' Alexander pulled a face, 'Don't believe a word she says, Amber, please.'

They all laughed and Amber sat down and pulled out her drawing book. They drew close and studied the drawings carefully. Amber could tell, now so close to Alex, that his face was young and strangely odd against his dark grey hair. She thought about what Zoe had been telling her and wondered how he had been widowed and whether that cast a shadow on his youth. With all that Zoe seemed to have done since leaving university it would seem that she was probably about the same age as Amber. Maybe Alex was a few years older. Amber thought how different life could be when marrying young and for a fleeting second she imagined how it would have been if Rob had turned up at the church. Then she realised that Alex was asking her a question and she quickly brought herself back to the present moment.

'I think this last drawing is fantastic, everything I wanted and more so. What do you think, Zoe?'

'Absolutely, I love it!'

Amber looked at them both with delight, 'Yes, I think that one works best, but just now, coming down in the lift...' Amber hesitated for a moment as she remembered that actually she had been thinking about Luc when she was in the lift. The colour rose to her cheeks she continued hurriedly, 'Well, actually it was seeing Zoe in the lobby and then you, Alex, sort of towering over her and with your arm round her shoulders... her obvious bump... well, if you look at the group of figures in this corner of the field... in my drawing... I was thinking I could sort of personalise them... use you as outline shapes for the farmer and his wife... then Calinda would be the grand lady overseeing everything from her carriage and Daniel would be this man...' Amber tapped the drawing lightly with the tip of her pencil, 'loading the grapes onto the wagon. What do you think?'

'I think it's a great idea... such fun... we'd be immortalised, Alex! But could you add a little girl standing beside the farmer and his wife? I could send you some photos of Delphi. She'd simply love to be in the painting, too!' Zoe nodded enthusiastically.

'Yes, of course, that's a great idea!' Amber nodded, pleased with Zoe's enthusasm.

'Well, it is certainly an original idea,' Alex agreed, 'yes, I like it too. Just the one twin then, Amber... not adding Luc to the scene?'

'No, I think that would be confusing!' Amber laughed and thought to herself that she really wouldn't object to Luc posing for her.

'How about using yourself as a model for this girl with the basket on her head? We'd like to have you in the scene, too, don't you agree, Zoe?'

'Definitely... that would be perfect. Then I hope you'll visit us and see your work in situ, Amber. You'd be welcome any time to Villa Sognidoro.'

'Thank you, I'd love that. Right now I'll finish off this drawing and tomorrow I should be able to start on painting the actual tiles. Dani has it all prepared.'

'Great, now, if you'll excuse us we should hit the road.' Zoe stood up and stretched. 'Come on Alex, finish your coffee, we're going!'

Alex swallowed the last of his coffee and stood up. 'All this pregnant energy, Zoe, how will I ever keep up with you.' He shook hands formally with Amber and then they left. Amber watched them walk away along the length of the terrace. Again, Alex had his arm around Zoe's shoulders and she leant toward him as they walked. Another good marriage, Amber thought to herself, wondering if she was envious. Maybe there was a vestige of envy lingering in the air around her but right now she really did want to begin work.

To: amber@hotmail.com
Cc:
Subject: Still in Sussex
From: William Marsden - wmarsden@talktalk.net

I am so sorry to hear the sad news from Sam. Poor lad has a lot on his shoulders now and it seems his dream of research in the Med have come to an end for now. I am sure you will have spoken to him by now. Back here in Sussex I have some real news at last about Calinda's kidnapped sister. Giles found real evidence at only the third convent he visited in Malaga. It seems almost certain that the girl, known now as Marissa, was adopted by a Spanish family just a few months after she was taken in by the convent. Giles is making careful enquiries as obviously this was a dubious adoption involving a large donation to the orphanage. If Marissa is found to be the sister then we have to decide how to proceed. The good thing is that the adopted parents are living in Barcelona... the mother is a lawyer and the father a doctor. It all seems very respectable but, of course, there is a lot that has gone on in the past that was outside of the law. I think we should still keep it from Calinda until we know more. Obviously the final proof will be a DNA test with Calinda or her parents. What do you think about it all?
Best love, my dear... I can't help thinking sometimes how Provence has changed both our lives! Grandy x

To: wmarsden@talktalk.net
Cc:
Subject: hi Grandy
From: Amber Marsden - amber@hotmail.commail.com
OMG Grandy... this is getting very serious, isn't it? I hardly know how to take it all in. If this girl does turn out to be Calinda's sister it will be so ... do you know, I can't even think of the word I need... shattering just about comes near. I

agree the most important thing is to be quite sure before we raise Calinda's hopes. I know she seems quite calm but I think underneath she is very fragile and I don't know how she would cope with the let-down of it NOT being her sister… you know what I mean… I've just googled DNA testing and it does seem to be quite a simple thing now. Supposing I could send you a sample of Calinda's DNA… like a hair or something. Would that work. I can hardly believe I am writing this. How right you are… Provence has changed everything. Must go now… I am going to spend the day painting the tiles for Tuscany and I shall be able to think it all through. Will try to Skype you about six-ish your time this evening. We really need to talk. Amber x

Amber had spent all day working on the tiles. It was detailed work and she painted slowly, using fine brushes and delicate strokes. The atelier was cool, on the north side of the barn complex and with narrow windows over-looking the lavender fields. The work brought its own calm and she enjoyed the slow pace of the day. She began to think more calmly about Grandy's hopes of finding Calinda's sister. If the girl was found then it could only be a good outcome, however hard it might be at first. She tried to imagine how a reunion scene could be best played out but it was hard to even contemplate. Amber's own life had aways run along such smooth lines of normality… until the moment that Rob had let her down at the door to the church. In the grand scale of disasters it began to seem relatively trivial to Amber. All she could be certain about was that they must be absolutely certain, one hundred percent sure, that this girl, well… she would be a woman now, just two years younger than Calinda. Amber stopped painting for a moment as she thought about this… for some reason the stolen child had stayed in her mind as a child. Obviously the truth was that the girl would now be grown woman living in her own adult world. Did this make it easier? Amber began to paint and lost herself once more in the tranquil scene of the grape harvest in Tuscany that was coming to life in front of her.

By six in the evening she had worked her way across the whole landscape in outline. She stood back and felt unusually pleased with her work. The figures were lively and worked well in the harvest scene. Zoe had sent photos of Delphi to Amber's phone and now she was particularly pleased with the small figure of a little girl, holding her father's hand and looking up at him. It added a small but poignant feature. Then she looked at the figure of the peasant loading the grapes into the wagon. The man's back was heavily muscled and yet arched gracefully as he heaved the large basket of grapes. Definitely representative of Daniel although Luc had been in her mind all day. She cleaned her brushes and went to look out of the window. It seemed as though there would soon be a real harvest scene right outside. A few men were walking along the long avenues of lavender, brushing the flowers as they walked. Dani had told her earlier that today they would be deciding when to begin to harvest the blooms. She turned back to her work and carefully laid the tiles in the correct order and left them to dry. Tomorrow she would be able to begin shading and toning. She stretched her tired arms and flexed her shoulders, deciding whether to go for a run or take a swim. Leaving the atelier she walked back across the courtyard and stood for a moment by the well. She remembered how she had seen Luc standing on the same spot... then she sighed. She had to stop all this thinking about Luc. He was miles away, playing his flute to an audience in Holland and probably with the beautiful jazz singer at his side. Amber was unsettled by the way that Luc had so obviously hinted at returning as soon as he could to the Hotel Lavande... and then he had kissed her. Not just a fleeting brush of his lips across her cheek but a full kiss on her mouth. Even now she could remember the heat of his lips against hers. She kept telling herself it was just his way and that it meant nothing, nothing at all. Quite possibly she wouldn't meet him again for months as his work took him away from Provence. She simply had to forget him. The man had a dangerous way of making her feel edgy. Fortunately, she was brought out of her thoughts by the arrival of Calinda and Fleur.

'There you are Amber, I haven't seen you all day. Have you been working on the tiles?'

'Yes, I've just finished for the day and thinking about taking a swim or going for a run.'

'It's still so hot… why don't you take a swim? Did Dani warn you that the pool will be emptied on Monday? I told him to tell you. We always close the hotel for the first three days of July to clean the pool and totally revitalise the hotel before the madness of the summer season hits in.'

'No, he didn't mention it, but I have hardly seen him today. I think he's been checking on the lavender.'

'Oh god, that too… yes, it's that time of the year again. Hopefully he'll decide to begin the harvest when the hotel is empty as the tractors make quite a noise… not ideal for hotel guests trying to enjoy the peace and quiet here.'

'Well, I suppose some of the guests would be interested… I can well imagine that Grandy would be.'

'Well, your grandfather is definitely not a typical holiday-maker. Anyway, that's the other thing I wanted to talk to you about. Will you come up for dinner with us tonight. It seems you grandfather is making good progress with his research.'

Amber looked at Calinda in alarm, thinking that Grandy had told her something about his attempt to find her sister. Then she realised that Calinda must be talking about the pending purchase of the Hotel de Plage.

'Yes, that would be great. I know he is ready to go ahead. I think I will take a swim then. What time tonight?'

'Maybe early… about seven? I know Dani will want an early night if he's in harvest mood.'

'Lovely, suits me too. See you later then.'

Amber walked quickly into the hotel and up to her room. If she hurried she would be able to Skype Grandy and have a quick swim.

It was just seven when Amber took the lift up to the top floor. She was nervous and yet pleased with herself. She had spoken at some length with Grandy and now felt more confident on how they would go ahead. The main part of their conversation had naturally been about the search for Calinda's sister but they had also managed to talk about the purchase of the Hotel de la Plage. Grandy had explained the division of the ownership and Amber felt ready to talk about it all with Calinda and Daniel. Apart from that she had an idea of her own. She had decided that somehow she would obtain Calinda's DNA that very evening. She felt a tremor of fear as she thought about it again and whether it was some sort of abuse of Calinda's privacy… but no, she was determined it was the right thing to do and the only way to protect Calinda from the possibility of a dreadful disappointment. Then once again the lift doors opened onto the next scene of Amber's life in Provence.

A player in the game of love or...

To: wmarsden@talktalk.net
Cc:
Subject: hi Grandy
From: Amber Marsden - amber@hotmail.commail.com

I did it, Grandy. I had the perfect opportunity last night. I went to dinner with Calinda and when we finished eating, Calinda asked me again if I would look after Fleur while she and Daniel went for a walk. The lavender harvest is about to happen any day and they were going to check it out or something. As soon as they had gone I slipped into their bathroom and Calinda's hairbrush was just on a shelf by the basin. I managed to find a few hairs and put them in a little plastic bag that I had taken specially. OMG Grandy, I was shaking all over by then. I went and sat down by Fleur's cot until they came back in. She was sound asleep the whole time. I was still so strung up that I told them I would have an early night and thanked them and fled. I felt so guilty and it was like they could see the bag in my pocket. I'd never make a cool detective. Anyway I drove into town and sent it to you express by the first post. Now it is over to you and Giles, thank goodness there is nothing more I can do here. Back to the quiet life of painting for me. Oh yes, of course we talked most of the evening about the Hotel de la Plage and they are as excited as I am about your plans. I wish you were here... life would be SO much easier x Amber

To: amber@hotmail.com
Cc:
Subject: Still in Sussex
From: William Marsden - wmarsden@talktalk.net

Well done, my dear. I think you are a lot tougher than you believe yourself to be. You always have been since a small child. First the fear and then your shoulders go back and in you plunge! I already have the DNA report from Malaga so as soon as your sample arrives it will be just a matter of hours. We can but hope. The only other news I have from Giles is that he has found out as much as he can about Marissa. She has an honours degree in history from Cordoba university and now working in a museum there. Not married but living with a boyfriend… he's a young lawyer. It sounds like she has a good established life.

Any more news from Sam?

BTW (do you see how good I am getting at email language lol) I am thinking about coming out the second week of July if the conveyancing for the hotel is ready. I'll let you know of course.

Back to your painting now… BTW I hear you sold one of your own… congrats… BTW I saw Kim for lunch in London and she told me that they are packing up your goods and chattels BTW that means 'your gear' fyi ha ha lol BTW etc etc and lots of love Grandy

PS I am never going to sink to sending those nasty little smiley faces… never!

Amber smiled as she read Grandy's email and allowed herself a moment of childish comfort at the thought that he might soon be back in Provence. She hadn't told him that last night's conversation with Calinda and Daniel had also touched on the motorbike menace. Daniel had been out early and heard the high whine of the bike as it came over the hill and then roared past. By the time he had run out of the lavender fields and down to the road it had disappeared. He had checked up and down the sides of the road for a cigarette stub but found nothing. Amber thought about the awkward conversation that followed.

'Well, I guess it was just a random moment when I saw him drop that burning cigarette.' Said Amber.

'Hmm, well maybe,' shook his head doubtfully. 'You remember Leon, from the Bastide de Rosefont? I phoned him yesterday about it. Did you know he was a private investigator before he worked at the Bastide?'

'Yes, yes, you told me and that he knew the previous owner here… a nasty piece of work who ended up in prison or something.'

'What could that have to do with the motor-biker?'

'Well, we're not sure really.'

'But, anyway, he's in prison in Marseilles, isn't he?' Calinda and Daniel looked at each other and then at Amber. Calinda spoke quietly, 'Apparently he escaped when he was being transferred from Marseilles to a prison hospital.'

There was silence in the room as they all thought about the possibility that the biker could be this Pascal Mazin. Then Danilel spoke again. 'Leon told me that this Pascal had the mad idea that he, not Michelle, should have inherited the Bastide as he was the illegitimate son of the deceased Comte. It was only by a DNA test that Leon had managed to prove otherwise.'

Amber drew in her breath sharply and managed to stop her hand moving over the pocket in her jeans where Calinda's DNA lay hidden. She struggled to reply, 'But, but… I don't get it… how did Leon even have the proof?'

Calinda answered, once again quietly and calmly, 'When this Pascal came to the Bastide he threw a cigarette out of the window of his van… Leon kept it. He used it to prove that the man had no blood relationship with the Comte, who was indeed Michelle's birth father. On top of that Leon checked police records and found that Pascal Mazin had a record for receiving stolen goods.'

'So how did he end up in prison in Marseille? Was it because of the attack on Michelle?'

'No, no… there was nothing they could do about that… she was hardly hurt and there was no proof, of course. I think Leon and a neighbour called Sven, apparently a hulking Swede, well, I think they threatened him with the police and he disappeared. Leon has now found out that he was later caught smuggling drugs into the port of Marseilles … that's how he ended up in Baumettes prison.'

'Then he escaped.' Calinda added and once more there was an awkward silence.

Daniel stood up and began to clear the table.

'Anyway, I have told the police the whole story and they are keeping watch now on the road. If you see an old car parked at the end of the drive it will be them keeping watch. We shouldn't worry any more.'

That had ended the subject and over coffee they had returned to the more pleasant and interesting subject of the Hotel de la Plage. Amber had still felt ill at ease with the DNA evidence hidden in her pocket and had left earlier than usual.

Now, standing on the balcony of her bedroom she looked out at the calm, quiet landscape shimmering in the mid-morning heat. She had missed her early run as she had driven into town to the post office. She decided to swim to clear her head before she began work on the tile landscape again.

The water in the pool was so warm it was hardly refreshing. Amber swam a few lengths and then decided to give up. As she began to pull herself out of the pool she saw Daniel standing on the edge holding out his hand to her. She blinked up at him, the chlorinated water blurring her eyes, and took his hand. Springing out of the water and standing close to him as the water ran down her body she drew in her breath sharply as she realised this was not Daniel but Luc. She almost reached out her hand to brush his forehead to make sure the mole was definitely absent. Gathering herself together hastily she managed to stumble out a few words,

'Why, hi Luc... I thought you were in Holland!'

'I was in Holland but for some reason I just couldn't stay there. Something was drawing me back to Provence... in fact, right to this very spot.' Luc still held her hand in his and slowly pulled her slightly closer to him. 'I haven't been able to think about anything else. I just wanted to see you again. I've never skipped a performance before... never once.'

'But, but...' Amber couldn't think what to say but she managed to pull her hand away and take a step back. 'What happened about the concert?'

'Well, of course I like to think I am not replaceable but in fact the second flautist just took over. No big deal, really, but I have never done it before. Not even a day's illness. It's all your fault Amber, you have bewitched me.'

'Now you are being ridiculous, Luc. Anyway, it's very good to see you but I really have to go to work now.' Amber spoke defiantly, expecting Luc to object.

'Of course, I understand… I can spend time practicing my new work for next week. I just wanted to see you and check you were for real… not going to disappear like Cinderella or something. Do you take time off for lunch? Perhaps we could eat together?'

Amber looked at him in surprise. She had never been with anyone who actually understood that her art was also her work. She thought briefly of Rob's lack of interest in her work at the museum and total disinterest in the watercolours she painted in the Scottish Highlands. She looked up at Luc and tried to resist the desire to quickly agree. She wanted to hold on to some line of resistance and maintain her calm but instead she found herself saying,

'Actually I was out really early this morning and missed breakfast. Do you feel like grabbing a bite to eat now at the poolside bar?'

Luc nodded eagerly and held out a towel for Amber. As she wrapped herself in it he gave a quick nod and then dived into the pool and swam to the far end. Amber watched as his body moved through the water… so very like Daniel and yet so different. Then she thought about Sam, now far away in New York. Was she ready for this new man to swim into her life and stir her emotions? Despite the heat of the sun on her skin she felt a cold shiver of fear. Rob had hurt her so deeply and Sam had somehow helped her over that. But Luc, yes, now there was Luc waiting for her at the far end of the pool. Was the man dangerous or exciting? A player in the game of love or… just maybe… the real thing? Then she threw the towel onto a bed-chair, dived into the water and followed Luc to the other end of the pool.

'What will you have, Amber?' Luc looked across the table at Amber, his dark eyebrows raised in question. Amber looked down quickly at the menu to distract herself from the strong ache of desire she felt just from his glance.

'I think just a tomato panini and a glass of juice, please. I do have work to do and this is actually my breakfast.'

'*Aussi moi… avec mayo et sans beurre, comme d'hab!*' Luc flashed a smile up at the waitress as he gave his order and Amber sighed as she noticed the effect it had on the young girl. Was Luc a serial flirt? Then the waitress brought a cd out from her apron pocket and, blushing deep red and squirming with embarrassment, she asked Luc if he would sign it. Luc smiled and there was a rapid exchange in French that Amber could not understand. Then he signed the inside cover and added a few words. The girl giggled and thanked him and ran back into the hotel. Luc turned to Amber,

'Excuse all that… just a performance! I have to keep my fans happy!'

'I'm sure,' Amber nodded and sighed, 'Especially all the pretty young girls, I can see that.'

'No, you misjudge me, *mademoiselle*! I am trying to encourage anyone from the younger generation to study music. I am making a name for it and it is one of the few things I pride myself on… I try to bridge the huge gap between young people's modern music and the classics. My master classes are all for young people already studying at the Conservatoire and already engaged with classics. I am trying to draw in a young public who may never have heard of Poulenc or even Mozart.'

Amber thought about what he had said and wondered how true it could be. Surely he enjoyed the flattery of attention too? But he was still talking,

'The thing that always amuses me is that nearly everyone ask me to sign for a friend or relative… like they never want to ask for my autograph for themselves… funny really.'

'Is that what the waitress was asking?'

'Yes, she asked me to write something for her sister who is studying piano in Aix.'

'What did you write?'

'I told her to try the flute as it's much easier to carry around. Made her giggle anyway!'

'I feel so stupid not speaking French. I shall start taking lessons next month.'

'Why worry? Everyone around speaks English or likes to practice it on you. I nominate myself as your French teacher, it will make a good change from teaching music. Anyway, you do speak some French, I've heard you and with the most provocative English accent.'

'Provocative? Really? I always thought an English accent would sound dumb. Whereas foreigners speaking English sounds so cool. Sexy sometimes.'

'Then I hope I have a strong accent when I speak English.' Luc laughed at her and held his hand on his heart. Amber laughed but thought to herself that it was a good thing he didn't realise just how attractive he sounded to her. Before she could think any more on the matter she realised he was asking her a question.

'How is your work progressing with the harvest scene? Isn't it difficult, or rather different, painting on ceramic surface?'

'Well, I am using oxides and a fine brush, the surface is very porous, too but Daniel is running some glaze tests so that I can get an idea in advance.'

'Is it based on Tuscan art or Provencal? Alex told me you had been interested in his research… but then he is the customer… how does that work?'

The conversation continued and Amber was pleased to be able to discuss her new work. Part of her still held on to the idea that he was showing interest in order to win her over in some strategic love play, but, by the end of their meal, she was impressed by his obvious knowledge. She was also surprised, although not sure why, to find that Luc was a vegetarian. Why should this fit oddly with his worldly extravagant life style? The only thing she could still be certain of was that he had to be the most physically attractive man she had ever set eyes on. At one point in the meal she had laid her hand on the table, almost willing him to take hold of it but he just talked on, munching his sandwich. Finally they finished coffee and Amber rose to leave the table. She would go to the atelier and work and try to forget that she would rather spend a long afternoon in bed with this annoyingly beautiful man. Luc stood up too and then said,

'I wonder if it would disturb you if I practiced my flute in your atelier? I have a new piece to learn… would you be able to stand it?'

'That would be great!' Amber answered almost too quickly, 'The atelier is beautifully cool as it's on the north side of the hotel. I usually play music as I work but live flute playing would be wonderful.'

'Great, I'll go and get it now and see you there.'

'OK, I'm going up to my room to change but I won't be long.'

They walked slowly back along the path by the pool and into the cool of the hotel foyer. Luc pressed the lift button and then asked Amber which floor she was on… then they entered the lift and stood side by side as it flew upwards. His bare arm brushed lightly against Amber and suddenly she turned to him and leant her body against him. His arms encircled her quickly and he lifted her off her feet as he pressed into her. She wrapped her legs around his waist and began to kiss him ardently. When the lift doors opened, they were both breathing hard and kissing more and more fiercely. Luc carried Amber along the corridor to her room at the end. Amber fumbled for her key and managed to open the door, still in his arms and with his mouth now buried in her neck as he carried on kissing her. Once inside the room he slammed the door shut with his foot and they fell against the wall. His hands pulled at her bikini and as her breasts fell loose he dropped his head to cover them with kisses. Amber moaned in pleasure and began to pull at the string knotted in his shorts. Then with a groan he swung round and carried her to the bed, falling on top of her. They made love urgently and fast, their bodies slicked with sweat as they moved together in a frantic rhythm. When the first passion was spent, they lay side by side across the bed, not talking but still breathing hard. Luc took Amber's hand and kissed it and she pulled his hand to her mouth and kissed the inside of his palm. Then his hand moved down her body, caressing her stomach and then down again. She moved on top of him and they began to make love again, this time, slowly and sweetly.

      And so it was that Amber did spend a very long afternoon in bed with Luc. The atelier remained empty and the tile landscape unfinished… the flute unpracticed. As dusk began to fall they finally fell asleep, still together and wrapped in each other's arms.

To: kimS@gmail.com
Cc:
Subject:_WISH YOU WOZ 'ERE
From: Amber Marsden - amber@hotmail.com
Kim… I really need you to talk too. I know I have been ignoring you for ages but now I need you, my best friend… tell me what to do? I am falling totally besottedly in love with the flute-player and I feel I am on a roller coaster… you know… the sort that makes you scream and you can't stop. I mean, I don't want to stop… anything…it is all so wonderful but i am so so scared that is all too wonderful to be true/real? I think if this man dumped me I would never ever recover. What should I, can I, ought I to DO???? your desperate friend,
Amber x
PS How are you?

To: amber@hotmail.com
Cc:
Subject: Wow…err…
From: Kim Simpson - kimS@gmail.com

What to reply? OMG Amber, why can't you live a quiet ordinary life just for a month or two. I am still reeling from your non-wedding and here you go again, jumping in the deep end. Anyway, having written that because I thought I ought to as your responsible good friend… now all I can really say is why not go for it? It doesn't seem that you can help yourself anyway. If this Luc the Flute is a player then, yeh, you will be hurt but what if he isn't??? You know me, always the optimist. Shall try to Skype you tonight about 7 French time though doubtless you will be running around the lavender fields stark naked and chased by a man waving his magic flute or some-such at the time what's not to enjoy?
K x
PS I am very well thank you.
PPS All your stuff is now in your parent's garage.

To: kimS@gmail.com
Cc:
Subject:_WISH YOU WOZ 'ERE

Omg… thank you very much for shifting all my gear…or 'goods and chattels' as Grandy calls it…btw he is starting to write emails like a teenager all 'lol' etc…so funny! He may be coming out here again soon… I wish you could, too. Once I get settled you have your holidays planned for life. Not to mench I would like you to meet Luc and see what you think of him. I haven't told anyone else, but when I first clapped eyes on Daniel I really really fancied him but of course he was married to Calinda. It just seems sort of ridiculously lucky that he has a twin brother… arty too. He played the flute again last night… it has to be heard to be believed. Just adds up to the surreal stuff going on all around me.

Must go now… have to catch up on work I delayed yesterday… can you guess why?
x Amber

'Will you come down to Nice this weekend? I have a class to give to students on Monday but apart from usual practice I have nothing planned.'

Amber and Luc were in the atelier together. Amber was working in the light from the narrow window and Luc was standing behind her. Before she answered, he resumed playing the flute. Amber thought for a moment, carefully dipping the tip of her finest brush into the dark iron oxide and laying a coat of shadow down the figure of the farmer. She was still very pleased with the work. The figures were animated and spaced well across the strong diagonal lines of the vineyard. She bit her lip in concentration and added a touch to the figure of the small girl. Then she laid down her brush and turned to Luc.

'You know, I'd love to but I really must finish this work as Daniel is waiting to glaze fire it.'

'Yes, I thought you'd say that... then, I'll stay here and go down to Nice early Monday morning. Anyway, Dani is going to start the lavender harvest tonight... he's worried that a storm is forecast.'

'A storm?'

'Yeh, it's the dread of every farmer in the area at this time of the year. I'll help Dani later although he never lets me to do much.'

'What do you mean?'

'Well, it's partly because he regards himself as my older brother... by two minutes in truth... also because my hands have to be insured for a fortune.'

'Really? I never thought about it but I suppose that is your life work.'

'Yes, true and also I am pretty useless at anything else!' Luc laughed and returned to playing his flute but Amber could sense that he felt a truth in his words.

'I'm sure that's not true... you could be good at dozens of things but you are especially gifted with your music. By the way, I don't mind if you do want to go down to Nice. I'm sure you have friends there you want to catch up with... I don't mind, honestly.'

Luc stopped playing so abruptly that his flute let out a high squeak of protest. He shook the flute and then put it down in its case. 'Amber, what are you on about? Of course I don't want to go to Nice without you. To be honest I don't want to do anything without you ever again but I realise that sounds pretty pathetic. And what do you mean my friends? What are you trying not to say, my love? Tell me, *s'il te plaît*.'

Amber stayed silent for a moment as she carefully laid a line of pale shadow behind the figure of the farmer, then she put down her brush again and turned to face Luc. 'When I first saw you, actually I thought you were Daniel, I mean, I had no idea then that he even had a twin brother. You were with a very beautiful jazz singer at the Bateau Noir club in Cassis and...'

'Hold it right there, Amber, *attends un moment*, you saw me with Arlette at the Bateau Noir? Is that even possible. I didn't see you.'

'Well, you were just leaving, it was late and you were so... obviously a couple.'

Luc looked at her in amazement, 'You seriously think I would go down to Nice after being with you and meet another woman. Are you quite mad? *Tu es folle ou quoi?*'

'Well, it's all been so sudden... no, of course I didn't really think that I just felt... I don't know, scared or vulnerable or something. I mean being here with you, painting and listening to your music... looking out the window at the lavender blowing in the breeze... it's like some beautiful dream.'

Luc came closer and put his arms around her, holding her close to him. 'I know, Amber, I know just what you mean. I do really. I'm guessing you weren't at Le Bateau Noir on your own either. The past is the past and all I want is the future with you... here by the lavender fields, down on the coast ... anywhere in the world you want.'

Amber leant back against him and felt the tension seep from her body to be replaced by a sharp stab of desire. Luc ran his hand lightly over her shoulders and cupped her breasts in his hands. 'One thing that worries me though, Amber, is how we will ever get any work done.'
She was about to turn around and embrace him when the atelier door flew open and Daniel burst into the room, bringing the heat from the air outside and the smell of fresh hay.

'What are you two up to in here? Sorry to interrupt but I need your help, Luc.'

'Now? Right now?' Luc looked reluctantly at Amber, his cheeks slightly flushed under his dark tan.

'Yes, right now... in fact, half an hour ago. I've been looking for you everywhere. One of the tractor drivers is off sick and I need you to follow the pickers. The forecast is for rain tomorrow so we shall be picking all night. I've only just got enough pickers as all the farms around are doing the same, of course.'

'Maybe I could help pick the lavender?' Amber asked.

Daniel looked at her with a wide smile. 'It's kind of you to offer but it's not as easy as all that. But thanks anyway. Maybe you could help Calinda. She's going to organise the kitchen to make food for all the harvesters. She's in the hotel kitchens now.'

'OK, I'll go straight over there now.' Amber quickly washed her brushes and gave a quick glance at Luc. He smiled and shrugged his shoulders and she knew that he too was thinking about what else they would be doing if the forecast had been different.

Amber found Calinda in the hotel kitchen, surrounded by several of the catering staff. She was carrying Fleur in her sling as usual. Amber waited until Calinda had finished writing a list and giving orders for the food then went over to join her.

'Is there anything I can do to help, Calinda? Dani has already told me I'd be no good at harvesting.'

'Oh god no! It's a dreadful job even though it sounds so nice and rural. The truth is that the lavender is full of biting insects and really quite sharp and prickly. The stalks have to be kept long, too, so it's back-breaking work. Anyway, I would be grateful if you would look after Fleur for half an hour... would you mind?'

'No, I'd absolutely love to. Shall I take her up to my room to play or up to your flat?' Calinda looked at Amber doubtfully before answering, 'I think it would be best in the flat... she has her toys there. Do you have your mobile on you?'

'Yes, of course, and I'll ring if I need you at all.' Amber carefully took Fleur from Calinda and was pleased that Fleur seemed happy to be with her.

'She really does seem happy with you.' Calinda's words reflected Amber's thoughts. 'Thank, Amber, it gets too hot here in the kitchens and I just want to organise the supper for the harvest workers later tonight. It's quite a traditional feast. I won't be long and I'll come up to the flat and find you both.'

Calinda kissed Fleur on the top of her head and Amber left the hot, steamy kitchen and walked to the lift.

The penthouse was pleasantly cool with an unusual breeze blowing through the shutters and lifting the white voile curtains. Amber held Fleur so that she could feel the breeze and watch the curtains move. Fleur clapped her hands in delight and Amber looked around for something else to amuse her with. There was a musical mobile hanging above the cot and Fleur was obviously well-accustomed to the sound it made as it turned. Soon losing interest, Fleur stretched her arm toward a shelf and Amber realised it was a stack of cd's. 'Did you want some music, then?' Amber asked and began to flick through the stack with one hand. Then she stopped in surprise... at least five or six of them were flute music and played by Luc Rabin. Fleur bobbed up and down in excitement, impatient for the music to begin so Amber quickly played the first one she had found. Soon the room was filled with the melancholic sound of a flute leading an orchestra. She moved around the room, slowly dancing to the music as Fleur burbled with delight. As she made a last turn toward the door she realised that Calinda was standing there watching them and smiling. Fleur reached out her arms for her mother and Amber passed her to Calinda. The music played on and Amber stood still in the middle of the room feeling slightly silly and missing the warmth and weight of Fleur in her arms.

'Amber, that is exactly what I do with Fleur. We always have a little dance to Luc's music, don't we, Fleur.' Calinda held Fleur up in the air and turned a slow circle. 'How we love his music. Now, let's have a cup of tea... or would your prefer coffee or maybe a glass of wine?'

'Tea would be great! I used to drink gallons of it in England. It's funny I haven't missed it at all but now you offer it... well, I can think of nothing better.'

They took the tea tray out onto the balcony and watched the lavender harvest get under way. Calinda sipped her tea and then looked at the tea cup with a critical eye.

'You know I was thinking about the design you showed me... the sprig of lavender on white porcelain. I think it would be perfect. Daniel thinks it would work with cobalt blue blurring into a magnesia matt white glaze. As soon as the Tuscan fountain is finally despatched he'll start testing for glazes to fit a fine white porcelain clay. That fountain has just taken far too long but we really like Zoe and Alex so we're making the best of it.'

Amber grimaced, 'I'm afraid I haven't really helped. I should have had the decoration of the centre piece ready for firing by now but...' Amber couldn't think how to end the sentence.

Calinda suddenly giggled, 'It's Luc, isn't it! I knew when he cam he back early from Amsterdam that something was in the air. And I could tell by the way he looked at you at dinner... so, is it serious?'

Amber blushed and was surprised to hear herself reply quite decisively 'Yes, it's serious.'

'But what about the cute American guy you were with in Cassis... what's happened to him?'

'Oh, you mean Sam. Well, yes, we did have something going but he had to go back to the States as his father died and now he is back with his fiancée.' Amber realised this didn't sound very convincing and that, in fact, Calinda was concerned about Luc. As if she read her mind, Calinda then said, 'I know Luc comes over as an outrageous flirt... all flamboyant and extrovert but really he is a very gentle guy and I wouldn't want to see him hurt. He's not so different from my Dani... if or when you meet his parents, you will see that they have been brought up with very strong moral principles. Quite an unusual family as they're not religious but have very determined ethics. I mean, Luc won't even eat meat because he's so soft about animals... and he's such a great uncle. Anyway, I've said what I wanted to say and more...so I'll leave it at that. I trust you, Amber, to understand me.'

Amber nodded quietly, 'I do, Calinda, I really do.'

Calinda suddenly giggled again, 'How serious I sound! Really sorry about all that, Amber. But Luc is so important to us... and he's such an idiot sometimes, pretending to be so … you know, show off. Maybe it's all the attention he gets with his work. I think he puts on a show to cover his feelings, whereas what he likes most is to be somewhere quiet and write his music and play his flute. In a way his fame makes his life complicated and I absolutely understand that. If I hadn't met Dani when I did I think I would have gone crazy and burnt out. I can imagine your calmness would be wonderful for Luc…even though neither of you have got any work done lately. By the way, don't worry about the tiles… Dani will be too busy for a day or so to even think about firing the kiln.

25   *a rapid charcoal drawing of him in the rumpled sheets*

To: To: wmarsden@talktalk.net
Cc:
Subject:_Lavender, lavender everywhere!

Well, Grandy, it's Sunday afternoon and I have a moment to write to you at last. Things moving fast here in hot Provence. The whole weekend has been given over to the lavender harvest. A wind blew up... nothing that would even be noticed by a Sussex farmer... and it was all hands on deck to cut the flowers before it rained. Then the wind died down as quickly as it came and it didn't rain a drop! Anyway, the lavender is beautifully bundled in the barn... the perfume fills the whole hotel... and everyone happy and resting. I have managed to finish the tile decoration and tomorrow it will be fired. For once I am actually pleased with my work... not sure what that means! Calinda has asked me to look after Fleur several times while she went down to the harvesters and tonight she has actually agreed to go out to dinner with Daniel to a harvest celebration and to leave me with Fleur. Actually, her uncle Luc will also be with me. So what do you think of all that news and what news do you have for me?
x Amber

To: amber@hotmail.com
Cc:
Subject: Still in Sussex
From: William Marsden - wmarsden@talktalk.net

Dear Amber (you see I am back to letter style emails and giving up on all this silly acronymic email language btw and fyi)
I was very pleased to receive your news. I wish I had been there to see the lavender harvest even if I am now too old and

decrepit to help. Also delighted to hear the Calinda is trusting you more and more to look after little Fleur. Is there a subtext or something I should be reading between the lines about this young flute player, Luc??

My news: nothing much yet as your envelope not arrived but hopefully it will be in the Monday morning post. Giles is standing by and ready to take the sample to a lab.

Your mother says you haven't Skyped for a few days and I told her that you had some new work. Why she refuses to email I have no idea. I find it a wonderful way to stay in touch with my favourite grand-daughter. Look after yourself out there in wild Provence!

from your loving Grandy x

PS Your mother very pleased with your photos of me and my panama… I had to download them for her…she is quite a determined technophobe but certainly enjoys Skype.

Amber read Grandy's email through twice then closed down her iPad. She smiled and looked across at her bed where Luc lay deep asleep. Had Grandy guessed that she was in love again? He had told her to look after herself. Amber stretched and massaged her back, feeling the sweet ache of long love-making. She ran a cool shower and stood under it, letting the water run over her body. Soon, if he didn't wake she would have to leave Luc and go up to the penthouse to be with Fleur. Luc needed to sleep now, he had worked two nights and days driving the tractor back and forth and then spent the last of his energy in bed with her. She wrapped a towel around herself and went quietly back into the bedroom and looked at him. Her artist's eye took in the long, graceful lines of his muscled back. Quickly and quietly she pulled out her sketch pad and made a rapid charcoal drawing of him in the rumpled sheets. She began to fill in the dark shadows and was lost in her work until he moved and pulled himself up onto one elbow, he looked around for her and then looked at his watch.

'What are you doing, Amber? Drawing me? Why didn't you wake me? It's time to go up and look after Fleur. Hurry up!' His voice was anxious but blurred with sleep.

'I am ready! I've had a shower. Take your time... I can go up and you can join me.'

'No, I'll be one minute.' He heaved himself out of the tangled sheets and laughed as he looked at Amber. 'You have wrecked me. I don't have an ounce of energy left. Fancy snatching the opportunity to draw me... you're scandalous, Amber. I am beginning to worry that you only want me for my body... I am just your sex-object, aren't I?' He wrapped the sheet around himself and pretended to look hurt. Amber laughed until the tears rolled down her cheeks and managed to say, 'You should see yourself, at least one part of your body doesn't look altogether worn out yet!'

Luc flung the sheet at Amber and chased her round the room, jumping over the bed to catch her and kiss her, holding her hard against him.

'If my little niece wasn't waiting for us upstairs I would show you how tired I am or not!' He let her go suddenly and ran into the shower. 'But I am responsible Uncle Luc and you will not lead me astray, you little witch!'

An hour later they were standing on the balcony of the penthouse looking down and waving to Calinda and Daniel as they set off for Aix and the harvest dance.

'I was beginning to think they would never go.' Luc said as he carried on waving to Calinda. 'Good thing you are here, Calinda would never have trusted me on my own.'

'Well, she has left me a few times with Fleur, but I really had to work at it. But I understand why.'

Luc looked at Amber in surprise as they went back into the cool of the penthouse living room. 'Calinda has told you about her childhood?'

'Yes, about her lost baby sister. So dreadful.'

'I don't think she has told anyone else apart from Dani and me. It's tragic and has had such a terrible effect on Calinda.'

There was a moment of silence and then, suddenly, Amber found herself telling Luc everything about Grandy's search. Luc listened to the whole story in silence and even when Amber came to the end, he said nothing. Then he stood up and said,

'I'll just check on Fleur and make sure she's still asleep.'

'I'll make a pot of tea, I think.' Amber was trembling now, wishing she had kept the secret to herself. She went in to the kitchen and waited, busying herself with filling the kettle and finding cups but her hands were shaking. Then Luc came back and stood beside her. It seemed he was struggling to speak,

'Amber, I don't know what to say… how have you managed to keep this secret? How long has the search being going on?'

Amber tried to answer his questions but her voice was shaky. Then Luc put his arms around her and took the cup from her trembling hand and placed it carefully on the worktop. He kissed the top of her head and held her gently.

'My dear, brave, little Amber. Why did I never think to do what you are doing?' Amber was crying now with mixed emotions. Relief that Luc approved of the dangerous steps that she and Grandy had taken and that she could now share the fear that it might all go very wrong.

'It was all Grandy's idea… I just went along with it. I am so scared that we are doing something we have no business to be doing.'

'No, no… you have done all the right things, obviously your grandfather is a powerful man and can use his influence, but keeping it from Calinda and … that is the most important thing you have done and all on your own. Now I can share it with you. Calinda and I have a very good friendship and normally I tell her everything but this, this is so important to keep from her until we know if this girl is truly Calinda's lost sister. Calinda is very calm on the outside but she is a very fragile person.' He stopped talking for a moment as though thinking something through, 'And if I told Dani then it would be laying a hard burden on him to keep it from his wife… no, it is best we keep this secret until your grandfather has absolute proof. *Mais oui, la preuve définitive.'*

Amber leant against Luc, thinking how close his thoughts were to her own. They stayed quiet a few minutes, Luc gently stroking Amber's shoulders until her tears subsided. Then he patted her briskly on her back and said, 'That's better, shoulders back again. Do you know, my love, you have the sweetest way of pulling your shoulders back when you decide to do something. It amuses me but the problem is that is does make me very aware of your beautiful body. Now, you had better go and check on Fleur and I will try and make you a …what do you call it… cuppa?'

Amber managed to laugh and went through to see Fleur. To her surprise she found Fleur awake and waving her hands in the air. She seemed delighted to see Amber and held out her arms to be picked up. Amber carried her into the living room and sat with her on the sofa, suddenly wondering how she would keep her amused for the next several hours until Calinda and returned. Then, Luc came in, carrying a tray. He put it down on the table and said, '*Ma petite Fleur, tu as decidé a joindre la fête?'* He clapped his hands and Fleur imitated him, bouncing up and down on Amber's knee.

'She doesn't seem very sleepy.' Amber looked down at Fleur doubtfully, 'Do you think she will miss Calinda?'

'In my totally uneducated opinion she sleeps far too much!' Luc laughed, 'She wants to party sometimes!' Fleur gave a wide, dribbly smile and gurgled in agreement. 'Maybe she's teething or something, don't they dribble a lot when they're teething?'

'Do they?' Again, Amber looked down at Fleur and began to jig her up and down a little. 'She does seem to like being up! Anyway, how do you know anything about babies?'

'Oh, I don't… except the first violinist has a baby that often travels with us and I carry her around sometimes. She's been teething lately… she was crying a lot in Amsterdam.'

'Goodness, your concert tour doesn't sound like anything I imagined. But Fleur never cries... Calinda doesn't want her too.'

'Oh, I know, and of course it is completely up to her but a small part of my brain does tell me that it is natural for a baby to cry just a little sometimes... you know, it's there way of communicating or complaining.'

'I guess Fleur never has anything to complain about then!' At that very moment Fleur let out a small cry of discontent and her bottom lip began to wobble.

Luc immediately stood in front of her and began to sing and dance. Fleur stopped crying at once and clapped her hands again.

'Well, that worked!' laughed Amber, 'Mind you, that was quite a performance!' Luc sat down beside Amber and said,
'OK, clever girl, pass Fleur to me and drink the lovely cuppa I made you.' Amber passed Fleur to Luc and sipped her tea and then grimaced, 'Oh, it's horrid! What did you do?' Before he could answer there was another small cry of complaint from Fleur. Amber put down her cup and leapt to her feet, dancing and singing in front of Luc and Fleur. Once again Fleur clapped her hands and stopped crying.

'Oh, that was good, Amber, really classy dancing and I love your choice of song, Baby Love!' He stood up and began to sing, then danced around with Fleur. Amber joined in and they sang together until ending in helpless laughter.

'Fleur really is wide awake now!' Amber laughed, we'll never keep this up.'

'Especially for me in my weakened state...' Luc laughed and then added, 'I know, I know what she'll like... just a minute. He ran from the room and Fleur reached her arms after him and made another small cry. Amber hastily distracted her by going back to the cot and finding a squeaky toy for her to play with. Then Amber heard the first sounds of a flute warming up. Fleur immediately dropped the toy and turned toward the sound of the music. Luc came into the room playing the slow jazz opening notes of 'Ma Petite Fleur'. Fleur clapped her hands again in delight.

'She seems to recognise it… have you played it to her before?' asked Amber, holding Fleur against her shoulder and feeling her begin to relax.

Luc nodded his head as he played and raised his eyebrows at Amber.

'Is it something I should recognise?' Again Luc nodded his head as he carried on playing, raising his eyes to the ceiling in mock exasperation.

'Oh, of course, it's Ma Petite Fleur… it sounds so beautiful on the flute.'

Luc nodded and gave a small bow, still playing but changing the notes to a different melody. Amber recognised the lullaby that Luc had written for Fleur. She nodded at Luc, realising he was going to play her to sleep. Amber rocked slowly back and forth, in rhythm with the sweet music. She eased Fleur slowly down from her shoulder and held her in front of her, rocking her as she had seen Calinda do so often. Fleur's eyes closed, blinked open again and then closed. Luc played on, repeating the same refrain. Slowly Amber lowered Fleur into her cot but immediately Fleur opened her eyes and gave a small cry. Amber quickly picked her up again and went back to rocking her gently in her arms. She looked at Luc as he carried on playing and suppressed a burst of laughter. On the third attempt to lay the sleeping Fleur in the cot, Amber was at last successful. They crept from the room, Luc still playing soft notes of music until they reached the living room. Then they both sat on the sofa and burst out laughing.

'Oh my, baby Fleur has us both dancing to her tune!' Amber said, wiping tears of laughter from her eyes, 'I'm exhausted and we've only been babysitting for three hours. However do mothers manage?'

'Well, I guess some mothers manage very differently. You know the old school where baby is left to cry and is fed every four hours…something like the opposite of everything Calinda does.'

'Yes, I suppose so. Maybe there's a happy medium somewhere? Anyway, Fleur is Calinda's baby so I definitely believe that we should do it her way as best we can. Oh god, you don't think Fleur was hungry, do you? Calinda said she wouldn't need anything more this evening but then she didn't know she would wake up. Should we have given her a bottle or something?'

Luc shook his head, 'I don't think so, but what do I know? Calinda would have left something if it was needed, surely. Anyway, she is fast asleep now. Maybe if she wakes again…' They both looked at each other in dismay at the thought of her waking again. Luc looked at his watch. 'Well, it's nearly ten thirty and they said they'd be back by eleven so we must be able to cope until then.'

Amber nodded in agreement, 'I could phone and ask Calinda but I really don't want her to worry or think I can't cope. Anyway, I'll just check on her again and let's hope she's asleep. There's a lot to know about this babysitting, isn't there?

'Basically it has to be common sense and instinct. It will be easier when we have our own.'

Amber had been about to stand up but his words kept her seated. She looked at him to see if he was joking but his face was very serious and he continued,

'I'm not joking, Amber. One day I want to have children of my own and now I know you are the only woman in the world that I want to be their mother.'

an uncanny way of guessing what she was thinking

To: kimS@gmail.com
Cc:
Subject:_YIKES!!!!
From: Amber Marsden - amber@hotmail.commail.com

Kim - things are getting out of hand here in hot Provence. I don't know where to begin except maybe to start by saying that Luc wants me to have his babies… yes, honestly, he said so last night. I didn't have time to reply as just then Calinda and Daniel came home. Did I tell you that Luc and I were babysitting for them? Anyway, the thing is… I don't know whether it was being with baby Fleur or what… but now I am feeling like it could be what I want too… then the next minute my brain tries to tell me I am definitely only one month into rebound from being jilted at the altar… what am I thinking???
Help, this man is so so wonderful… sweet and tender, interested in my work too… and yes, the sexiest item everrrr… how can I resist? Do I want to resist and the answer is coming up NO. Anyway today he is going down to Nice to give his give his master class to some students and staying over night. I held out against going with him as… well, I want some time to think. Also Daniel and Calinda's car broke down in Aix last night and I said I'd stay with Fleur (more time to get broody, sigh) this evening while they take Calinda's car to go and get it from the garage. Do you begin to see how my life rockets on here??? Anyway, how are you and Mike… are you getting serious? Are we actually growing up ha ha??? best love, your scared friend, Amber x
PS The only thing Luc can't do is make tea.

To: amber@hotmail.com
Cc:
Subject: Wow…err…
From: Kim Simpson - kimS@gmail.com

OMG… do you have to keep dropping these bombshells in my inbox. I am at work right now and sneaking a quick email back… but what can I say? You can't be serious about this Luc the Flute man if he can't make a decent cup of tea? Could you please just try and have an ordinary quiet week or few days at least. Go into an empty field and paint… keep out of trouble just for a day or so while you catch up with yourself. BTW Mike makes the best tea in the world and yes, we are both very grown up and serious… does that make you feel any better? Also I now wear a dark, navy dress to work and hand out instructions to my assistant and she makes ME coffee… howzat for maturity?
Stay safe and …oh, I dunno… sound? x Kim
PS Your Ma has had all your photos of Grandy printed b/w and framed… they hang in the hallway…très super!

      Amber watched Luc's car disappear down the drive. She smiled, thinking how typical it was of him to drive such an old car. He had proudly showed her the car papers with his grandfather's name showing the date of purchase.

      'You see, Amber… this car is a classic… well, almost.' They had both looked at the slightly rusty cream paint and the worn leather interior.

      'I like the walnut dashboard… and the steering wheel's lovely.' Amber had struggled to find something to praise about the ancient Citroën.

      'I can tell her beauty is lost on you. You know, Leon, from the Bastide, he has one similar. They found it in a garage when they restored the Bastide. Now, he understands what I'm talking about.' Amber nodded and tried to look more interested but they had soon moved on to other subjects.

      Now, as she watched him disappear she realised they always had so much to talk about. Not just that, but Luc had an uncanny way of guessing what she was thinking. When he had told her he wanted children… and with her… somehow even though she had not time to reply, yes, somehow she knew that he was thinking that she wanted it too. Amber realised she was still looking at the empty road and suddenly she remembered the motor biker. Nothing more had been said or even thought about him. It was still early and the heat not yet built up so she thought she'd go for a run. Even running was different now as she missed the sound of Luc beside her. Pushing her shoulders back she resolved to fill her day with everything she needed to do and to forget Luc for a few hours at least. Not an easy task when even pulling her shoulders back made her remember his blatant gaze of desire.

'This has to stop!' Amber spoke the words aloud to the empty room.

Amber ran along the drive and down to the road, determined this time to go further toward the blue hills. The only sound was the strident rasping of the cicadas as she ran through the olive grove. No sound of a motor bike or any traffic at all. She ran on, trying to ignore the heat that was building up. She reached the end of the olive grove but jogged to a halt. There was a dried river course to cross if she was to go any further. Amber reluctantly gave in to the power of the sun beating down and slowly jogged back to the hotel for a swim.

The rest of the day passed quickly and Amber had little time to think about anything but work. First she helped Daniel to load the tiles into the kiln and watched as he set the thermostats. The studios were all empty and already swept and clean.

'Time for a last swim.' Daniel said, 'Calinda and Fleur will already be at the pool. IT Will be emptied out by tonight.'

They walked back across the courtyard and through the foyer. The hotel was strangely quiet without new guests arriving. Staff were leaving in ones and twos, pleased to have a few days holiday. A cleaning company was booked for the next day so there was a pleasant lull in activity.

'It's only now the hotel is closed that I realise how much you both do every day.' Amber said as they all sat on loungers by the pool.

'Well, this is a strange week... more the calm before the storm really... the rest of July and August will be fully booked hell!' Calinda laughed and stretched out her long legs. 'The strange thing is I really enjoy it all. Since your grandfather pulled me up short about running away from my celebrity, well, life has just been so much easier. Instead of lurking in the shadows or pretending not to notice people looking at me... well, I don't know, I just regard it as part of my job and actually enjoy it.'

'Luc seems to have his share of the limelight, too.' said Amber, 'I hadn't realised a flautist could be famous... you know, people wanting his autograph and stuff like that...'

'My brother is something of a phenomenon in the music world. Maybe more in France than in England but now he is really becoming an international name. Of course, I tease him but really I am very proud. He's joining the group of musicians who want to bring music to young people... classical and popular. He plays jazz, too, did you know?' Daniel looked at Amber and gave a small wink.

Amber blushed and said, 'Well, I didn't know he played jazz but I did see him once at a jazz club in Cassis.'

'Oh, that would be the Bateau Noir... I think Luc had a fling with a singer from that club but it didn't last long.' Suddenly Calinda looked at Daniel, 'What's going on? You're teasing Amber about something, tell me!'

And so, at last, the story of Amber mistaking Luc for Daniel finally came out. To Amber's surprise, Calinda just couldn't stop laughing.

'But I was so awful.' Amber protested, 'I really hit hard... I was so out of order... I hit him really hard.'

'Where did you hit him?' Calinda said, struggling to stop her laughter as she could see Amber was upset.

'I hit him in the lavender fields.' Amber said miserably and Calinda curled up with helpless laughter, 'I meant...' she tried to speak, 'In the lavender fields, oh Amber, you are too much! I meant where on his body did you manage to hit him... oh my, in his lavender fields. Oh stop, don't tell me any more. I can just imagine it all!' Fleur was looking up at her mother, burbling and bouncing up and down with excitement. 'Honestly, even Fleur sees the joke! Don't worry, Amber, it's not the first time the boys have been mistaken. They used to play dreadful tricks… it serves them right.' Daniel stood up and lifted Fleur from Calinda's lap and passed her to Amber. 'Excuse me, Amber, would you hold my daughter for a moment while I deal with my naughty wife?' Amber took Fleur and the next minute Daniel had picked Calinda up in his arms and thrown her in the pool. Then he dived in and bobbed up beside her as she surfaced. Calinda swam to Daniel and said, 'Ah, my big strong husband, I deserved that, now kiss me!' Daniel swam toward her and when he was about to kiss her, Calinda pushed him under the water. He came up again spluttering and laughing. Amber watched them play like children and Fleur bounced up and down with delight, clapping her hands.

After lunch, Calinda and Daniel took Fleur back to the apartment for a siesta. The heat was more oppressive than usual. Amber decided it was too hot to work outside so she went back to the cool of the atelier and spent the afternoon working on the design for the porcelain. The perfume of lavender was everywhere, almost cloying now that it was picked and drying in the barns. She had several sprigs and bunches laid on the table in front of her and she began to copy them carefully. The atelier was even quieter than usual with all the resident artists away and the hotel closed, even the lavender fields were now bare and flattened to red earth. Amber began to let her mind wander as she worked on the minute detail of the lavender design. The work reminded her of the time she had spent in the studio of the museum in London… which turned her thoughts to Kim. Had she really decided to settle down with this Mike? The thought of Kim wearing a neat, navy dress and having an assistant brought a smile to her lips. How she wished she could introduce Luc to Kim and to meet Mike. Well, maybe soon. There was lot to settle before then. Inevitably her mind turned to Grandy and his search for Calinda's sister. The deep relief she felt from sharing the problem with Luc once again swamped over her.

Would they always be able to share all their fears and problems in the future? Then she thought about the way Calinda had picked up on Daniel winking at her. The only surprising thing was that they had kept quiet about the whole ridiculous matter for so long. Obviously they were so sure of each other that any thought of infidelity was ludicrous to them both. How sweet that must be, she thought. Is that what would grow between her and Luc? Would they be able to trust each other the same way? Had Rob stolen Amber's belief in true love the day he had left her standing at the church door? Amber sat up straight and stretched. She couldn't let Rob do that to her. If she let the damage he had done to her stay with her then he had won some cruel game. No, she would forget him and move on to a better place. She sighed heavily. How difficult it was waiting for news from Grandy. Wherever else her mind travelled the same problem returned to the front. Was this girl, Marissa, to be found as Calinda's lost sister. When that was settled, Amber decided, then and only then would she think about her own life and its small problems and decisions. For now she was safe and happy, surrounded by new friends and with interesting work… and she had found Luc. Amber yawned and began to wash her brushes and clear away the stalks of lavender. It was no good, she couldn't work any longer. She needed a shower and to find something easy to wear and get up to the penthouse to be in time to look after Fleur.

The hotel foyer had just the emergency lighting on behind the desk when Amber made her way across to the lift. The air-conditioning was still working but the hotel was now completely deserted. Amber was pleased to get out of the lift on the first floor and find Calinda waiting with Fleur and the apartment light and airy.

'Wow, the hotel is spooky when it's closed like this.' Amber laughed and ducked her head to give Fleur a small kiss on the top of her head. Fleur burbled with delight and reached out her arms to Amber.

'*Bonsoir*, Amber, thank you so much for coming up. You can stay up here with us tonight if you like. I know it is strange in the hotel when it's closed. We get used to it in the winter, of course.'

'Oh no, I'm fine. My room is great and I love it. No, I'm not all the scared type!' Amber laughed and looked down at Fleur, 'We'll be fine, won't we, Fleur?' Fleur clapped her hands as though in agreement.

'Then if you don't mind I'll dash off. Dani is down in the yard already. We won't be long. I phoned the garage and the car is repaired… just a fuel pipe or something. We shouldn't be more than an hour and a half.'
'Shall I get Fleur to bed… has she had food? Last night I wondered if she needed a drink or anything?'
'No, don't worry, she has already had her evening meal. If she seems sleepy then it would be great if you can lay in her cot… only if she's really sleepy though. There's a bottle of her juice in case of emergency but honestly she never seems to want it… I've got my mobile, of course.'

'Don't worry, we'll be fine. Off you go. Stay in Aix for while if you want?'

'Oh no, we had our night out last night… I don't think either of us could cope with another for a month or so! There's so much planned for the big clean-up tomorrow and Dani will want to get back to check the kiln. OK, I'm off… sooner I go sooner back again.' Calinda went quickly to the lift and Fleur looked up at Amber.

'OK, Fleur, let's see what we can find to play with tonight?'

The lift doors closed and the apartment seemed very quiet. 'How about some music? No live flute player tonight but we'll find something. Amber carried Fleur into her room and found one of the cd's recorded by Luc. 'How about this? Peter and the Wolf… I loved this when I was a child. My grandfather told me the whole story. Shall I tell it to you?' Amber set the music to play and then sat in the wing chair by the cot with Fleur on her lap. She flicked through the leaflet in the cd cover and saw a photo of a very young Luc. Her heart fluttered as she looked at it. So young and already famous enough to make a recording with Decca. Certainly some sort of child prodigy. Fleur reached out a plump finger and traced the photo. 'Clever girl, you know that's your Uncle Luc, don't you? And now he's playing to us and I shall begin my story. Once upon a time there was a little boy called Peter, he lived in a forest far...' Amber looked down at Fleur and realised she was already asleep. 'So is my story so very boring? Or is it Luc's flute playing? Well, let's see if you like your cot?' Amber stood up and very carefully laid Fleur in her cot. To her surprise, Fleur made no complaint and, after a moment or so, Amber crept from the room. The music still played and Amber went out onto the balcony to breathe some air. The wind was blowing up again. She stood for a moment enjoying the strong breeze that seemed to be coming from the hills to the west. This must be the Mistral in all its force. The air was too hot to be refreshing so she went back into the apartment and pulled the shutters back. The curtains were blowing now and the wind seemed to get stronger every minute. Her mobile bleeped and Amber saw it was a text message from Grandy. She read it quickly then drew in her breath sharply.

'unable to contact you - is your tel/internet down? Have definite proof that marissa is calinda's sister. please call.'

Amber quickly pressed Grandy's number but her phone showed no signal. She ran to the landline in the kitchen but that too was buzzing out of order. Not sure what to do next she decided to check on Fleur. The wind was now whining and the shutters banging to and fro. Despite all the noise, Amber was relieved to find Fleur still sound sleep, her little mouth slightly open as she breathed deeply. Just as Amber was thinking how she could get in touch with Grandy she heard, above the roar of the wind and the rattling shutters, the sound of a motorbike engine. Amber ran out onto the balcony but the yard wasn't all visible from the top floor. She strained to listen but now there was just the whining of the wind again and clattering of the shutters. She struggled to fasten the shutters back against the wall but it took all her strength to force them to lock tight. It was still daylight but the sky was overcast and dark. She looked out across the lines of the mown lavender field and first saw a dark swarm of bees moving toward the road... then, her heart stopped, as she saw a plume of smoke snaking toward the hotel. Even as she watched the blue-grey smoke turned to sparks of fire. Amber ran into the apartment and picked up the sleeping Fleur. She ran through the apartment to the lift and then stopped. Would it be dangerous to use the lift? Supposing the power went down or was already down? Amber hesitated for a moment and then ran to the fire escape. It was on the north side of the hotel and curled down the wall for four long flights. Smoke was now blowing across the whole area and the air was stifling, hot and acrid. She ran back into the kitchen and grabbed a fire blanket that hung on the kitchen wall. Surprised to see that Fleur was still asleep, she wrapped the blanket hastily around her and began the descent. The staircase seemed endless and Amber regretted wearing her thin leather pumps. She held Fleur tight in one arm and slid her hand down the thin metal banister as she ran down, terrified of slipping. Finally she reached the ground and immediately ran round the building to the yard where her car was standing. Then, she stopped short and almost screamed aloud. Her car door was open and the cobbles all around were soaked in petrol. She backed away quickly, realising it was impossible to use the car... a car which had become a bomb ready to explode. She pulled the edge of the fire blanket right over Fleur and ran back into the hotel lobby and to the fire alarm by the lift door. She hesitated for a brief second reading the warning 'FEU-ABAISSER-PULL DOWN. Still clutching Fleur tight in one arm she snatched at the lever and pulled sharply. Immediately the air was full of deafening noise. Fleur cried out in terror and Amber could do nothing but cover her with the blanket. The smoke was thickening now and she began to panic. She remembered a fire hydrant at the end of the drive but surely that was only for the fire engines? Amber thought longingly of water, gushing water, to save them from the heat and the smoke that was drawing nearer and nearer. Even the swimming pool was empty. The hot wind blowing in her face brought the smell of burning. Fleur's loud cries had now turned to a constant sobbing. Amber held her close in front of her and began to run. She ran into the wind and downhill. She knew she had little chance of winning against the speed of the fire but it was all she could do... hoping that if she ran into the wind the fire would be spreading in the opposite direction, that the smoke would blow away from her. Even now the gusts of wind whipped in circles and choking smoke would enclose her and then clear again. Still she ran, her feet already sore from the gravel and tarmac. Was it her imagination or was the road melting hot under the soles of her feet? As she ran, Fleur's crying ceased and Amber looked down anxiously. She moved the blanket aside for a brief moment and almost cried out with relief as she saw Fleur smile up at her. Now, all she could do was to keep running but the smoke was stinging nostrils and her breath came harsh and gasping. She turned for a moment to look behind her and then wished she hadn't. Dense smoke now covered the lavender fields and flames were catching hold, sparks flew high in the air and then settled, catching alight to the dry grass at the edge of the road behind her. Amber ran on but with a feeling of dread. The fire was catching fast and furious and her breathing now tore through her throat, painful and rasping. Still she forced her feet to pound on in a relentless rhythm, her only hope was to keep running. Fleur made a small murmur and Amber realised she was clutching her tight, maybe too tight. Another fleeting glance down to the bundle held in her arms and Amber gave a sobbing cry of relief as she saw Fleur's little face peeping out of the blanket. Her dark eyes were bright and she was still smiling up at Amber. Tears began to pour down Amber's cheeks as she ran faster now, her bare feet pounding the sandy road in a regular rhythm. How long could she last running at this speed? Everything that Amber knew about running was against what she was doing... she should be pacing herself, this all out speed would not, could not last... but still she ran full pelt down the hill, away from the fire above her and into the wind. Just when she felt she would fall to the ground helpless she saw, over the edge of the next hill, a car coming toward her. Then it dropped out of sight. With the last remnant of her energy Amber ran on... had she imagined the car? She had only caught such a brief glimpse, only the top edge of the car roof, glinting white in the sun, could it have been an ambulance coming to her aid? Had it been a cruel mirage of hope? Still she ran, her legs trembling now and her feet slipping, the pain in her lungs unbearable. Then, suddenly, at a bend in the road, she heard a car engine. Her ears were singing with pain but she was sure she heard a motor... and then the car was screaming to a halt in front of her. A man jumped out and Amber managed to cry his name and pass Fleur to him before she fell to the ground.

in the half light of the room

Suddenly in the blackness there was a flash of light and searing pain. Amber's breath rasped in her throat as she struggled to breathe. She blinked open her eyes and saw Calinda leaning over her, looking down and smiling but with tears in her eyes. They were surrounded by a shimmering pale light. Amber forced out the one word 'Fleur?' The one word was a question and Amber strained every fibre of her body trying to stay out of the dark that was beginning to surround her again.

'Fleur is perfectly well and fine, thanks to you Amber, now you must sleep and rest. You will be fine soon. Rest.' Calinda's words were spoken softly but with so much conviction that Amber felt a deep, sweet relief sweep over her as she sank once again into the darkness.

The next time she awoke it was to the sound of music, the light notes of a flute. She lay still, her eyes still closed, enjoying the sound and feeling little pain. If she took small short breaths she found she could breathe without the searing agony that she remembered from the darkness. Cautiously she opened her eyes and looked through her lashes. The shimmering grey light had gone and now the only source of light came from the edges of a large window. There was a dark figure standing outlined against the shafts of light shining brightly each side of a drawn blind. Was it morning? How long had she slept? Where was she? Suddenly everything flashed back into her head and she saw in her mind's eye the billowing smoke clouds sweeping across the Provençal landscape, the agony of running and running with Fleur in her arms, Fleur crying in fear. Agitated now, she tried to sit up and then, the blood pounding in her head and coughing painfully, she fell back onto the pillow. The figure at the window turned quickly and the music stopped.

'Amber, Amber, are you awake? I'm here, it's Luc, everything is alright. You must rest now.' He gently stroked Amber's hair back from her forehead, 'Just rest.' Then a nurse appeared from nowhere and gently placed an oxygen mask over her mouth. The relief was almost instant and she regained a regular pattern of breathing.

Amber looked first at the smiling face of the nurse and then to the worried, frowning face of Luc. There was so much she wanted to say, so much she needed to know. Her eyes filled with tears as she felt weakness swamp over her. She wanted to sleep but she needed to know. Luc gently dabbed the tears from her eyes and the nurse muttered something to him and then disappeared again. Luc leant close over Amber and smiled as he spoke softly,

'Shall I tell you all I know about what happened? Don't try to speak yet, the nurse said you must rest and you have been given pain-killers so you will feel sleepy and muzzy, of course. I'll talk and you can listen to your own story.'

Amber nodded gratefully and closed her eyes, listening to his quiet voice beginning,

'Once upon a time there was a beautiful girl called Amber...' Luc took Amber's hand in his and squeezed it gently, 'but I mustn't tease you, Amber... the story could be long but I know you need to sleep so, for now, I shall just tell you that you saved the life of Fleur. Remember, you were looking after her at the hotel when Calinda and Dani went to collect their car...' Amber's eyes flashed open at the memory but before she could try to speak, Luc kissed her forehead and continued, 'Don't try to talk yet, Amber, not yet. The doctor told me not to wake you...' His voice was so gentle and quiet that Amber drifted in and out of sleep as he carried on, 'you must have seen the fire and you were alone in the hotel, you sounded the fire alarm and then, finding the cars in the yard in pools of petrol... you just began to run. No shoes, clutching Fleur in a fire blanket, you just ran... and ran downhill, into the wind and away from the fire. I was coming up from the coast and had my car radio on a local station and heard that the road from the south was blocked by forest fire. Then I remembered a small road that looped around from the other side... through the blue hills that you have always wanted to see up close. Remember, Amber?' Amber briefly opened her eyes and nodded, then gave a small smile. 'Ah, Amber, your wicked

little smile is coming back. We shall take a trip to those blue hills together very soon, I promise. Anyway, I drove toward the Hotel de Lavande and there you were, pounding toward me, in the middle of the road, with my little niece, Fleur held in your arms. You saved her, Amber, you saved her life. The fire-fighters arrived, by air and road and soon the fire was brought under control. Only the lavender fields were burnt. The hotel is fine, apart from some blackening of the back walls of the ceramic studios… that's how close the flames reached. There's a lot of red dust around still, apparently some flame retardant that is sprayed everywhere by the aircraft… but that's being cleared up now. But, Amber, it was the smoke, suffocating smoke that you ran from, carrying Fleur safely wrapped in a fire blanket. So brave, Amber, so brave…'
Amber shook her head, wanting to explain that there was nothing more she could have done. She remembered then the pool of petrol around her car and wanted to explain to Luc why she hadn't been able to use it. She shuddered at the thought of how near she and Fleur had been to being in the centre of a fire ball and silent tears rolled down her cheeks. Again, Luc stroked her hair away from her forehead, as he continued quietly, 'Don't think any more now, Amber. Sleep again, Fleur is with Calinda and Dani, they want to visit you soon. Now you need to sleep and rest and next time you wake you will feel stronger. Now, I shall enchant you with the only real skill I have and play my flute to you. I shall play you a love song, Amber, because I do love you.' His last words were whispered softly into her ear. Amber lay still, her breathing easier now as it slowed to a calmer rhythm. The sound of the flute filled the air with a soft, lilting melody. She tried to concentrate on the sound, slightly familiar and yet unknown… then she fell into a deep sleep.

The next time she awoke she felt remarkably better. She sat up in bed easily, her breathing almost back to normal and her throat just tight and dry. She looked around in the half light of the room and saw for the first time that it was obviously a plain hospital room but improved with a vase of flowers and… her new breathing came to a brief halt as she saw a chair in the corner with Luc fast asleep. The small wooden chair was impossibly uncomfortable for the large shape of Luc. He was sitting with his legs stretched in front of him and his head resting against the wall and grasped in his hand was his flute. Amber was just wondering whether to leave him to sleep, however uncomfortable he looked, when he awoke with a start and stumbled over to the bedside.

'Amber, you're awake, how do you feel?' His voice was thick with sleep and his dark eyes anxious as he leaned to kiss her forehead.

'I feel fine, absolutely fine.'

'No, you're not fine. I have been told that you must rest at least another day. You're not fine yet.'

'Well, I feel fine, I can breathe perfectly normally and nothing hurts at all… right down to the soles of my feet.' Amber inspected under her feet, 'In fact whatever it was the doctors have been putting on my blisters should be marketed as a beauty cream. My feet look better than before. Maybe I am just a little drowsy still. How are you?'

'Absolutely wretched, I feel dreadful.' Luc stretched and rubbed the back of his neck.

Amber moved over in the narrow bed and tapped the space. 'Why don't you lie down beside me for a while?'

Luc looked at the gap and then carefully laid down on his side, facing Amber.

'Are you sure there's room? Amber, my beautiful girl you have been scaring the life out of me.'

'Everything is so muzzy… I can't really remember what happened… but Fleur was crying so loud…'

Luc stroked Amber's pale ash brown hair away from her forehead. 'Don't worry, I'll tell you all about it. The fire started…' and then he fell asleep. Amber looked at his face so close to hers and studied every part of it. She kissed his forehead and stroked his hair and then, she too, fell asleep.

'I can't believe you've arranged all this without telling me!' Amber looked across the breakfast table at Luc, 'How many people will be coming?'

They were sitting on the terrace of the Hotel de la Plage in La Ciotat. The sun was already high in the sky and the Mediterranean sparkled in the bright light.

'Well, *ma princesse*, now you have had a few days of convalescence, involving sunshine, sea, sand and constant sex, it is time to meet your admiring family and friends again.'

'What are you talking about?' Amber sat back and looked up at the fringed palm tree outlined against the blue sky. She screwed up her eyes and said thoughtfully, 'That would be good, yes, I could paint that in acrylic or maybe make a screen print...'

'Tomorrow and every day of your life after you can paint anything in any way you want but today, I have it insist, today we celebrate.'

Amber looked away from the tree and back at Luc. He was sitting forward and excited as a child. 'So you've arranged a lunch? You may as well tell me... is it Calinda, Dani and Fleur?'

'Amber, don't look at me like that. You know I will tell you everything if you do. No, *oui et non*, it's a surprise party and how can it be a surprise if you ask me to tell you everything?' Luc looked away from Amber and kicked the gravel. 'I shan't look at you or I will crack. You can get anything out of me when you look at me with your turquoise blue eyes. No, you should just go and get ready as it's nearly eleven thirty and at noon everyone...'

'Everyone? Who else have you asked then?'

Luc sighed heavily and turned his back on her and looked down to the sea. 'I'm going for a swim, you are a wicked temptress.'

'Oh well, if you're going to sulk... I only asked who else was coming. Anyway, Calinda always looks so very beautiful, I will go and find a pretty luncheon on the Côte d'Azur style frock. I guess this kaftan is a bit hippy.' She laughed and ran into the hotel.

As she changed she thought back over the last few days she had spent at the Hotel de la Plage with Luc. Long nights and sweet days of loving words and hours of understanding all that had happened. At first, Luc had been reluctant to talk to Amber about the fire but as the days passed and her health really returned to normal she insisted he should tell her all that he knew.

'Well, if you really want to begin at the awful beginning I suppose it was the night that Calinda and Dani went to the harvest feast in Aix.'

'You mean the night we stayed with Fleur... but nothing happened...'

'No, not really but remember Dani's car broke down in Aix. Trouble with the fuel hose. Well, now it seems that Pascal Mazin, the guy with the grievance... the one who had owned the lavender farm... well, he attempted to... how do you say... *saboter*... sabotage their car that night. Of course they took a taxi home and the garage repaired the car and nobody thought any more about it. Dani always drives old bangers and is used to breaking down.' Amber looked at Luc in horror as she imagined what could have happened that night. 'Anyway, as that didn't have any effect,' Luc hurried on with the account, trying to sound matter of fact and not waiting for Amber to imagine more, 'the wretched Mazin came back the night you were all alone with Fleur. This time he managed to disconnect the petrol pipes of the truck and your car,' Now it was Luc that shuddered at the thought of how near Amber and Fleur had come to being blown up. He struggled to continue and took Amber's hand in his, 'but you were too clever for him, even in the panic of the approaching fire you realised there was petrol on the ground and...'

'The first thing I saw was that my car door was open... if I hadn't seen that then...' Once again they both paused and looked at each other, their eyes wide with the fear of recollection. Then Luc continued, 'So you must have set off the main alarm...'

'Oh yes, I remember that now... I pulled the alarm lever in the fire alarm in the hall and there was the most tremendous din and poor little Fleur cried aloud.' Tears rolled down Amber's cheeks as she thought about the dreadful sound of Fleur's wailing cries and the deafening noise of the alarm. Luc gently kissed Amber's tears away and said, 'Shall we talk more tomorrow? You are still in shock and...'

'No, I want to hear everything... I shall feel better when my memory clears... at the moment I just can't join all the pieces together. Please carry on, Luc.'

'*Très bien,* if you are sure it's a good thing... well, of course the alarm is direct to the fire station so they were alerted but you couldn't have waited where you were... you did the right thing by running... and running to me.'

'I remember the running, of course, it was hard to breathe as the smoke was catching up with me in gusts and my feet hurt dreadfully. Fleur seemed to get heavier and heavier and... yes, then I remember seeing a white car roof over the hill... I didn't know it was you... I thought it might be a rescue ambulance... then, I remember seeing you get out of the car... in fact, I wasn't sure if it was you or Daniel... I was so confused by then and my eyes streaming.'

'Well, you almost threw Fleur into my arms, all wrapped in the fire blanket and then you said my name and fell to the ground. I was so concerned with holding Fleur that I couldn't catch you... sorry about that!' They both smiled at each other as his ridiculous apology and he continued again, 'You didn't really fall, you just sank to the ground. I took Fleur to my car and then carried you and put you in the back seat. It was all crazy... I remember thinking that Dani would tell me off for not having a car seat for Fleur... then I came to my senses and wheeled the car round and drove away like a bat out of hell.'

'I don't remember anything about that... next thing I knew I was in hospital.'

'Yes, we made down to Aubagne, the Edmond Garcin and I drove straight to the *urgence,* emergency entrance... suddenly everyone took over and I was left sitting in the corridor. Not long after that Calinda and Dani arrived in a dreadful panic but by then Fleur had been thoroughly tested and found to be absolutely unharmed. At one point I thought they'd be checking Calinda in as she was in such a state. You, poor thing, had to sleep in an oxygen tent the first night and it wasn't at all pleasant. You looked so very fragile and tiny but it turned out you're as tough as nails!' Luc laughed and kissed Amber's hand.

'Oxygen tent... yes, I remember now something sort of shimmering around me when I first came round. So then you stayed in the hospital all night or what?'

'Well, you didn't expect me to go home, did you? One nurse told me I could only stay if I was a close relative so I told her I was going to marry you and she took pity on me.'

'Did you indeed, now that we can discuss later but now I want to know what happened next... did the police catch this Pascal Mazin guy or what? Do we have to watch our backs for him to come back and try again?'

'No fear of that, my love, don't worry. The gruesome truth is that he died in his own fire. It seems he was carrying the usual arsonist gear... the police said it is something like a homemade bomb... apparently just a box of matches wrapped in synthetic wadding that can be lit and thrown into dry grass.The police and the fire brigade were quickly on the scene because they were ready, waiting for trouble. When the Mistral starts up it excites pyromaniacs and the like... the fire brigade were ready with their helicopters, small planes and the usual fire engines ... anyway, he must have been slow in getting away and perhaps panicked when he heard all the action in the air and on the roads so he took off onto a small path and managed to skid. Well, that is really all I am going to tell you except he died by fire... fire of his own making.'

Amber shuddered and shook her head sadly. 'So horrid. I'm ashamed to say all I can feel is huge relief that he can't come back again. I remember Leon from the Bastide...

do you remember that night at the dinner party… he said something about the man trying to run over his friend, Michelle… some sort of identity crisis. I suppose he was very disturbed.'

'Yes, and very drunk and when he wasn't drunk he was high as a kite. Sad but true.' They sat in silence for a moment and then Amber said,

'What bout the Hotel Lavande…was there much fire damage?'

'That was unbelievable… only black sort of sticky soot all along the back walls of the studios. It's already been sandblasted clean and looks better than before. Dani has turned over the earth in the lavender fields and will be ready to replant for next season. Even this year's crop was safely stacked in the hay barn… phew, if that had caught… the stalks are full of oil, lavender oil, of course.' Once more they were silent, then Luc took Amber in his arms and they held each other close.

'It's all over now, Amber… and…' She knew he was going to say that she had been so brave. He had said it so many times already and she couldn't make him understand that she had only run away. She smiled and ruffled his hair and very soon words were no longer necessary.

Now, standing on the balcony, Amber smiled to herself as she left her thoughts behind and came back to the present. She looked out to sea and could just make out the figure of Luc swimming strongly, parallel to the beach. What had he been planning? Several times she had found him on his phone, talking rapidly and waving his hands in the air. When he saw she was listening he would end the call. He just told her he was planning a surprise for her. She hoped that Luc had invited Calinda and Dani to lunch, it was time now to talk about it with them. More than anything Amber wanted to hold Fleur in her arms. Amber took a deep breath, delighting that it was now so painless, and drew back her shoulders. Time to dress up… Luc had obviously planned a celebratory lunch.

At twelve noon Amber and Luc were standing in the hotel foyer waiting. Amber could feel him tense with excitement. What had he been up to? Then a car rolled into the hotel driveway and Amber gasped and ran out into the sunshine.

'Grandy, I don't believe it. Grandy!' Amber threw herself into the arms of her grandfather and began to sob.

'There, there, my Amber. Don't cry, you have been a brave girl. I am so proud of you.' Grandy held her in his arms and patted her back, then added, 'Now, dry up your tears, there's another car behind mine.'

Amber looked up and saw a taxi, the same wild-haired taxi driver that had taken them that day to Cassis in the driver's seat and then, Amber drew in her breath so sharply that she gave a small cough. Yes, just getting out of the taxi now, her mother and father. Amber ran to meet them and soon, with more tears, she was between them both, wrapped in their arms. Slowly the family made their way toward the hotel steps where Luc stood waiting. Introductions were made and then her mother spoke.

'I feel I already know you, Luc, the number of times we have spoken on the phone.'
Luc kissed Amber's mother on both cheeks and then put his arm around Amber, 'Now I see where Amber gets her amazing turquoise eyes from… please, come into the cool shade and have a cold drink.' Amber's mother reached up and smoothed her hair, 'Well, I think we need a strong drink after that taxi ride. Grandy was ahead of us as he had flown into Marseille the night before and had a driver from his hotel. We took pot luck with the cabs at the airport and managed to choose a complete maniac. I began to think we would never get here in one piece.' She laughed and Amber's father put an arm around her saying,
'Well, we're here now and very nice the place is too. We've heard all about this Hotel de la Plage, of course. I had no idea it would be in such a splendid location. The gardens are wonderful… although I see that the hotel does need a lick of paint!' They all laughed and walked into the cool lobby. Luc stood in the middle of them and said,

'Well, I have champagne on ice waiting on the terrace... follow me!' Amber saw the look of barely concealed excitement on his face.

'Luc, there's more to this than iced champagne, isn't there! You're practically hopping up and down with excitement now... I bet Calinda and Daniel are with Fleur on the terrace right now!' She pushed past him and ran through the hotel salon and out onto the terrace, then she stopped short and put her hands up to her face in shock as she saw a couple sitting at a table, waiting.

'Kim, I don't believe it!' Amber ran up to her friend and hugged her, 'When did you get here? How did you keep it so secret. I had no idea!'

'Your Luc the Flute is quite a mover and shaker, Amber. He has been arranging flights and arrival times and ... oh yes, this is Mike, my man!' The young man who had been standing aside watching Amber and Kim with a broad smile, now held out his hand,

'Pleased to meet you at last, Amber. Believe me I know absolutely everything about you!' Amber shook his hand and laughed. Before they could say more there was movement at the other end of the terrace and Calinda made her entrance. She glided down the length of the terrace, her ice blue dress swirling around her. Then, she held out her long arms and Amber ran to her and held her close, feeling the sobs shaking Calinda's body.

'Amber, I can't talk yet, I'm sorry, I don't want to cry at your party.' Calinda brushed away her tears with back of her hand and made a brave attempt to flash her world famous smile.

'Where are Dani and Fleur?' Amber asked, blinking away her own tears.

'They are waiting to come to see you but I wanted to tell you first, prepare you for yet another surprise. My sister, Marissa is with them, too.'

Amber gasped in shock. 'Oh Calinda, I can hardly believe it! You mean...' words failed Amber and she looked at Calinda who simply nodded. Then Daniel came out onto the terrace holding Fleur and followed by a dark-haired woman in a red dress. Then Amber saw that Fleur was stretching out her arms to her and babbling 'Mba, Mba!' Daniel grinned with delight. 'Fleur is calling your name, Amber!' He passed Fleur to Amber and she held her close, feeling her warmth and weight in her arms once more.

'Now,' Amber said, looking around at her family and friends, 'now, at last, I feel the nightmare is truly over and everything is well in my world. Thank you all for coming, and you, Luc, thank you for arranging it all… very clever and a very well kept secret.' Amber looked across to Luc and saw he was holding his flute. He smiled at her and then gave his answer in music.

EPILOGUE

Two young women are sitting side by side under a deep blue umbrella. The Mediterranean, exactly the same colour blue, is a shining line in the background.

Kim: How did we get here, Amber?

Amber: And both of us four months pregnant, how did that happen?

Kim: Well, you surely know the answer to that question.

Amber: You know very well what I meant. Isn't it rather amazing that we are both expecting babies at the same time?

Kim: Spose so, but we've always have done everything together. I always thought we'd have a double wedding too.

Amber: Did you? Yes, I suppose I did , too, when we were kids and dressing up in net curtains for veils and stuff. Then, Rob came along and it all changed.

Kim: Did you ever hear any more from him?

Amber: Well, not directly but a friend told me he had gone to live in Canada.

Kim: Sounds perfect. Can't be far enough away as far as I'm concerned… the way he hurt you back then.

Amber: I spose so, but he'd had a horrid childhood, you know. I feel sorry for him really… especially as it all ended up so well for me. I'd never have met Luc *(waving hand around in air)* and none of this would have happened.

Kim: True enough. And our double wedding at Christmas time in the Bastide near Aix en Provence. Now that was amazing!

Amber: Wasn't it just… such a great day. Only in Provence could it have been such a blue sky day in December.

Kim: Well, there probably are other places in the world but who cares… this is just the best place ever.

Amber: Do you think it will all be different when we have babies?

Kim: Well, that's another silly question. Of course it will... we shall have babies.

Amber: You know what I mean, do you think our lives will change much... basically?

Kim: Of course not, we shall still be best friends and we shall still love our husbands and even more because we shall have children. Anyway, I really don't get what you are on about. Can't you just sit quietly and enjoy the view? I don't worry about things like that.

Amber: What do you worry about then?

Kim: Nothing really. I am perfectly happy and content. Mike is my dream husband and will be a good father. My business now runs on smooth lines and I can get away for a week like this. My family are all well and happy... what should I worry about in my own little way?

Amber: Dunno, same here. Luc is the best thing that ever happened to me and he can't wait to be a father. He's already bought enough baby kit to fill our flat. Oh yes, that's another thing not to worry about... we have a wonderful top floor flat over-looking the Med and I have a studio all to myself. Luc's work takes him away sometimes, but only long enough for it to be wonderful to have him home again. Bonus being... I paint far more when he's on tour. My family, Mum, Dad and Grandy are all well. Grandy visits often and loves it here. No, I can't think of anything to worry about in my little life either.

Kim: There is one thing though...

Amber: (*looking anxiously at Kim*) What?

Kim: I'm simply dying for a cup of tea.

Man's voice in background

Voice: Would you two girls like a cup of tea brought out there?

Both women laugh and say in unison.

Amber/Kim: Yes please!
Kim: I hope Mike is making it. Your Luc the Flute makes the most diabolical tea.
Amber: I know, (*dreamily*)… it's his only fault.

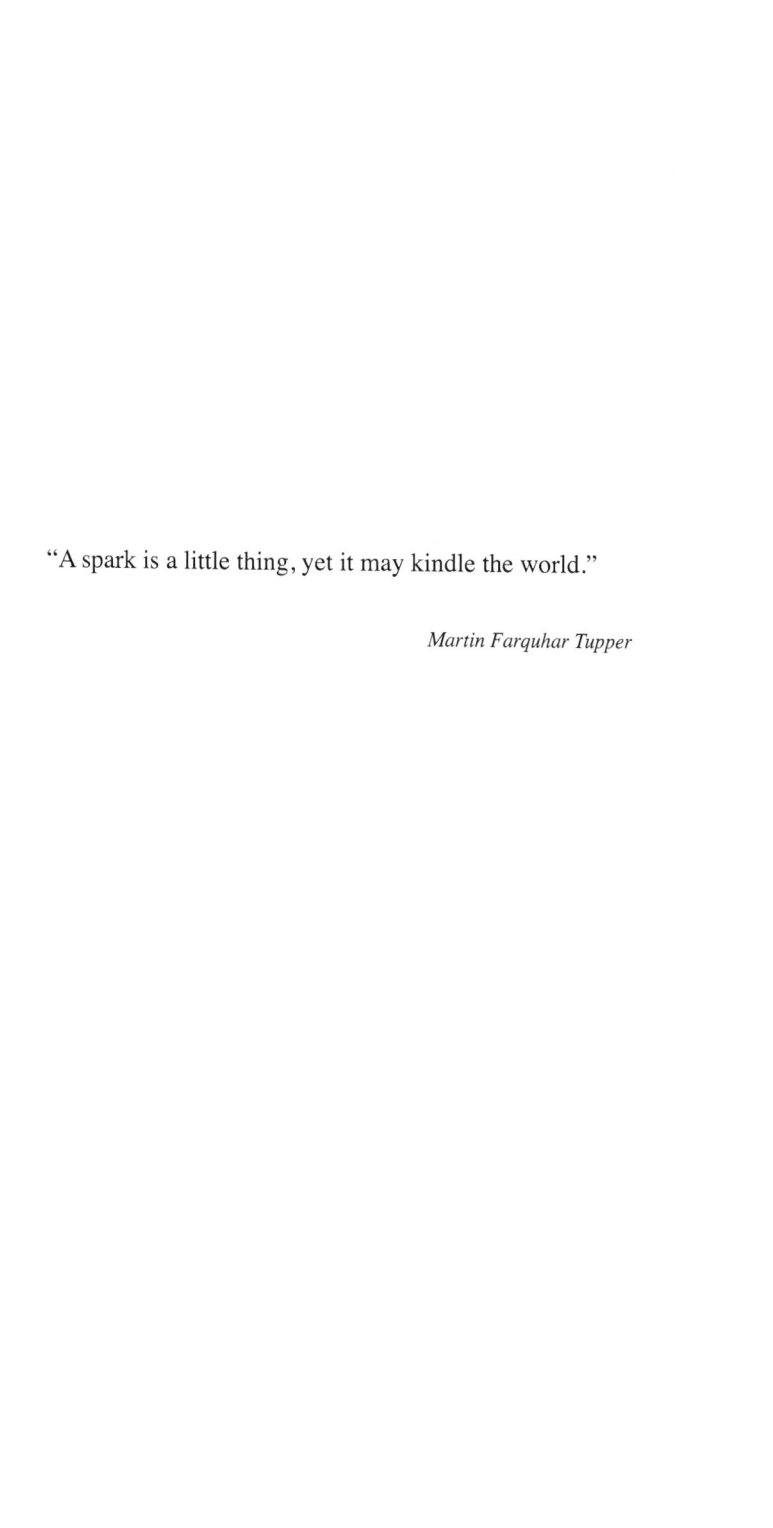

"A spark is a little thing, yet it may kindle the world."

Martin Farquhar Tupper

Have you read my other titles?

Perfume of Provence

Provence Love Legacy

Dreams of Tuscany

My next book is in the pipeline and will once again bring together some of my favourite characters. At the back of my mind there is also a Christmas title lurking and I am planning a double wedding with a guest list from all former titles.

You are formally invited to reader-attend!

Printed in Great Britain
by Amazon